Over a Thousand Hills
I Walk With You

Hanna Jansen

*translated from the German
by Elizabeth D. Crawford*

Andersen Press
London

First published in Great Britain in 2007 by Andersen Press Limited,
20 Vauxhall Bridge Road, London SW1V 2SA.
www.andersenpress.co.uk

Published by arrangement with Carolrhoda Books, Inc., a division
of Lerner Publishing Group, 241 First Avenue North, Minneapolis,
MN 55401, U.S.A. All rights reserved.

Original German language edition,
Über tausend Hügel wandere ich mit dir
published in 2002 by Thienemann Verlag GmbH, Stuttgart, Germany

British Library Cataloguing in Publication Data available.

ISBN 978 184 270 673 2

Printed and bound in Great Britain by
Cox & Wyman, Reading, Berkshire

This is the story of Jeanne d'Arc Umubyeyi, daughter of Florence Muteteli and Ananie Nzamurambaho, sister of Jean de Dieu Cyubahiro, called Jando, and Catherine Icyigeni, called Teya.

Jeanne was born on the second of January 1986 in Kibungo-Zaza.

In April 1994 her parents and siblings were victims of the genocide in Rwanda.

Jeanne also lost her aunts, uncles, and cousins, as well as neighbors and friends. Nearly all the Tutsi people who lived in Kibungo at the time were killed.

Jeanne was the only one in her family to escape the massacre.

Two years later, in February 1996, she was brought to Germany by an aunt who was living there.

Since April 1996 Jeanne has had a family again. Now she is the daughter of Hanna and Reinhold Jansen, sister of Niklas, Fatia, Bob, Bobette, David, Samia, William, Katharina, Michel, Sali, Maurice, and Jano.

*The book that follows was written
with the help of my daughter Jeanne d'Arc,
who wanted to remember and tell.
I have listened to her again and again
and afterward written her story . . .
As well as I am able to feel it.
I dedicate my work to Jeanne's first family
and to their memory.*
—Hanna Jansen

PART I

il y avait une maison sur la colline
there was a house on the hill

I listen to you.

I have always believed that horrors can seal the mouth. And not only the mouth, but also the heart and mind, at least for a long time. That there are horrors that let all stories die because the words refuse to come.

But you wanted to tell. Me. And, with me, or through me, others too. I am going to listen to you, as I have several times already. I am going to try to conceive of the inconceivable and see what happens to me.

When it comes to the point, I may cry for help. As loudly as you did.

Or did you not cry out? You will tell me.

We will put our words together, and I will write them down. Perhaps it is even true that once a thing is contained in words, it leaves us. Or turns into something from which we are able to take a step backward.

If we succeed, perhaps your pain, embedded in a whole, may be put to rest.

Whenever I try to imagine the extent of your pain, I can find no dimension that makes it conceivable for me. And so

9

I am also afraid of what we are attempting.

But you trust me. And I you. I firmly believe in your strength.

There was a time before. There will be a time after.

Let us build a bridge. A bridge that will carry us over the unbearable.

I am certain that as we walk back and forth, we will find love on both sides.

Jeanne was sitting in the small tin bathtub, which had been brought outside into the inner courtyard in the afternoon so that the sun could warm the water.

The children had carried the water to the house themselves. During the course of the day they had several times followed the narrow path to the distant, carefully guarded place where you could buy it at a kiosk. They walked there mornings, noontimes, and evenings in the company of the bigger children and some grown-ups to secure the supply needed daily. Once, during one of the many trips, Jeanne had counted much more than a thousand steps.

Chattering, sometimes singing, too, they made their way home in the shadow of the banana palms that lined the path left and right, passing a bamboo field whose arm-thick stalks towered three feet high, a little later through a small eucalyptus wood that concealed a large frog pond. The dirty surface of the pond never receded, even during dry periods, for it was constantly fed by several springs burbling out of the ground. Here was where people who couldn't pay for water got theirs.

A great deal of water was needed if banana juice was going to be processed. The younger children, of whom Jeanne was still one, balanced the small plastic cans on their closely cropped heads, held by a wreath of banana leaves or a cloth tied around, in which the hard bottom of the can sat as if in a nest.

The older children—among them Jeanne's brother, Jando—and the grown-ups carried the big cans between them, hung over a long, sturdy stick held up on each end. Sometimes even several cans at a time.

The water came from the mountains. There was enough of it. But it had to be brought to the houses. And so fetching water was just as unalterable a part of the daily routine as waking up and going to sleep.

As Aunt Pascasia's strong hand approached with the sponge, Jeanne pulled in her head and arched her back like an angry cat. Squeezing her eyes shut as tightly as she could and inwardly fidgeting with impatience, she endured being soaped from head to toe and scrubbed until her skin glowed.

Aunt Pascasia showed no mercy toward the day's dust. Jeanne hated this unavoidable evening cleansing ritual and, besides, she found it beneath her dignity. She was six and no longer wanted to be washed.

At home with her parents, she had once succeeded in convincing Julienne, the still very young housemaid, to let her do this job herself. But then she'd earned the noisy scorn of all present when—obviously—she'd forgotten one of her feet. And Julienne had gotten into trouble.

Here, however, in the country with her grandmother, where Jeanne passed the long summer vacations from June to September with all the rest of the grandchildren every year, there was no escape.

Jeanne heard her little sister whimpering in a second tub beside her. And mixed in was the irritated voice of her cousin Claire, who was already allowed to do women's work.

"Then hold still, Teya!" she commanded.

Teya had gotten soap in her eyes, Jeanne guessed and squeezed her eyes even tighter shut in precaution as she felt the burning suds running out of her hair over her face.

Secretly she was glad that she had gotten Aunt Pascasia for the bath this time. Of course her aunt's hands grabbed hard and firmly, but all the same, they were much more practiced than Claire's, and so Jeanne had a good chance of getting finished sooner than Teya today.

Being first at every conceivable opportunity was the ongoing battle between her and her younger sister, and it never came to an end. Not seldom, Jeanne lost, which galled her terribly because the two years she had on Teya should really have ensured her a constant advantage. But Teya was smart, also a little beast sometimes when it came to winning over the grown-ups and getting them on her side.

When Teya deployed her weapon of relentless, piercing crying, Jeanne had to yield the field, just because she was the oldest.

"Don't you hear how your little sister is crying!" her

mother would reproach her in such instances. "Then why can't you humor her?"

And Jeanne would yield, even though she was resentful inside. It isn't fair, she would think. But she never said it out loud.

Aunt Pascasia dropped the sponge and scooped up water in both hands to pour it over Jeanne's head and rinse away the soap. This was done a few times in succession, for the sake of thoroughness. Jeanne straightened up and stood there. Now she would soon have it all behind her. The lukewarm water streamed from her head down over her body, and some of the stinging suds got into her eyes. They burned horribly, but Jeanne pressed her lips together and didn't utter a sound. After all, you could also win in matters of bravery.

Besides, she didn't want to attract Aunt Pascasia's displeasure, to avoid the risk of being kept here any longer than absolutely necessary. She could hardly wait to gather with the others near the fireplace, where the smallest children assembled evening after evening before supper. They sat down on straw mats at the foot of Grandmother's chair—all spotless from head to toe and in their bathrobes—and listened to the old woman's stories, while the aunts and Véneranda, the housemaid, busied themselves around the fire preparing the evening meal.

Jeanne loved her grandmother's stories.

She would close her eyes while she followed the quiet, dark flow of the old voice, so that she saw everything right in front of her. She swallowed the sentences almost greedily, filled with the desire to fix them in her mind word for word until she knew most of the stories by heart. Sometimes she annoyed the others by suddenly interrupting a story and anticipating something.

"Your fingernails need cutting, Dédé!" Stern-faced, Aunt Pascasia interrupted her thoughts.

Though they were still burning, Jeanne opened her eyes in horror, and a fat tear washed away the rest of the soapsuds. Cutting fingernails meant a loss of time that could never be made up.

"Whatever do you do to get yourself so dirty every day!" grumbled her aunt.

She lowered her broad, energetic face dangerously close to Jeanne's, but she received no answer.

Aunt Pascasia knew perfectly well how a person got so dirty.

From roaming through the banana grove, from attempts to cook with sand and freshly plucked leaves, from hide-and-seek, from climbing on the widespread branches of the avocado trees behind Grandmother's farm buildings.

Today, running away from Jando, Jeanne had been a little too fast and too careless while climbing down from a tree and had fallen from a low branch onto the dusty ground. Happily, Aunt Pascasia's critical eyes had so far missed the scrapes below her knees.

ling, Jeanne hid her hands behind her back. "My
cut!" she declared.

had scarcely passed her lips when Aunt
hizzed down and landed with a painful

smack on Jeanne's small, curving behind.

Jeanne silently dropped her head and peered out of the corners of her almond eyes at her aunt's face, where she could discover nothing but grim determination. Respect forbade further objection, and besides, it was useless and could even lead to banishment to the house or a prohibition against taking part in the story hour. With heavy heart she resigned herself, looking enviously over at Teya as she did so. She, now toweled dry, was at that moment being rubbed with milking fat.

The light brown skin of her sister's small, round face shone in the deep light of the evening sun and her blindingly white little teeth beamed in a triumphant smile.

Jeanne was only able to restrain her tongue with difficulty. It wanted to poke from her mouth like a sharp dagger and stick out at Teya full length.

Some time later Jeanne joined the circle of clean children, last of all.

They were sitting close together on the straw mats, eyes turned expectantly toward their grandmother's house. Until they were called for supper, they were not allowed to stir from that spot.

Jeanne was relieved to see that her grandmother hadn't appeared yet. Ordinarily she was already sitting there and greeting the children who gradually gathered around her. But today her chair was empty. This quieted Jeanne's gnawing feeling of having been done out of something, and also her secret anger.

She lifted her chin and looked over the circle toward the front row, where for a second time she encountered Teya's victorious smile. Directly at the foot of Grandmother's chair.

"Puh!" Jeanne said. With exaggerated slowness, she let herself sink into the only place still free, next to her cousin Saphina, stuck out her lower lip, and turned her face away, to the fireplace, where Véneranda was stirring something in one of the oversized kettles.

Before her bath, Jeanne had found out, through a quick peek into the pots, that there were sweet potatoes and vegetable sauce again today. She didn't like sweet potatoes at all. Therefore she'd taken the precaution of gobbling down a few sugar-sweet red bananas and a juicy ripe mango. Later, when she gathered with the small children around the big common bowl for supper, she intended to fish out just a few beans with her sharp fingers when the grown-ups weren't looking.

Véneranda put down her stirring stick and wiped her forehead with the back of her hand. She had been Grandmother's housemaid for many years, and Jeanne had known her ever since she was born. But Véneranda's time as housemaid was coming to an end, for she was already twenty—much too old for a housemaid—and she would soon marry.

Jeanne could hardly imagine summer at Grandmother's without Véneranda. She just belonged there. Usually good-humored, she freely took part in practical jokes with the children, laughed constantly and louder than all of them,

16

and let the really small ones ride on her shoulders when she cantered along the path to the water place, her long legs swinging in great steps. Her movements seemed to follow a secret rhythm. Often she danced or sang, and she couldn't keep from drumming on anything that came under her nimble fingers.

The children loved to tease her, and she mostly took it good-naturedly. But if ever someone went too far, she got respect by grabbing the pest on the spot and setting him straight with an authoritative slap.

Véneranda was the only one of the housemaids allowed this grown-ups' right. The younger housemaids were strictly forbidden to raise a hand, and they often found it hard to restrain themselves.

Mournfully Jeanne watched the young woman, so familiar, who would no longer be there a few weeks from now. Véneranda's small, dark profile stood out like a silhouette against the evening sky, where the gigantic ball of the sun, sinking slowly behind the hills, had spread its lush orange, now, as on many summer evenings, suffusing the colors of the land: bathing the green of the gentle row of hills in deep ochre and making the earth swim in gold.

Véneranda was singing now, too. Or rather she was humming a melody that Jeanne had often heard from her. The young woman's crinkly hair, twisted into thin, short braids, stood out from her head belligerently, like the thorns of a cactus, and the wild flower pattern of her dress challenged the day to hold out a little longer yet, until pitch-dark night descended over all.

When Véneranda noticed Jeanne's gaze, she gave her an enigmatic smile, which had the color of the evening. It worked like milking fat on Jeanne's small soul, chafed with the defeat it had just suffered. She returned the smile with a slight trembling at the corners of her mouth.

At that very moment the sound of the opening door announced Grandmother. Jeanne turned around and immediately joined in the greeting of the others.

"Good evening, Nyogokuru!" the children cried.

Upright, one hand supported on her polished, carved stick, holding her pipe in the other, the unusually tall old woman walked out of the house, approaching the crowd of her grandchildren one step at a time. As she moved, her face wore a tense expression of suppressed pain.

She had a serious disease in her bones, which confined her to her bed from time to time and made each movement torture for her. She had not been able to do the work in her fields herself for a long time, and other activities demanded so much of her strength that her daughters or people who were temporarily living with her had to step in for her.

However, year after year the grandchildren gathered during vacation on her farm outside the town of Kibungo, and she still took joy in the task of looking after the children and keeping them awake with stories before the evening meal.

As always, Nyogokuru had dressed carefully for the evening. Today she wore a brilliant blue *umucyenyero*, a cloth gown that wrapped around the body and fell to her feet, which were inserted into comfortable slippers. Over the *umucyenyero*, the *umwitero*, a broad sash tied diagonally across the shoulder, on whose warm yellow and earth tones a bird pattern of brilliant blue repeated the color of the dress underneath. The same colorfully patterned material was used for the *igitambaro*, a cloth wound around the head, which Grandmother wore like a turban.

Before Nyogokuru sat down in her chair, her eyes traveled carefully over her grandchildren's heads. They were alert, dark brown eyes under broad, prominent cheekbones in an almost wrinkleless face. The unusual form of the cheekbones, which made the lower part of her face look like a triangle, was a characteristic of the women in the family. Jeanne had also inherited it and therefore her face already lacked any childish roundness.

After Nyogokuru sat down, she lit her pipe with deliberation. Turning her clear gaze on the children, she took a deep drag.

They all waited eagerly for what she would say. When she finally opened her mouth to speak, Jeanne saw her words sail away into the evening with a little puff of smoke.

"Now, how did you spend the day?" Grandmother asked.

Many mouths opened at the same time, jabbering excitedly, and over the babble of answers Teya's clear, bright little voice, distinctly audible to all, announced: "Dédé fell out of a tree!"

Traitor, thought Jeanne, filled with stormy thoughts of vengeance. Well, just you wait!

Quickly she dropped her eyelids to conceal the spark of

anger in her eyes. For if she challenged fate or the anger of her grandmother too much, it could happen that she would have to pack her things and return to her parents early.

It wasn't always easy for Jeanne to behave the way a girl of her age was expected to. Gentle and yielding she was not. And not always obedient, either. Protest dwelt in her, a small, steadily flickering flame, which could suddenly flare up brightly and burst out of her in hot words. Words that were better left unsaid.

Now Jeanne surreptitiously pulled the hem of her dress over the scrapes on her knees and bent her head, because she expected a sharp reprimand to rattle down on her the next moment.

But the reproof didn't come.

Instead, Nyogokuru asked, "What would you like to hear today?"

Jeanne lifted her head in surprise and saw her grandmother smiling.

"The fairy tale of Snow White!" crowed Teya.

"Not that again!" Saphina grumbled. "Instead, let's have the story of the girl from the Kalebasse who had to stay with her prince. We haven't heard that one for a terribly long time. Please, Nyogokuru!"

Lionson, one of the only two boys in the group, jumped up. He was Aunt Pascasia's youngest, a half a head smaller than Jeanne, but he acted like his name, "Son of the Lion." Nothing could be gruesome or dangerous enough for him.

Now he bared his teeth and bellowed aloud. "The story of the monster that ate up his ten children!" he demanded, rolling his eyes wildly.

"Eeeh, no, not that one!" squealed the girls.

The ringing of a bell and the dull trampling of hooves joined in with the noise. At the same time, a slight vibration of the ground revealed that Gatori, the herdboy, was back from the mountains with the cows and would be coming through the big gate any minute. The children forgot the argument about their story. They turned their heads to watch the drama that was about to unfold.

A little later Nyampinga's brindled head, with its long, curving horns, appeared in the entrance. As the oldest cow of all, she was the leader. She walked heavily ahead of the others. Her huge udder, full to bursting, was obviously a burden to her. She headed purposefully for the barn, where she was already awaited by Muzehe, the old farmhand with the big feet.

Muzehe was one of those who had to earn the right to live and eat with Grandmother by working. He had come one day and stayed. His job was primarily the milking of the cows.

He received Nyampinga and led her into the stall, in the quiet certainty that the other three would follow her, as would the two calves.

Now Gatori also appeared. He strode smartly through the gate, a lanky fourteen-year-old, whose bare arms and legs were covered with a thick layer of dust. He drove the calves ahead of him with a small stick, carefully watching to see that none of them danced out of line. His day's work was done. Right after washing, he would join the big boys.

Jando and his two cousins were already waiting for him at the fence. When Gatori raised his stick in greeting and grinned at them, they called back something and waved.

Jeanne watched the cows vanish into the barn and sent a longing look after them.

Even more than sitting quietly on the straw matting at Nyogokuru's feet she would have liked to be in the barn now. She wanted to stroke her favorite cow, Tsembatsembe, and let her run her rough tongue gently over her head. Tsembatsembe had the loveliest eyes in the world.

"Today I am going to tell you a story that you don't know yet," Nyogokuru announced.

Jeanne turned around, wrapped her arms around her knees, and raised her face attentively. And a second time she met the smile of her grandmother.

"It is the story of the drums," said the old woman. "Today I am going to tell you how they came into the world."

She was silent for a long moment, as if she wanted to give the children time to prepare their minds for what was about to follow. Their eyes were eagerly focused on her lips, but those were again closed around the stem of the pipe.

The ensuing stillness was pierced by Jando's shout to Gatori, followed by the croaking voices of the many frogs in the little pond nearby.

Jeanne imagined the sturdy little fellows jumping straight out of the water and lining up around one of the ponds, looking like little soldiers in their spotted camp uniforms. She saw them before her, chests out, cheeks blown up, croaking out orders on all sides. Or perhaps one of them was even trying to strike up a song, in which the voices of the others joined in a giddy chorus.

"Once, a very, very long time ago, there lived a king who ruled over all of Africa," Nyogokuru began. "It was a time of peace and well-being, for everyone in the land had enough to live, and even the king had everything he needed. Because he was a very wise and just king, he always wanted to be sure that all his subjects were doing well and that no one had to be envious of others. But the kingdom was enormously big, and so it often took much too long before a message from afar reached the king or the king's message to his subjects living far away reached them. If help was needed somewhere or something special had happened, his messengers often came too late. Over and over the king thought about how he could create a remedy, but he still didn't know how to do it. So one day he raised his voice to the great King of Heaven and put before him an urgent request to give him and his subjects a way to send news all over the country quickly, so that everyone would hear it in time to be useful.

"'Yes, I have something for you,'" said the great King of Heaven. 'And I will gladly fulfill your wish, if you send to me the cleverest and bravest of your messengers so that they can receive the gift from me. It will not be easy for them to find me, for they must walk up hill and down, over a thousand hills until they reach the one that leads directly into Heaven.'

"The ruler of Africa thanked the great King of Heaven from the bottom of his heart and immediately summoned ten of his best messengers in order to send them to him. He gave them plenty to take to eat and drink on the way and ordered them to approach the great King of Heaven peacefully and humbly.

"Their leader, however, thought about the dangers they could meet on the way. 'We're going where no one has ever been before,' he said. 'Who knows what will happen. It's better if we carry weapons with us so we can fight if anyone attacks us.'

"They set off, bristling with spears and machetes, against the orders of their king. They walked uphill and downhill, day after day, week after week. They walked over one hill after another, but they never reached the mountain where Heaven and Earth touch, although they saw it before them the whole time. And they never returned.

"After the king had waited in vain for them for a long time, he again chose ten of his best messengers, to send them after the others. Again he gave them an urgent warning to approach the great King of Heaven peacefully and in humility. But their leader also disregarded his order. He armed himself and his people as if they were going to war. And like the ones before them, they were never seen again."

Nyogokuru stopped and drew on her pipe with enjoyment. After a while she continued: "So the king decided to go himself. Once more he called together ten of his men who were to accompany him. And because now he was the leader, they went unarmed, according to his wish. Seven days and seven nights they walked uphill and downhill, until on the evening of the eighth day they finally came to the foot of that hill where Heaven and Earth touch. And since they didn't know what to do from there on, they first lay down to rest for a little and soon fell asleep from exhaustion. When the king and his men opened their eyes the next morning, however, they were frightened out of their wits, for in front of them, at the top of the hill, they saw a giant spider, whose body darkened the sky. It was staring down on them threateningly with eight glowing eyes."

Nyogokuru fell silent. A loud sigh of exhaled breath rippled through the rows of her listeners. Lionson poked little Blando beside him, who had stretched himself out full-length on the straw matting during the story and fallen asleep. Blando sat up, blinked briefly, and dropped back again. Lionson shook him by the arm indignantly. Finally it was getting really exciting! Jeanne felt a tickling in her stomach. She found spiders horrible. And this hideous monster up there on the hill was certainly very dangerous. How was the king supposed to be able to conquer it without weapons?

"The king had to pull all his courage together," Nyogokuru continued. "He rose from his bed and began to slowly climb the hill. Eye to eye with the repulsive brute, which seemed to be waiting just for him. Filled with fear, his men followed him, though only hesitantly. When the king finally reached the top, he realized that it would be an easy thing for the spider to crush him under one of its feet, and he was very much afraid. But it merely sat there, unmoving. He stared bravely back at it.

"'What do you want?' cried the spider. Its voice echoed

over the chain of hills a thousandfold and then reechoed a thousandfold, so that the men threw themselves to the ground in terror. Only the king remained upright.

"'I am the king of Africa and come with friendly intent,' he announced courageously. 'The great King of Heaven expects me. But unfortunately I do not know how I am supposed to reach him. Can you help me?'

"The spider said nothing at first. It seemed to be thinking.

"Finally it asked craftily, 'And if I help you, will you then give me something for it?'

"'I would like nothing better!' cried the king. 'Only tell me what you want, and it is yours.'

"'Something that is especially valuable to you,' answered the spider. 'When the time comes, I will choose it.'

"'I give you my word,' promised the king with a light heart. 'Before I return home, you may ask something of me.'

"Then the spider began to spin a web, and in a very short time it reached from the earth to Heaven. And the king and his messengers climbed up it to the entrance to Heaven, where the great King of Heaven was waiting for them and received them gladly. He asked them in and gave a great feast in their honor. They celebrated with music and good food for three days and three nights. And at the end, the great King of Heaven took the earthly king to one side because he wanted to speak with him alone.

"'I promised you something,' he began solemnly. 'And you have come yourself to get it. That was very clever of you. I know that you are a wise and just king. Therefore I will give you something that in the future will hold all the parts of your great kingdom together. I am going to present you with the voice of Africa. Its sound will be unequaled. And as you wished, it will spread every bit of news as quickly as the wind. It will tell you when a child has come into the world, it will accompany the dead to their kingdom, it will call you when a bride and bridegroom are joined. And you will dance when it speaks with you.'

"After the great King of Heaven had said this, he clapped his hands three times. In the wink of an eye there appeared ten servants bearing before them ten drums, carved of fine wood and with splendid animal hides stretched across them, each more beautiful than the last. But the greatest of the drums they set down at the feet of the earthly king.

"'That is Kalinga, the king's drum,' said the King of Heaven. 'It belongs to you now and will spread your fame everywhere.'

"Then one of the servants began to play on his drum, another joined in, and soon the next followed, each drummer in his very own way. It was a call and answer, a conflict and agreement, until all voices flowed into one another and joined together in a tremendous harmony that filled the heavens.

"'Take them all with you!' said the great King of Heaven. 'From now on, whatever happens can always be heard everywhere in the voice of the drums. Everyone will understand it, for it speaks to the heart.'

"The earthly king threw himself to the ground and thanked the great King of Heaven a thousand times for the wonderful present. Then he called his messengers together to take the drums for him and carry them home. Soon afterward they left. The spider was waiting for them at the exit from Heaven, again ready to spin its web, this time from Heaven to Earth so that the visitors could return home.

"The king and his men climbed down. When they were at the bottom, the king turned to the spider.

"'I thank you for your help,' he said. 'Now is the time for you to tell me your desire, which I will gladly fulfill.'

"'Bring me your daughter,' commanded the spider, 'and give her to me for my wife!'"

Here Nyogokuru stopped speaking for a second time to fill her mouth with tobacco smoke, which she let seep out between her lips in a yellowish-gray streamer.

Jeanne was already expecting that. Grandmother had a great fondness for breaking off just when things were getting unbearably exciting. Saphina groaned. Lionson clenched his fists grimly, and Jeanne swatted in vain at a big mosquito, which had been whining around and around her for a while and now settled itself on her foot. Jeanne slapped her hand down on it with a smack. Too late. The bloodsucker bit at that very moment. Very soon there would be a fat, light weal, and it would begin to itch terribly. Jeanne quickly smeared some spit on the bite with her fingertip. She was dying for Nyogokuru to continue the story.

But this time Grandmother let the pause drag on end-lessly, until the smallest ones finally began to fidget and someone squealed impatiently, "Go on!"

Nyogokuru cleared her throat and went on. "The king sank to his knees in horror. 'Oh, no!' he pleaded. 'You cannot ask that of me! Take what you want. I will give you one hundred of my best cows, you shall have my most beautiful piece of land, and if you want, my house and my court as well. Only please leave me my daughter!'

'You promised me!' insisted the spider, its voice raised to a powerful storm, so that the men froze in horror. 'Will you now break your word? The word of a king? You have received what you asked. Now pay your price. Go and bring your daughter right now. I will wait for you here.'

"The king didn't know what to say to that. For the spider was right. The word of a king was sacred. It might not be broken. With a heavy heart he made the long journey back to his kingdom, along with his messengers. He walked over the thousand hills, uphill and downhill, to fetch his only daughter and marry her to the hideous spider. But he dared not tell his daughter, who was following him in utter trust, what lay ahead of her, for she was very delicate, and he feared that she might die of fear on the way. It took them seven days and seven nights, and the closer they came to their journey's end, the unhappier the king became.

"'I cannot do it!' he kept lamenting to himself. 'No one should ask it of me!'

"'What's the matter, Father?' the girl would ask then.

"He didn't answer her.

"When, on the eighth day, they finally reached the foot of that hill where Heaven and Earth met, it was already evening, just like the first time. The king looked anxiously around him, but he couldn't see the monster anywhere. So he lay down to rest with his daughter, and soon both fell asleep with exhaustion.

"The next morning, however, they were awakened by an unfamiliar voice.

"'So, you really did do it,' the voice said in a friendly tone.

"The king and the girl opened their eyes. They saw before them a gigantic young man with powerful limbs and perfectly regular facial features. His night-dark skin gleamed like ebony, and his eyes were like dark jewels. His loins were wrapped in a finely tanned animal hide, his legs and arms richly ornamented with costly pearl bracelets. And he smiled as he spoke again.

"'You have brought me your daughter so that I may take her for my wife. I will lay my life and all I possess at her feet, for she is very beautiful.'

"'What are you talking about?' replied the king in confusion. 'I don't understand you.'

"'You see before you the son of the great King of Heaven,' the stranger explained to him. 'As guard of his realm I sometimes take the form of a spider. It is my task to inspect visitors who want to go up. If they are welcome, I spin my web for them. You were welcome to us, and your daughter will be also if she will marry me and follow me. She shall decide for herself.'

"The girl, who had fallen in love with the handsome young man at first sight, agreed joyfully. And the king did too. In this way the families of the great King of Heaven and the earthly king were united, and there began a blessed, peaceful time. . . . So, now you know how the drums came to Earth. You can still hear that they are a gift from Heaven. For the drum's voice spreads as far as Heaven does."

At this point Nyogokuru's words sank to their darkest tone and faded away. From that moment on the old woman's mouth remained shut like a closed book.

Jeanne sighed deeply. As always, she felt disappointed. Not over the outcome of the tale, which she couldn't have wished any better, but because it had come to an end much too quickly.

She had a burning desire to learn more. Especially about the wedding! How it was celebrated and how things went afterwards. Whether the son of the King of Heaven and the daughter of the earthly king had children and whether they were happy.

She stretched and yawned involuntarily.

Imperceptibly at first, the darkness began to mount over the hills. It had become cooler. The light in the sky was long extinguished and the orange of the sun appeared to have fallen into the fire, where it slowly died out.

All over the courtyard small groups were sitting down on the ground to eat. Blando had fallen asleep again.

When Véneranda approached with a large bowl, Nyogokuru rose stiffly from her chair.

"Good night, children," she said clearly. "It is time to eat." And with these few words she went back into her house, where she would have her meal with Aunt Pascasia in peace and quiet.

Can you forget a sensation?

For instance, the sensation of an entirely different, much stronger sun on your skin?

Or is it lost even when, for the third year now, you're once again immersed in this gray, all-obliterating soup of a cold, damp November day?

How do you feel at such a moment, far away from your own sun? Here, in a strange country, with which you've become so familiar that it has slipped its own pictures over memory like opaque rippled glass.

A day like this, which will never brighten at all, which grips you with cold fingers until the last bit of warmth oozes out of your veins, can make you forget what the sun is like.

And do you forget the taste of sweet potatoes? The way they are supposed to taste? Really!

Not far from our house is an Asian shop that has been there for a short time. You can buy almost everything the world has to offer there. Also sweet potatoes.

"No, they didn't really taste like that," you tell me, after we've eaten them for the first time. "A little bit like that, yes, but still very different."

You like them better these days.

"But how did they taste?" I ask you. "Can you describe it to me exactly, so that I can taste it too?"

You say that I'm your twin. Your name is mine in French.

So I walk back with you and, with you, immerse myself in the days you experienced far away from us, before our time.

We are now eating from a pot.

And reaching for the childhood days of your life as if for sweet potatoes. We're looking for stories. They too are no longer just the way they once were, but still we get them near enough for us to taste them.

Jeanne d'Arc of the thousand hills, you are a fighter!

Your country in the heart of Africa: hardly bigger than a heart, measured by the size of that continent. A land where milk and honey once flowed.

And blood.

Urugo ruhirwe—blessing on this house—was written on one of the basketry plates that Jeanne's parents had received as wedding presents and that decorated the wall of the salon next to the framed family photos.

Her parents' house lay a little beyond the edge of the town of Kibungo. Still, you could reach the center of town on foot in a very short time. A center where there was everything that was important: churches, convent, hospital, and schools, small businesses, restaurants, two banks, a market field, post office, drugstore, the town hall, a community center, a small stadium for public celebrations, and finally a jail.

The image of the people in Kibungo was defined by uniforms.

The inmates of the jail, whom you met on the street when lines of them were being led to work in the outlying fields or at construction sites, wore loose, baby-pink prison uniforms. The guards patrolling at their sides, rifles on shoulders, wore respect-inspiring dark blue uniforms and black berets. The village police presented themselves as stern law enforcers with rubber truncheons, green police jackets, and matching visored caps. Soldiers from a nearby military support post turned up now and again in round helmets and spotted camouflage clothes; nuns dressed in white carried out their duties in the hospital, their faces enclosed in black, stiff nuns' coifs. Churchmen appeared during Mass in priests' robes of various colors according to their level of rank; road builders in signal-red, visible a long way off, labored as pavers of the way; bank employees looked urbane in suits, shirts, and ties. And the schoolchildren joined in prettily in the uniforms of their schools.

Girls at the state school wore simple cornflower-blue cotton dresses, the boys khaki trousers and safari shirts; the girls and boys at the private school, on the other hand, were fitted out with noticeably more elegance, but therefore less comfort: the girls with short, dark-blue pleated skirts, white blouses, and black bow ties, the boys with dark-blue trousers, white shirts, and black-and-yellow striped ties.

Women, with the exception of the Europeans living in the town, appeared only in dresses or colorful wrap-arounds. On feast days they danced through the town in traditional costumes, hair teased high into a pouf and held away from the face with a circlet of bone or raffia.

Even the street boys, who lived outdoors, were recognizable at first sight because they wore the uniform of poverty.

Jeanne encountered all these people in the company of her mother, Florence. On the way to the private grade school where Florence taught grades four to six, on the way to the post office if they had received a letter or wanted to send one, Sundays at Mass, or during one of the frequent visits to the hospital.

For Florence dragged her children there at even the tiniest sign of an illness. These measures were often completely unnecessary, of course, as Jeanne knew perfectly well.

For example, when the reason for a terrible stomachache was to be found merely in the excessive enjoyment of fresh sugarcane from the garden. Rather than admit to this harmless, self-induced cause of her ailment, however, Jeanne put up with the tiresome examinations, especially because the visit to the doctor ended, as a rule, with a small reward. After all, one needed to be comforted when one was sick.

Jeanne observed the people in Kibungo attentively, but

she never actually met any of them—unless they were friends or colleagues of her parents or children she knew from school.

Florence warned her children over and over to keep their distance from strangers. For friendly faces could conceal evil itself: wicked old women who offered poisoned food, rapists who lured little children with candy, or people who could put a spell on you for a bad sickness.

Never accept anything! Never use a strange toilet! Never stay alone with someone who didn't belong to the family! And for the girls, not even with the houseboys. You could never be sure.

The lives of Jeanne, Teya, and Jando were spent in a charmed circle within the protection of the dense cypress hedge that fenced their parents' house on all sides and securely shielded them from the outside. They weren't even allowed to go to the neighbors' unless they'd been invited there. That was simply unheard of.

But the house was large, the yard gigantic, and life was full of adventure.

Their small housing development lay quiet and secluded on a hill outside the town. It wasn't connected to the public electricity system. Jeanne's father, Ananie, had compensated for this deficiency with their own power plant: In a small shed there was a large gas-driven outboard motor, which was linked to the house with several cables and, when darkness fell, was turned on with a pull cord. It provided electricity until it was time to go to sleep and thus for light in the house, which Jeanne's parents, who were both teachers, needed for reading or correcting papers. However, only Ananie was allowed to start the motor, because no one else had the strength to pull the cord hard enough to turn the reel and get the motor running. When Ananie was away, the rest of the family had to make do with the meager light of candles, flashlights, or kerosene lamps.

One day in May, almost a year after the summer visit with Grandmother—the last, because Nyogokuru died of her serious disease shortly after Christmas—like every school morning, Eugène, the chauffeur, drove up at about six in the official car to take Ananie to his school, a private secondary school about thirteen miles away. The roads, which went through the country, were in such bad condition that you had to drive slowly. Therefore Ananie had to get up at the crack of dawn if he wanted to get there in time.

Jeanne and Jando stood companionably at the garden gate and watched the tall, thin figure hurrying down the paved walk in great strides.

The sun, just risen, still hung deep in the sky and spread a gentle glow over the shadows. When their father turned around and waved to the children, it flashed promisingly on his glasses.

Shortly afterward Ananie reached the car. He bent, pulled in his head, slipped into the passenger seat, and slammed the door behind him. The car, a five-seater with an open cargo area, roared away. It would stop on the way a few times to pick up passengers: pupils who lived in the town of Kibungo and couldn't afford accommodation in the boarding school. Or also neighbors who wanted to be taken a little way.

Very few people owned their own cars. Therefore many depended on being able to get a lift. Ananie was lucky to have the official car and chauffeur at his and the family's disposal all the time. He himself did not drive a car, just a motorcycle.

Jeanne had the feeling that her father was always a little distant. His greetings were brief, although friendly, whenever he came and went. When he was there, he was usually hidden behind a book, usually enclosed in a calm silence. When they went on walks, he was a step ahead of everyone or else towering close to the clouds, high over the heads of the children, whence he let fall on them his long-winded lectures on connections in nature.

It was only when Jeanne sat close behind him on the back-seat of his motorcycle that she could even—must, really—grab him to hold on tightly. But even then, his back was toward her.

"On your mark, get set, go!" Jeanne commanded, poking her brother boisterously in the side, and she darted off, because she wanted to be the first to reach the house.

But Jando caught up with her in a few steps. He grabbed her by the neck of her T-shirt and pulled her toward him with a jerk.

"Where did you hide my shoe this time?" he asked angrily. His eyes flashed like his father's glasses.

Giggling, Jeanne stared down at his unmatching feet.

One was shod comfortably in the sandal, while the other was forced to greet the day naked and unprotected.

"Look for it yourself! Look for it yourself!" she shouted, laughing.

Jando swiftly flung both arms around her chest and put her in a headlock. "I'll count to three!" he hissed.

"Oww, I can't breathe," she gasped and turned, but it wasn't a serious attempt to free herself, for she knew that Jando would never do anything to hurt her. The headlock was part of the game. She would tolerate it and enjoy it at the same time and, of course, never reveal the hiding place of the shoe with even the tiniest word. Sometime or other Jando would let her go and, in a rage, begin to search. This time it would take a long while for him to find the shoe! If ever. But they had time.

Because today was a special day, one of the rare days in the middle of the week when they didn't have to go to school, because there was a teachers' conference. Only Florence had to go, leaving the children behind in the care of Julienne, the housemaid.

"Dédé! Jando! Where are you? Can you look after Teya?"

As always just before she left, Florence sounded excited and breathless because she was running out of time. Before school started she went to Mass, and day after day the morning seemed to defy her plans. Often she got into such a rush that she didn't even have time for breakfast.

Jeanne knew her mother only as a calm and controlled woman, who never became loud. Around this time, however, she was irritable, and you knew that even she could be upset by something.

Now she ran to the door, already in her bright summer dress for school. She was still combing her hair. Using the point of her steel comb, she tugged impatiently at her tangled hair, trying to smooth it strand by strand, so that it didn't stand out in all directions. The movements of her thin arms appeared angry, as if she wanted to punish the hair for its unruliness.

"Now, see where Teya is!" she commanded. "And after breakfast, please go to Zingiro, I just can't take time to talk with him now. Tell him he should make a banana casserole with chicken and peas for lunch. I'm bringing Bernadette home for lunch. He should buy the meat in the market."

Jeanne rolled her eyes. She had no desire to look for Teya. She also had no desire for breakfast, for so early in the morning her stomach rebelled against everything that might find its way into it. Above all, she had no desire to go to Zingiro.

He'd only been houseboy for the family for a short time, and she didn't like him. For one thing, besides the fact that the seventeen-year-old was a beginner and often unskilled and didn't know much about his job, he had something enormously lazy about him. Apparently without drive of his own, he dragged himself through the day and always seemed sullen.

"Now, get moving, you two!" Florence commanded. "I have to leave right now."

They were spared looking for Teya, for at that very

moment she strutted out of her room completely dressed and wearing an expression of fierce determination. She was in her school uniform.

A five-year-old, Teya did not attend school regularly, or was taken by her mother as a guest only, as Jeanne had been too in earlier years. But Teya had insisted on having a school uniform. And, as usual, she'd won out.

Now Florence looked at her youngest in astonishment. "What do you think you're doing?" she asked.

Teya opened her eyes wide and directed a piercing gaze at her mother. "I want to go with you," she answered unwaveringly.

"Nonsense," Florence said. "You can't go with me. I have to go to a conference."

"Me too," asserted Teya.

Florence suppressed a smile. Then a sigh escaped her. "Now, get yourself into the house and take that uniform off again!" she ordered.

Teya did not move from the spot. "But I want to go with you!" she persisted.

Florence frowned. Her face was transformed into a danger warning. "Te-ya," she said. Nothing more. But the tone said it all.

Teya, who always had to have the last word, ignored the signal. "Why can't I go? After all, you're going too!" she whined.

Wordlessly and with full strength, her mother slapped the answer on Teya's behind.

For the first moment of horror there was complete

silence. Jeanne and Jando exchanged meaningful looks, then put their hands over their ears, because they knew what was coming now.

And immediately thereafter the usual siren wail sounded.

Teya screamed and wouldn't stop. Her round cheeks quivered as she expressed her fury in shrill tones, her small, sturdy legs rammed into the ground.

Annoyed, Florence grasped her by the shoulders and shoved her into the house. "Julienne!" she called. "Come and take care of Teya, I have no more time."

Without honoring her screaming daughter with another glance or word, she turned and ran quickly into her study, where she hastily began combing her hair again.

When Julienne rushed out of her room, Jeanne and Jando shrugged, turned away, and unhurriedly made their way toward the cookhouse, Teya's screaming still in their ears.

That would stop by itself eventually. At the latest, when Teya realized that there was nothing more to be gained by it.

Jeanne and Jando left the house through the door at the back and sauntered across the terrace into the large back courtyard.

Here there were a few additional smaller buildings:

The generator house lay between the cookhouse and a storehouse with a spare room in which the houseboy lived.

A narrow path led to the tiny outhouse, where there was a one-holer.

The back courtyard was the supply center for the family. Right next to the cookhouse, Florence had laid out a lush vegetable garden, from which everything necessary for meals could be freshly harvested as needed: Tomatoes, onions, cabbage, lettuce, carrots, string beans, spinach, and celery thrived here under the care of the houseboy and Florence's watchful eye.

Beside the terrace towered an avocado tree, which provided shade and fruit all year round.

As Jeanne and Jando crossed the courtyard, Jando bent over the low wire fence between the yard and the orchard, stretched his hand out for a *coeur de boeuf* that hung within reach, and pulled it from the branch.

"Give me some too!" Jeanne begged. She wasn't hungry, of course, but she could never resist a *coeur de boeuf.*

Obligingly Jando broke the soft, light-green fruit into two parts and offered half to Jeanne, who dug her fingers deep inside it to remove the hard, shiny seeds.

They looked like black tears, she thought as she flipped the seeds carelessly on the ground. In times gone by she had zealously collected the little things and saved them, for you could do a lot of things with them: bargain and calculate, have spitting contests, or use them for "cooking" when playing house.

Jeanne pressed her lips against the sweet flesh and sucked it out of its skin. A few of the fine fibers remained stuck on her cheeks. She tried to remove them with the tip of her tongue. Then she caught sight of Jando, who, like her, was running his tongue busily around his lips. She grinned at him.

Meanwhile they had reached the cookhouse.

Teya's screams, which had been following them without a pause, now ceased. Probably Florence had just left the house.

"Let's see what he's doing," said Jando. He meant Zingiro, whom they had often caught doing nothing.

It was the houseboys' job, early in the morning, before everyone got up, to get the fresh milk from the farmer and prepare breakfast. They had to shop and cook, fetch water, keep the kitchen in order, and make sure that the food was stored in an orderly fashion and kept away from mice. At night they were supposed to guard the house.

Housemaids took over the rest of the housework: the polishing, cleaning, washing, and the occasional care of the children.

Jando flung open the door.

Zingiro sat at the worktable in front of the window, his powerful back toward the door. He was having breakfast. The smell of fried eggs—and loud music from the cassette recorder—filled the room.

When they called his name to let him know they were there, Zingiro turned his head and looked at them under half-closed eyelids. His expression didn't change.

"Mama said to tell you that you should make banana casserole with chicken and peas," Jando said. "She's bringing her friend Bernadette home to lunch. And Teya and I would like our breakfast now. I want an egg too."

Muttering something under his breath that they couldn't

hear, Zingiro coolly turned to his breakfast again.

At her brother's side, Jeanne dared to enter the large kitchen for once. It excited her to poke around in what was forbidden territory to them. After a careful side glance at Zingiro, who was shoveling in his fried eggs and refusing to be disturbed, she headed straight for one of the high wall cupboards. Jando followed her.

Curiously Jeanne lifted a wooden board over a large bowl, looked under it, and made a disgusted face.

Sour milk.

Even the thought of it made her feel sick. She stood on tiptoes and stuck her nose into a clay pitcher, in which, as she'd hoped, she discovered *maracuja* juice. But when she tried to take the pitcher from the shelf, she almost tipped over backward. It was much too heavy for her.

"Could you pour me some?" she asked Jando.

He gave her a glassful.

While she drank it in small sips, she let her eyes travel around the room, inspecting. Her gaze stopped briefly on a large bunch of cooking bananas hanging from a hook screwed into the ceiling. Supplies for a whole week.

The kitchen hadn't been cleaned up. Besides the frying pan there were piles of pans and dirty cooking utensils.

A few sacks of dried peas, manioc flour, and rice stood around on the floor, open and not hanging up in the cupboards, as they were supposed to be, where they were safe from dirt and thieving little animals.

Empty water and cooking-oil cans were piled in one corner in a loose tower.

There was a lot of work waiting for Zingiro, and he would have to hurry if he was going to be done with cleaning up and cooking in time for Florence's return at midday. Florence would not tolerate such disorder under any circumstances.

"Besides, you're supposed to go to the market and buy meat," Jando completed his commission.

Zingiro got up heavily. Although he was already a young man, he was only a head taller than eleven-year-old Jando. Instead of height, he appeared to have grown in breadth. He shuffled to the window and turned up the music.

"*Inyenzi tuzitsembatsembe, inyenzi tuzimene Umutwe,*" the cassette recorder sang. "Cockroaches must be exterminated. Cockroaches must be beheaded. . . ."

At the sound of the familiar melody, Jeanne's hands and feet gave an involuntary twitch.

The song was very popular and was frequently picked in music class at school when children were allowed to choose what they wanted to sing. You could bellow it out at the top of your lungs, the catchy rhythm got into your arms and legs and made them clap and drum.

But for some inexplicable reason, Florence and Ananie had forbidden their children to sing this song in their presence.

"It's not a good song," her mother had explained sharply and curtly. And as she said so, she had such a forbidding expression on her face that none of them had dared to argue or even ask why. Even Teya had kept her mouth shut.

". . . We'll squash the Cockroaches' heads. The snakes are poisonous. We must cut off their heads. We've already gotten rid of the Cockroach boss . . . " now sounded deafeningly through the room.

"Bring me and Teya breakfast right now!" Jando demanded.

"Get it yourself!" Zingiro growled. "I have too much to do."

He only permitted himself this harsh tone when Florence wasn't around.

"I would like an egg," Jando repeated firmly and left the kitchen with Jeanne.

After the door had shut behind them, Jeanne breathed a sigh of relief. "Wow! Was he ever in a bad mood!"

Jando nodded darkly. "You have to keep an eye on him. Tonight, when everyone's asleep, let's sneak into the garden and see what he's doing!" he suggested.

Jeanne agreed enthusiastically. With Jando at her side, she was ready for anything.

"After prayers, get dressed again and wait until I come for you. Can you manage to stay awake that long?"

"Of course!" Jeanne assured him. "What do you think about giving him a scare? With lightning bugs!"

Jando laughed. "Yes, we'll do that!" he shouted gleefully.

Around this time of year, after the heavy rainfalls in April, greenery was bursting forth everywhere, and the fireflies flitted out in droves in the late evening and danced as tiny points of light in the darkness of the garden. You only needed to stretch out your hands to catch several of them immediately.

The children took great pleasure in transforming themselves into little nightmare visions with the help of the insects.

They pasted the fireflies to their fingernails and over their eyebrows, jumped out from behind a bush or a tree with fingers spread and making horrible loud noises, and tried to frighten each other.

But Jeanne had no fear of ghosts. She lacked the imagination for magic and superstition. Her imaginative powers belonged to mathematics, in which she could maneuver very easily, and also to the logic of natural connections, whose backgrounds she wanted to investigate.

Once she and Jando had enclosed a few fireflies in a jar, so as to be able to examine them thoroughly next morning by daylight and find out the secret of their light. They had found light green, flylike insects, with a corn-yellow rear end.

This discovery had amused Jeanne and provoked a few improper thoughts in her.

"Imagine if your behind was a lamp . . . ," she murmured, and Jando had enthusiastically picked up the thread.

And as they'd pictured all the things a person could do with a lighted behind like that and to whom it might be especially impressive to show it, they almost choked laughing. They kept doing each other one better in silliness, stopping only when neither could think of anything more.

You called me.

After you didn't appear at breakfast this morning.

You don't want to get up, you say. You don't want to go anywhere, you say.

Anyway, where is there to go? There is no future, you say. How can there be a future when, in one day, everything can suddenly be completely gone. Gone forever.

What should I answer? I can't think of any sentences. Sentences have to lead to an end.

You are just fourteen and think that there is no future for you. I have no sentences. Not at this moment. Only words, single words aimed at your ear while I hold you.

Your life. A gift. Nevertheless. Now more than ever.

I feel that.

I hold you and pull you back. Only the shortest little step this way. Only the one little step to me.

Just yesterday you seemed to me as usual. You ate and drank. You left the house and came back. You talked on the telephone and laughed as if nothing were wrong.

And apart from that?

I don't know. Reading, perhaps? Staring out the window? Were you pacing back and forth in your room? I don't know.

I missed all the signs.

For days you've been wandering sleepless all night, you say. Because of horrible pictures from your memory that assault you in your dreams.

You don't want them. You resist. You weep. You sink ever deeper while you try to survive the night. The next day. While you try to act as if nothing were wrong.

Today, finally, you called me.

You should call me. Always, whenever things get to this point again.

Jeanne took off. Past the outhouse, around the house.

Jando was supposed to catch her.

He waited a moment before he set off after her. Ten steps lead. That was the arrangement. She ran as hard as her legs would go. Today she could beat him. With only one shoe, he was clearly at a disadvantage.

Later, when she was in bed and listing her day's sins, as required, in the quiet between the Our Father and the sleep prayer, she would confess it.

Because she wasn't supposed to run. She was forbidden to undertake any exertion at all. If she stressed herself too much, she could keel over in a faint. And wake up afterwards with a weight on her chest that took her breath away.

"You had polio when you were little," Florence had

explained to her. "And so you aren't allowed to exert your-self."

Jeanne didn't go along with that. It annoyed her that her left side, strangely stiff and weak, would not go along with her movements. That she had to look on when the others were romping, and even her little sister was faster than she was.

When there was no one watching who would stop her, she fought her weakness, not ready to resign herself to it.

Jando almost caught her just before she reached the front door. He was stretching out his arm to grab her. But at the last moment, she threw herself forward and slapped her palm against the wall.

"Safe!" she gasped.

"Wait until I get my shoe back!" he growled.

Side by side they reentered the house through the salon.

This room was not meant for them. It was the biggest room in the house, a sort of reception room, which was only used when their parents had visitors.

Comfortable, black-covered wooden armchairs and a large sofa were arranged in an inviting circle. A tall glass cabinet filled with glasses and good china stood right next to the door.

From the sofa you could look through the two windows into the front yard. But the line of sight was impeded by a heavy, diamond network of iron. Everywhere, on all sides of the house, there were grills over the windows to protect the occupants against intruders. The metal front door also had a grilled window. At night, when everything was locked up, the house was like a fortress.

Florence never failed to have flowers from the garden in the salon. Today there was a lush bouquet of pale pink roses in a large glass vase on the old drum that served as a little table, spreading their scent through the room.

The multicolored, sumptuously blooming rose hedge in the front yard, for which she was often envied, was Florence's great pride. She cared for it devotedly, immediately snipping out undesired growth with the pruning shears, diligently combating insects, and providing the soil with an abundance of fertilizers and water.

As Jeanne and Jando walked out into the hall, they encountered Julienne, armed with a bucket, a brush, and a dark look.

She was a pretty, petite girl. Not yet fifteen. Her light-blue summer dress ended just above the knee and showed off her slender, straight legs. Between the toes of her small feet stretched the red straps of her rubber flip-flops. Julienne placed great value on looking pretty. Her very dark skin, immaculate despite the daily housework, shimmered like matte velvet. She had a different hairdo every day. Now she had braided her medium-length hair, with colored ribbons, into three thick braids, all sticking out on one side of her head.

Wordlessly she put down the bucket, pulled out the dripping cloth, wrung it out, and wrapped it around the brush. She turned away and began to push the brush list-lessly ahead of her, head bowed. At each of her steps, which followed the track of the washing, the soles of her flip-flops sounded like slaps on the smooth surface of the linoleum.

"Do you want to have a reading lesson later?" Jando asked.

She whirled around. When she lifted her head to look at him, her face brightened miraculously. "If I hurry, I can be finished with the work in about two hours," she answered hopefully.

Jando had been giving Julienne lessons in reading and writing for the past several weeks.

Jeanne was deeply disappointed by his suggestion. On this free morning her brother was supposed to be there for her! Only for her.

"And where is Teya?" she asked challengingly.

"She's sitting in her room, still feeling insulted," Julienne replied.

"You can't have a reading lesson today. Mama said you're supposed to watch Teya!" Jeanne declared, with a clearly threatening undertone.

"And you!" answered Julienne serenely. "You can stay near us."

"Well, then I'm going to tell Mama."

"Oh, come on, Dédé, don't be like that!" Jando interposed. "We won't take so long this time. There'll still be lots of time to play afterwards."

"I'll sew with you afterwards, too, if you want," Julienne promised.

Now the door to Teya's room opened a crack. Slowly a small arm reached through it and remained outstretched between door and frame. Like a flagpole, at whose end, instead of a banner, waved Jando's sandal.

Jando made a leap forward and snatched the shoe. At the same time, Jeanne pushed the door open.

"Owww!" Teya screamed as she stumbled out. She was still wearing her uniform.

"You're mean!" Jeanne snapped at her. "You always have to spoil the fun for me!"

"How did the shoe get into my doll's chest?" Teya hissed.

Jeanne gulped. She hadn't figured that Teya would be rooting around in the chest today.

The doll's head was only a remnant of cloth tied around a ball of paper. Buttons fastened with a few stitches formed the eyes and nose; the mouth was a small slit cut underneath and embroidered around with wool thread. Cloth scraps and cotton for stuffing for the body, arms and legs made of fabric, all sewed on. The doll was finished. You proudly carried it around on your back with you for a while. Then finally you put it down to sleep, and that was it. You only played with such a doll once. When it was just made. Afterwards it lost its charm and landed in the chest with all the other forgotten things.

Jeanne had been convinced that Jando would never in his life find the shoe under Teya's mountain of dolls. In the evening he would have had to exchange it for a ransom, for instance for one of his many comics.

"You're dumb!" she raged and shoved Teya.

Teya hauled off and shoved Jeanne. Jeanne shoved Teya.

Teya Jeanne.

Jeanne.

Teya.

They stared furiously at each other. Jeanne knew for sure that Teya wouldn't give up until the exchange of blows was even to the exact number. But this time she didn't intend to give up, no matter what.

Finally Jando intervened. When Teya was just about to haul off again, he flung his arms around her and warned Jeanne, "Stop it, Dédé! Or do you want her to start howling again?"

"Come on, Teya," he said, turning to his little sister, "we'll go over to Zingiro and get our breakfast. I told him he should fry eggs for us. And after that you can finally take off your uniform."

Teya sniffled. She sent Jeanne one last furious look before she finally let herself be led out of the house, unresisting, holding onto Jando's hand.

During the quarrel Julienne had continued with her mopping with marked indifference. Now she let the rag drop into the bucket, dried her hands on her dress, and looked at Jeanne expressionlessly.

"If you don't want any breakfast, you can help me along with the washing!" she said. "Then we'll be done with the reading faster later."

Jeanne raised her eyebrows. She couldn't follow this logic. Reading took as long as it took. It had nothing to do with the washing. She was about to open her mouth to lecture Julienne to that effect, but she held back just in time.

Julienne was in a bad mood. And she wouldn't tolerate anyone's suggesting she was dumb. She was extremely sensitive about that and could get terribly angry. Besides, at that moment, Jeanne had no idea what to do anyway. Better washing clothes than being bored.

Willingly she trotted behind Julienne out into the courtyard, to the washing area, where the housemaid had put the washing into a zinc tub as soon as she'd gotten up so it could soak.

Julienne pulled one of Jando's shirts out of the cloudy solution, held it up to the sun, looking for spots, spread it out on the washboard and began to work the material vigorously with both hands.

"Take out your underpants," she ordered Jeanne. "It's long past time for you to be washing them yourself."

More than once, she'd let it be clearly known that in her eyes Jeanne and Teya were much too spoiled.

Jeanne looked for her own laundry and fished a pair of underpants out of the water. Teya's. She let them drop immediately.

Uncertainly, waiting for further instructions, she blinked in Julienne's direction.

But Julienne had her lips pressed together and was staring over the tub at an undefined point in the distance while her arms moved back and forth automatically.

Usually she chattered cheerfully at her work, but today she belabored the laundry without saying a word and without paying any attention to Jeanne.

After a while Jeanne broke the uncomfortable silence.

"Is this the right way?" She rubbed the material of the underpants between her fingers with all her strength, trying to emulate Julienne in order to put her in a better mood.

The girl didn't answer. Suddenly she threw the T-shirt that she had just kneaded back into the wash water and supported herself on the edge of the tub. Her knuckles showed pale.

"I have to go home. This weekend. Perhaps for longer," she said. "My mother is in the hospital. Malaria."

So that was it. Julienne was in a bad mood because she had to go home. She wouldn't be getting paid while she was gone, either. She had to give a part of her very small daily wage to her large family, but she was allowed to keep the rest for herself.

And Jeanne knew that she saved relentlessly.

Because Julienne had plans. She wanted to go to the capital, to Kigali. She needed the money for the bus fare and for emergencies in case she didn't find work at first.

She had often painted her future plans for the children in the most glowing colors: In Kigali you could earn much, much more as a children's nursemaid. Her sister lived there and had told her about it. If a girl was lucky and was placed with a rich family, she might not even have to clean anymore but only take care of the children.

"And someday I'm certain to get other work. In a fabric store. Then I'll save for a sewing machine, sew the most beautiful clothes, and sell them at the market. I'm telling you, I'm going to be rich. And someday I'll have my own shop. And a rich man. And my children will go to the best schools!" she boasted.

With the last words her voice would rise, a little frown would appear between her eyebrows, and the corners of her mouth would draw into a smile. But it was not a joyous smile.

Ordinarily Jeanne listened to such speeches from the housemaid with amazement. She didn't doubt that Julienne could make her dreams come true, but it was incomprehensible to her just why anyone would want to go to Kigali.

She herself knew Kigali from visits to her Aunt Rose, who worked for the United Nations there and lived in the center of the city. Jeanne wouldn't have wanted to stay with her for more than a few days for any money. There was no place to play, you couldn't move freely, and you always had to hold someone's hand if you were going anywhere. The people acted terribly refined and the neighbor children were stuck up.

"I don't like Kigali one little bit. You aren't allowed to do anything at all there," she'd said to Julienne one time, whereupon Julienne had replied with a scornful sniff, "What do you know about it!"

Julienne came from an eleven-member farm family. Two of her sisters worked as housemaids like her, one of her brothers as a herdboy.

Julienne's family had no cattle, only land on which corn and vegetables were grown. And although four of the children no longer lived at home, the meager harvest was hardly enough to feed the rest of the family. Very much to her regret, Julienne had never been to school. There was no money for tuition, books, or uniforms.

Because Jeanne, hidden in one of the fruit trees, had once overheard a conversation between Julienne and Zingiro, she knew besides that Julienne's father was regularly drunk. And he hit his wife and children.

Jeanne had not believed her ears when she heard that. It was unimaginable that her own father would raise his hand to hit anyone. He never even punished his children that way. And never had she seen her parents quarrel with each other.

She looked over at Julienne and wondered how long it would be until the girl had gathered enough money together. But at the moment Julienne appeared to be far from thinking about her future.

"I have to go home to take care of the little ones," she said gloomily.

She spread Jando's jeans out in front of her on the wash table. With a brush and an extra portion of soap she began to scrub back and forth to remove a few grass stains. The jeans were the last piece of washing that had to be scrubbed, but the grass stains resisted stubbornly.

Finally Julienne put down the brush with a sigh. "Grab hold!" she said.

With their combined strengths they tipped the wash tub to one side so that the dirty water spilled over the edge in a torrent onto the ground. There, where it soaked in every day, the ground was slimy and grass had long ceased to grow.

Jando and Teya were just leaving the cookhouse. They ambled across the courtyard with their breakfast. Jando threw Jeanne a cheerful "See you later?" but she pointedly acted busy.

Now began the exhaustive rinsing process, for which several large water canisters were standing ready. The laundry had to be doused with fresh water and rinsed through until finally the clear water showed that no more soapsuds were left behind.

Meanwhile the sun was now slanting over the avocado tree. Some of its beams worked their way under the edge of the thick roof of leaves, sat on Jeanne's shoulders, and brought out tiny beads of sweat on her forehead.

Julienne was also groaning in the heat, which had quickly increased during the last half hour. It was just shortly after nine. The day's heat had not yet approached its height, but the washing area was only partly in the shade, and the place where the clotheslines were stretched was completely in the sun.

Julienne filled the tub with fresh water again. Suddenly she struck the stream from the canister with the palm of her hand so that a cool rain shot Jeanne in the middle of the face. Jeanne squealed. With both hands she scooped up water and happily gave Julienne a return spraying. A small water fight began.

Again, something that she would have to confess tonight. For it was also a sin to waste water.

The door to the cookhouse was thrown open. Zingiro

came out with two shopping baskets, ready to go to market. But first he made his way over to the washing area and planted himself in front of Julienne, obviously trying to put on an amiable face.

"Can you peel the bananas for me if you're finished here now?" he asked Julienne. "Otherwise I'm never going to get the cooking done before twelve."

Julienne had often helped Zingiro out of a jam, for usually the servants stuck together. But now she shook her head decidedly.

Jeanne surmised that nothing in the world would make her miss her reading lesson, for which there weren't so many opportunities. Besides, peeling cooking bananas was an especially unpleasant job. You got black, sticky spots on your hands from it.

"Please!" Zingiro said.

"No!" answered Julienne brusquely.

"Why not?" he asked, surly. "You have time enough after the laundry. And the girl can help you peel them."

"I have my work, you have yours!"

"Please, Julienne," he began to press. "If I'm not ready today, I'm going to be in a lot of trouble. Mamam-Jando has already threatened to dock my pay."

"So?" Julienne returned coldly. "Then you just have to begin earlier. You're always asking me to help. Not today!"

"I'll remember this!" he yelped and stomped away in a fury.

She sent a scornful look after him.

"Quick, you hand me the wash and the clothespins!"

she commanded Jeanne.

Jeanne's stomach growled suddenly, but more than anything she was thirsty and wanting to know what Jando and Teya were doing. "I can't do any more now. I have to have breakfast," she said, and she went into the house.

After the noonday meal she slipped from her room unnoticed. She intended to escape the ordained daily nap. She couldn't sleep in the middle of the day. There was too much light for her, and it was also too warm, and her lively spirit wasn't ready to rest.

But Florence insisted that the rest period be observed. She needed it herself, too, so that toward two o'clock she could return refreshed to her afternoon classes.

Even when Jeanne remained obediently in the house, she didn't usually sleep but chatted with Teya or, if possible, with Jando, whom she reached in his room on a homemade tin-can telephone.

But sometimes Jando wanted to read during the siesta, and Teya, who still needed the sleep, often dozed right off. On such occasions, Jeanne often left the house secretly and hid in the orchard in one of the trees whose crowns towered into the sky. Some of them had branches so close together that it wasn't particularly difficult to climb up high and conceal herself among the dense leaves.

Inhaling the garden, Jeanne would listen to the manifold voices of the bird chorus sounding from the tree crowns all around, bite blissfully into a sun-warmed fruit, and enjoy the moment of stolen freedom—torn between a prickling feeling of exaltation and the gently gnawing fear of being discovered.

She had learned to estimate the time, even without a watch.

Shortly before the others got up, she would hurry back into the house, stretch out on her bed, and pretend to wake as if she were just emerging from deepest sleep.

Today Florence, less observant than usual, had already withdrawn into her study with Bernadette soon after the meal.

And so, with no misgivings, Jeanne had dared flight from the house, straight to climbing her favorite tree, the *amapera*, which grew very close to the fencing of the back courtyard.

Now she was sitting in the sturdy fork of a branch and letting her legs dangle, her back leaning against the mighty trunk.

Her perch gave her a good view in all directions: right to the extensive lawn in front of the cypress hedge—a gigantic playground for the children and Jando's soccer field—left to the courtyard and the outbuildings.

At the moment she was looking down into the courtyard.

In the meantime Zingiro had left the cookhouse twice with a panful of dirty water and emptied it into the washing area, not mindful that the splashes dirtied the clean washing on the line.

The houseboy was obviously in a rage.

As expected, he was not done with his work in time. He

had brought in the midday meal more than a half hour late, which Florence might even have forgiven if, to crown it all, the meat had not been half raw and so had been inedible. Florence, who in her tireless battle against dangerous disease organisms placed the highest possible value on absolute care, could not let such a mistake go. Besides, guests at the table deserved the very best. An unsuccessful meal was an insult.

During the meal, in the presence of her friend and her children, Florence had withheld her displeasure. She had merely removed the meat from the pot, put it on her own plate, and wordlessly set it aside. But later she had followed Zingiro to the cookhouse, her posture and gait unmistakable heralds of the mighty anger that would soon be directed against the negligent houseboy behind closed doors.

Jeanne, who had herself already experienced how pitiless her mother could be when someone made an inexcusable mistake, tried to imagine what might have taken place in the kitchen. This time, especially, Zingiro would not have gotten off with just a warning.

Serves him right, she thought with satisfaction.

Still hungry, because she'd touched hardly any of the casserole, she reached over her head for an *ipera* and pulled it from the branch. Dust sprinkled down, and something flew into her eye and firmly embedded itself there. She instinctively pressed her fist into her eye socket. She'd meant to rub the foreign body out again, but instead she just drove it in deeper. The stabbing pain was so unbearable that she had to close her eyes and only noticed her mother and Bernadette when their voices suddenly carried up to her.

She held her breath. The *ipera* almost fell out of her hand. She didn't dare move at all now. She watched anxiously through a haze of tears as the two, deep in conversation, approached the vegetable garden and stopped there. She stared down and prayed that her mother would not look in her direction. But the women turned to the vegetable garden.

"...I did wonder. Aliette has never been absent for so long before. And when she didn't show up at the conference today, I was afraid of something like that....To Burundi, you think?" Jeanne could just hear her mother say. Her voice sounded subdued, but so sharpened with tension that Jeanne could understand every word.

The two women were standing close together. Beside the plump back of her friend, Florence's figure looked even thinner than usual. The thin stuff of Bernadette's dress stretched over her broad hips. Her dress was caught up a bit in the back and with it a brilliant red flower, which now was resplendent in the middle of the spreading roundness of her behind. Bernadette was one of the people whose backsides Jeanne and Jando had disrespectfully imagined as unique lamps.

"I don't just think it, I know it," answered Bernadette. "Aliette wrote me. I got her letter yesterday. The housemaid brought it to me before she went back to her village."

"Do you think they both really had to leave?" Florence's question sounded unusually faltering, which disturbed

Jeanne.

"Yes, they were in danger!" Bernadette asserted. "There's no doubt about that."

"What happened, exactly?"

"For a long time, Theodore has been under suspicion of being connected with the Rebels."

"But how come? What did he ever do? As far as I know, he never had anything to do with politics."

"He had relatives in Burundi. That was enough to get him on the list of suspects."

Florence was silent. Shaking her head, she bent over a tomato plant and examined the fruits, which were reddening. They would be ripe soon.

In few words, Bernadette repeated what Aliette had written her:

The militia had forced their way into Theodore's house the first time a month ago. The men had turned everything upside down but didn't find what they were looking for. Still, after that they kept showing up again. They put pressure on Aliette and even the children and harassed them. Finally Theodore had blocked their way and tried to keep them from rooting through everything all over again. But they clubbed him down and injured him so badly that he couldn't go to work.

"Believe me, once they get someone on one of their lists, they won't leave him alone anymore. Even if he hasn't done anything!" Bernadette ended her report.

"Horrible!" said Florence. "I feel really sorry for Aliette and the children. When I imagine we might have to start all over again somewhere ...! No! That's all behind us.... Do you suppose that Theodore actually..., I mean, that he and the Rebels ... you understand ...?"

Jeanne's heart was thumping in her throat. It was impossible to sit still any longer. She carefully pulled her legs up. She absolutely had to change her position. With her extreme concern at being caught listening, she'd been so tense that one of her legs had gone to sleep. A thousand needles were stabbing her back, while the pain in her eye, washed away by tears, was gradually easing.

Although she didn't understand what it was about, her fear of being discovered had meanwhile turned into another feeling. Something constricted her belly and a strange chill spread through her.

She wondered about the meaning of what she'd overheard.

She knew Theodore, but only slightly. He was the doctor at the hospital in Kibungo. He'd examined her a few times. He had always been nice to her, and she couldn't believe that he belonged to the Rebels.

She didn't know exactly who or what the Rebels were. Only that they did bad things. And that there was a war with them. There were reports on the radio about them daily. "The Rebels have occupied Umutara..., the Rebels are at Akagera..., the Rebels were beaten..., we must fight the Rebels with every means...." Now and again Jeanne absorbed bits of such reports without, however, thinking about them. They interested her too little. The war was somewhere very far away from them.

But now, unleashed by a tremor in her mother's voice, usually so firm, the sense of an approaching calamity crept up to her like a predator and crouched beside her in the tree, ready to spring.

"How can one know? But to be candid . . . yes, I think it's possible that he's on their side," Bernadette now answered Florence's question about Theodore's ties to the Rebels.

"They say that the president is ready to negotiate with them," Florence remarked. "To end the fighting. Then it could only get better. . . ."

"No! I'm afraid it will keep getting worse! Theodore isn't just an exception. They're persecuting Tutsis everywhere again. You only have to listen to the radio, and then you know how they're stirring up trouble. Sometimes that makes me really scared. Many of us have already left the country."

"Nonsense!" Florence objected energetically. "Everyone knows us. We're respected people here. After all, many Hutus are our friends. What can happen if we quietly do our work and don't mix into politics?"

The door of the cookhouse opened. Zingiro stuck his head outside and the women fell silent. The houseboy immediately pulled back.

"I don't really know what to do about him," Florence complained. "He's good for nothing at all. Do you know a good boy who's looking for work right now?"

Bernadette shook her head. Then she let go a vehement volley of words about her own, also good-for-nothing servant. With that, the theme of politics was ended.

After a small walk around the vegetable garden, the two women moved away.

Just in the nick of time, before Jeanne would inevitably have revealed herself with an attack of sneezing.

After Bernadette had gone home, Florence sat down in the garden with a pile of school papers to correct. She didn't have to go back to school again today and her presence at home ensured that the afternoon passed peacefully.

Still under the influence of what she had learned in her tree hiding place, Jeanne was unusually quiet for a long time. The calamity beast had followed her from the tree and skulked around her. She would have liked to tell Jando about it, but there was no chance because Teya always stayed within hearing.

Of course she and Jando had made up a secret language, with which they could send each other messages in code, but communication was very limited. For the language was based on mere exchange of terms—a certain word would be put in place of another and vice versa—so there would be a few bits of doubletalk whose meaning they usually forgot after a short time, with the result that sometimes they didn't even understand themselves what they were talking about. But that didn't bother them, because it was lots of fun to do it while the others looked blank and got irritated. Especially Teya—they could bring her to white-hot fury. Or Julienne, who would threaten them with Hell.

Jando tried in vain to cheer Jeanne up by hinting about their plans for that night.

"Tonight I'm going to bed really early!" he announced to her, putting special emphasis on the word *early*, or "I'd better leave my shoes on, so you can't steal them."

She didn't react at all.

And she was still depressed when, toward six, she and Teya joined her mother in the courtyard.

Florence sat on the little low wall that separated the terrace from the courtyard. In her usual fashion, she was braiding her hair for the night.

Meanwhile she was waiting for the girls for a lesson, the reading glasses on her nose, the books piled beside her. And now, finally, at the sight of the familiar scene, Jeanne's fears evaporated into nothing. She gave a deep sigh of relief.

Everything was normal.

Florence wound the end of a little braid around the tip of her finger, pulled it taut, and wound it into a little snail, which she placed next to another one on her head. Later she would look as though she had big buttons on her head.

She waited until both girls had taken their places on her right and left.

"We'll start with French today," she said. "Dédé, do you remember what the parts of the body are called?"

Jeanne heaved a deep sigh. Of course she remembered everything very well. She knew the terms exactly, but she couldn't say them. Even in their own language there were some words for which her tongue just wouldn't obey her mind. She saw the syllables before her, formed them in her head, but when they left her mouth, something else came out.

When she had to speak French, she found it especially hard going with the R. Almost always, when she spoke fast, she made an L out of it.

La poitrine—the chest, *l'oreille*—the ear. She could never get them across her lips correctly. And the more she tried, the worse it got.

"Mama," she pleaded with a side glance at Teya, who was already burning to be able to show her up, "can't we start with arithmetic?"

In arithmetic she beat Teya every time. The times tables, forward and backward and crisscross, that was child's play for her.

"We'll do arithmetic later," Florence ruled quietly. "Come on, try it, Dédé."

Reluctantly Jeanne obeyed. She began with the simplest. *Le nez*—the nose, *la bouche*—the mouth.

This lesson outdoors before supper had taken place for as long as she could remember.

Florence was ambitious. She demanded as much of her children as they could accomplish, far in advance of everything that they were supposed to learn later. "If you want to become something, then you must be better than good in school," she said. And she gave each of the girls the opportunity to prove herself. Usually that was very fair. Jeanne got her mathematics problems with which she could excel, while Teya, on the contrary, could shine with her flawless French.

"*Il y a une maison sur la colline*," Teya read in her crystal clear voice.

The French picture book lay open on their mother's knees and the house on the hill, under which this sentence stood, was drawn large on one side. A beautiful house. Similar to theirs.

"Good!" Florence praised her. "And now you, Dédé."

Stumbling a few times over *il y a* and *sur la*, Jeanne wrenched the words out of herself.

"You see, you can do it," said Florence.

Finally, after the arithmetic, began the part of the lesson that Jeanne enjoyed most. Her mother read something to them. Poetry, stories, and songs out of a thick, illustrated reading book in which she first paged around a little with them so they could look at the pictures and choose something. Florence recited poems and songs several times. This way Jeanne quickly learned them by heart. Afterwards she pretended she could already read the text herself.

Florence opened the book.

Teya climbed onto her lap. Jeanne leaned her head against her mother's shoulder.

Although the sun had already gone down, the stones held its warmth. As they were paging through the book, a mild breeze blew up.

"That one!" Teya stretched out her index finger and pressed down a page that showed a woman with an elaborate hairdo. A baby lay in her arms.

Jeanne tried to turn the page. Babies didn't interest her. She would rather hear again the story of the clever rabbit who saved itself with honey wine during a famine. But

Teya's finger was holding the page down.

"I want to hear this!" she repeated.

"Very well," Florence agreed. "It's a poem for Women's Day. I think it's very beautiful."

With a gentle voice she began to recite:

Urimwiza Mama
koko urimwiza
s'ukubeshya,
singutaka
bimwe bisanswe.
Abantu benshi
Bakabya cyane.
Amezi cyenda
Munda yawe,
untwite ugenda
wigengesereye . . .

You are beautiful, Mama,
you are truly beautiful,
I do not lie,
I do not exaggerate
like other people.
Nine months in your belly,
you carried me.
You walked slowly,
so that nothing happened to me.
After my birth,
before I could see,

you kept me warm.
No cold touched me.
My nourishment was your milk.
For my sake you dropped your work,
I gave you my tears,
and you said: Cry peacefully, my child.
My very dearest Mother,
I will describe you
as you really deserve.

"Read it again," Jeanne pleaded as soon as Florence had ended.

"Do you want to learn it?" their mother asked.

The girls nodded; for once they were united.

And Florence began over again.

"*Urimwiza Mama*
koko urimwiza. . . ."

As she went through it, she left long pauses so that her daughters could say the words after her several times.

"Is that true?" Teya asked. "Was I in your belly for nine months?"

"Nine months and three days."

"And I?" Jeanne asked.

"A little less than nine months."

"I was inside longer!"

"I was here earlier!"

Florence laughed. "Is there anything you two don't fight over?"

"How could I have fit into your belly?" Teya wanted to

know. She measured Florence's narrow waist with an appraising look.

"At first you were smaller than a fingernail. And as you slowly grew bigger, my belly grew along with you."

"And how did I get in there—and get out?"

"The dear Lord made you," declared Florence, and she snapped the book shut. She stood up, a sure sign that she didn't intend to be questioned any further.

Jando, who already did his schoolwork independently and was now and then questioned by his father, appeared in the courtyard. "I'm hungry," he cried.

"Then tell Zingiro that you want to eat in half an hour," Florence told him. "I'll wait until your father comes home. And you two," she added, turning to the girls, "go to Julienne now. She should wash you."

When her mother came into Jeanne's room that night as usual to say good night to her, Jeanne was lying there in bed with her eyes shut, apparently clad only in her night-gown.

"I'm terribly tired," she murmured when Florence came in. She wanted to keep her mother from staying with her any longer than necessary, possibly even hearing her say her prayers.

Nevertheless, Florence came close, bent down, and gave her a kiss. "Sleep well," she said.

Shortly after she'd left the room, Jeanne leapt out of bed, produced out from under it long trousers, a pullover, and her shoes, and dressed herself completely.

Then she climbed back into bed, pulled the covers up to her neck, stuck her feet over the end of the bed so the shoes couldn't dirty the sheet, and waited for her brother's arrival.

The time passed without anything happening.

She said the Our Father. Then in the silence she began to list her day's sins.

. . . Hiding Jando's shoe, running too fast, pushing Teya. . . .

The list wouldn't come to an end. However, before she got to her greatest sin, which was still being planned and couldn't be confessed in advance, she fell into a deep sleep. And free of this last sin, she slept without interruption until the next morning.

You walked through our door.

One afternoon. At the beginning of April.

The first moment is very decisive. For when one says yes, it is a promise.

It's sometimes difficult to honor it in the long period afterward, when doubts arise and when one wonders whether that first moment might have been deceptive.

The moment comes only once, it lasts only seconds, and immediately after it begins the period of getting to know each other, which never comes to an end. Because one never reaches that goal.

It has been this way with each one of you children. There has been that first moment. And no going back afterward.

The first moment with you? Yes, I still remember it very clearly.

How you came through the door. Small and quiet. You struck me as being almost bodiless. You were in the company of your aunt. What an aunt!

Elegant and flawless. The face chiseled, well-proportioned. I could not believe that it would ever have a *wrinkle.*

If I hadn't been expecting you, I would probably have overlooked you next to her. Encountering the two of you outside somewhere, not as awaited visitors, I would have seen you as a tall, beautiful woman with a child. But here, in our small, narrow hallway, I encountered you as a serious child with a tall, beautiful woman.

You were just ten. Hair cut short like a boy's. Yes, one could have taken you for a boy.

And yet not. At a second glance, that view was no longer possible: the broad hips and the round bottom, those spoke against it.

And also your smile. It flitted across your face so very unexpectedly. A wonderful girl's smile.

Which your aunt beside you caused to disappear.

His steps springy, Ananie was walking up the narrow clay path that led along the crown of the hill above the terraced fields in gentle curves to the next valley. Around the bend, a view over a gigantic distance would open: A line of hill ranges grouped there around a deep depression, and over it—with good visibility like today's—could be clearly seen the tip of the big volcano, whose crater was often concealed in a cloud cover or in a layer of steam.

The children squeezed past their father, ran ahead, and immediately disappeared around the bend.

They reached the valley almost at the same time, and Jeanne immediately began looking for a hiding place.

It had rained this morning. Now a gentle, steady wind

was driving low, light-rimmed shreds of cloud before it like flying carpets over to the hills lying opposite. Behind the clouds the sky was unusually clear, its light sharpening the contours so that the landscape looked as if it were drawn.

Catching sight of her father, Jeanne slipped quickly behind a banana palm, pressing her arms to her sides and her legs together as if she could scrunch herself together to the circumference of a stick to make herself nearly invisible. Motionless, she awaited her father's arrival.

Her fingers clenched the fine, lilac-colored material of her ruffled dress and pulled it straight so that no corner of it could be seen and give away her hiding place. Only a few yards away from her, a yellow ruffle of Teya's Sunday dress was sticking out between the cypress branches. Jando had bounded up the slope and been swallowed farther up by a dense wall of banana leaves. Jeanne would have liked to hiss a warning to Teya, but it was already too late for that, for Ananie was going to appear around the bend any moment.

He would probably stop abruptly and shade his gold-rimmed glasses with his hand against the glaring burst of light. Then he would look for the children, his head turning in all directions, only to resume his walk after a while, shaking his head as if he had to resign himself, like it or not, to the children's having vanished into thin air.

As on many Sundays, Ananie had set out right after morning Mass on a walk over the hills with Jeanne, Teya, and Jando. Florence had stayed home; she wanted to take care of the meal preparation today herself. The menu included plenty of meat with various delicious sauces, for she was expecting guests. Bernadette and her whole family were coming.

Jeanne tried to drive the thought of it away.

Having visitors meant that you had to behave perfectly, especially to the children of the visitors. And sometimes you couldn't stand the children at all.

Besides, Sunday was a day that Jeanne would have preferred to do away with. This went for most Sundays, anyway.

For it was the day of ruffled clothes. Certainly she liked the one from Aunt Rose in Kigali that she was wearing today, but ruffled dresses were without exception prisons, in which you couldn't move. They attracted dirt as if by magic, and the fluttering ruffles caught on every possible obstacle, hooked themselves, and constantly threatened to rip off.

Besides, Sunday was the day to go to church.

It was tolerable at the beginning of the long Mass, during the singing, and Jeanne also liked to hear some of the stories. Especially the one about Zachaeus, a man who was too short, whom she had taken to her heart, although no one else could stand him. One day, when Jesus came into a city where he was awaited by a large crowd of people, the tiny Zachaeus climbed to the tip of a fig tree because otherwise he couldn't have seen anything.

Jeanne understood that only too well.

When important visitors were expected at home: Grandmother, Aunt Rose, or Aunt Pascasia, Jeanne also often climbed into a tall tree, which allowed her to look out

80

into the street all the way to the next little wood.

"I saw them first!" she would announce later, full of pride.

Whenever she heard the story of Zachaeus, it seemed to her as if she sat with him high up in the tree and waited for Jesus. He later even went to Zachaeus's house! Florence would certainly also have cooked something especially good for Jesus if he ever came to her house the way Zachaeus had.

After the Sunday story it was hard for Jeanne to sit quietly and patiently on the bench next to Jando and her parents until the drumming and little bells with the closing hymn ended the service. For she had to watch as Teya, dressed in angel white, moved among the holy dancers up front in the chancel. How she bent and waved her arms animatedly in the rhythm of the drumming. This sight twisted Jeanne's heart and gave her so much trouble that she could no longer listen devoutly.

She would have adored to have been among the dancers. She'd gone to try out once, but she hadn't managed to bring her movements into harmony with the others. Ashamed, she'd given up and afterwards told her parents, "I don't want to do that."

No, Sunday was not her day.

But after all, it was also the day that Ananie usually stayed home and took time for his children. Like now. And even if they didn't always start on the extended walks with him with enthusiasm, they often had quite a lot of fun.

Especially with the hiding game that went with them.

Holding her breath and conscious that the two others were doing exactly the same, Jeanne waited for her father's appearance. The equality of their activity and their feelings at this moment made them into a conspiratorial unit, which made Jeanne happy.

Finally Ananie turned the corner, whistling.

He had rolled up the sleeves of his white shirt and opened the collar. As expected, he stopped, looked surprised, raised his arm, shaded his eyes, and looked all around him. Shaking his head he went on his way, and Jeanne, nearest to the path, heard his steps as he passed her. She waited until he had gotten far enough away from her before she softly came out of her hiding place and waved to the two others.

That was the sign.

With a piercing three-throated scream they plunged after their father, saw him jump, clap both hands over his ears, and turn on his heel. His eyes widened in fear behind the circular gates of his glasses.

"Fooled you! Fooled you!" Teya squealed, while she hopped around his legs like a startled rabbit. Until finally he stooped, smiling broadly, caught her up, and clamped her under his arm, a bundle of yellow ruffles, with which he walked determinedly on. Only when she began to whimper and kick her legs vigorously did he, still laughing, set her down on the ground again.

There was no point in continuing the hiding game any longer. You could see far out over the valley here, and it was impossible to disappear from anyone else's view unnoticed.

Ananie walked with long strides. Teya, his index finger grasped in her little fist, tripped eagerly along beside him, and behind him Jeanne and Jando tried to follow his large footprints in the softened ground. Jeanne hopped from one depression to the next.

Suddenly their father stopped and pointed to the row of jagged volcano peaks. They stuck up behind the hills like teeth in the mouth of a gigantic dragon.

A long time ago it must have been a fire-spitting dragon.

"*Bon, mes enfants*," said Ananie, "today we can see them all very clearly." He had the habit of weaving French words and phrases into his sentences. "*Voilà le Karisimbi, voilà le Muhabura, et enfin le Sabyinyo!*"

Sabyinyo means "big, protruding tooth." The volcano so named thrust itself out of the line of the others and towered over them all.

As Jeanne let her eyes sweep over the valley, she narrowed them to small slits so that the play of its colors swam together and the landscape lay before her like a daubed picture: the dark green of the cypress groves, the strong, light green of the banana palms, the matte silver shine of the eucalyptus woods, the yellow-brown clay areas, and coal-black flecks all over where burned-out bushes were. In between, scattered like little occasional dabs of color, roofs of houses. Red tile roofs, well roofs of silver and colorfully painted tin.

"It's raining over there," Teya observed.

Jeanne opened her eyes again.

In front of the hills on the other side of the valley hung a dark rain cloud, a great tub out of which water would pour straight down onto the earth, while everything else beyond the edges of the cloud would remain dry.

This property of the clouds, of raining only within limits, often challenged the children to play a game with it. When the wind drove such a cloud toward them, they ran ahead of it, keeping an eye on it, just fast enough not to get caught and to reach a shelter or the house still dry, while only a few yards behind them the drops were already pelting the earth and bursting in fat bubbles.

Playing tag with the rain, they called it.

"How does the water get into the clouds?" Teya asked.

"*Alors*, the air consists partly of water," Ananie explained.

Teya looked surprised.

"*Mais oui*," her father continued, "there are water particles in the air." He loved to explain celestial phenomena, no matter what kind, whether asked or not. "The heat makes them evaporate into the air, where they crowd close together, like steam, which you already know. *Donc*, when it cools off later, the steam turns to water. But water is too heavy to remain in the air and falls to the earth as rain. It's that simple. *D'ailleurs*, on especially hot days so much power builds up in the sky that there are powerful thunder-and-lightning storms."

The children nodded. They had already experienced many evenings of thunderstorms. After some very hot days they longed for the torrential rains right afterwards.

At Grandmother's, in the country, they often secretly sneaked out the back door, despite all the warnings of danger from thunder and lightning, to dance in the rain and jump in the puddles and collect the small, round clumps of ice that struck the earth in between drops.

You just mustn't get caught doing it by old Muzehe, who regarded all such weather as bad spirits and would banish the hail forever by throwing peas between the grains as a charm.

Earlier, when Jeanne had still been small, the tremendous thunderstorms at night had frightened her. But now she had come to enjoy watching the display before her window. After every flash that chased across the sky and illuminated her room like daylight, she counted the seconds till the next thunder clap. When she grew tired, she pulled the sheet over her head and tried to sleep in spite of the noise. She felt completely safe in the house.

"*Alors*, it's getting to be time to go back," said Ananie with a glance at his wristwatch. "*Allons enfants!*"

The words were scarcely out of his mouth when the children ran off ahead of him to reach the bend long before he did, where they would once again repeat their hiding game before finally going home.

Something was holding down her eyelashes. Her eyelids would hardly open.

The sounds of Jando's calls and Teya's laughter had startled Jeanne out of an unusually deep, dreamless sleep. She fought her way to the surface, lifted her head, and blinked over toward the closed curtains at the window. Their confusing pattern seemed to have begun to move.

She felt a stabbing pain in her neck. Something was pressing full force against the inside of her forehead. Her head flopped back onto the pillow, and her eyes closed again.

Her time sense told her that the morning was already well advanced, but that wasn't so bad, for it was vacation, so they could sleep as long as they wanted.

As far as she could remember, this was the first summer vacation she had spent at home.

Jeanne missed the free life at Grandmother's farm, getting together with other children of the family, and she especially missed Nyogokuru and her stories.

It was boring at home. Every day was just like every other day.

Since Florence took the time during vacation to do the cooking herself and to get the household thoroughly in order, there was a lot of work in the house and garden every day, and the children had to help her with it. Especially Jeanne, who, as oldest daughter, was supposed to be gradually introduced to women's work.

"You'll need to know all this later on," she heard over and over again.

Her mother's frequent admonishments provoked Jeanne's indignation. Why didn't they also apply to her brother? He was even older. Just because he was a boy? Or to Teya? She was also a girl, after all. Just because she was younger? Jeanne couldn't understand such unfairness, no matter how hard she tried.

After the midday nap, the children sometimes played with the boys and girls from the neighborhood, taking turns in their own yard or in the neighbor's.

The only interruptions in this daily sameness were excursions to relatives or small motorcycle trips with their father. More than ever, Jeanne longed for the end of the vacation. After that she would be in second grade, while Teya still wasn't a proper school child.

She turned restlessly from one side to the other, but she felt strangely powerless, too weak to get up. Hovering between waking and slumber, she gradually fell back to sleep until Teya's enthusiastic squealing from outside pierced her ears and finally pulled her into the day.

She rolled to the edge of the bed and sat up. When she stretched out her legs, the floor withdrew in front of her. She put her feet down, swaying. It gradually dawned on her that something was wrong with her. Maybe she was sick. But she didn't want to be sick. That would mean passing the rest of the day in endless waiting in the hospital.

She swallowed. Her mouth was very dry. With difficulty she battled the feelings of nausea and weakness. She had to get herself together and act as if everything were the same as usual so that her mother wouldn't notice anything.

A cold shiver went down her back when she pulled her nightie over her head. She would have liked to put on long trousers and a warm pullover. But if she appeared in sweater and trousers in the heat, Florence would most certainly be suspicious. Still shivering, Jeanne reached for her skirt and blouse.

Firmly determined not to be sick, she stumped through the hall to the dining room. Her head was buzzing, and the longer she was on her feet, the worse it got. She was trembling. She had to have a cup of hot tea. Now.

The door of the dining room was open. Luckily Florence was nowhere to be seen. She was probably already outside in the cookhouse.

In the coolest corner of the room there was a shelf with food, where you could serve yourself anytime you were hungry or thirsty. There was always a thermos jug of runny, warm gruel and another with strong black tea, all ready to drink with grated ginger and powdered milk. When the jugs were empty, you had them refilled in the kitchen. Also, there was buttermilk in a tightly closed tin can and juice in bottles. In a small cupboard beside the shelf there were white bread, butter, honey, and various pastries.

Usually Jeanne took some millet gruel or tea. Today she wanted tea.

After she got the thermos jug, mug, and spoon, along with the sugar box, off the shelf and put everything in front of her, she let herself drop onto a chair, exhausted, and stared numbly for a while at the pictures on the wall opposite: Mother and Child, a large bird on a branch, a hilly landscape—all composed from raffia, leaves, and the bark of banana trees.

"I won!"

Teya's ear-shattering cry of jubilation startled her once more.

Jeanne poured herself a mug of tea. She filled the mug to the very top with the dark-brown brew, which had probably stood on the shelf for a few hours and would be sure to taste rather bitter. She took three spoonfuls of sugar, just in case. When she lifted the mug to her lips, the flowers on the plastic tablecloth began to dance before her eyes. She blinked and sipped at the tea. It wasn't too hot anymore. Slurping, she took the first swallow, felt the bittersweet drink run warming and enlivening through her throat down into her stomach, and drank without stopping until the mug was empty. Afterward she actually felt better. Anyway, strong enough to go outside and get a breath of fresh air.

As she left the house, she saw her father reading in the shade of the fruit trees. He didn't look up.

She slowly approached Jando and Teya, who were playing with marbles on the dusty side path. Teya was kneeling in front of the small marble pit dug out of the earth and had her back to Jeanne. She flicked the fat, gleaming glass spheres with her thumb and accurately sent one after the other into the hole.

"I win again!" she exulted, made a grab for the marbles, let them disappear, clicking, into her marble pouch, and jumped to her feet. Only then did she notice Jeanne, who had walked up behind her.

Teya's laughter died. Her eyes narrowed to slits, she placed her hands on her hips.

"*Udahari igiti nticyimugwira!*" she said sternly, punching the air with her index finger as she spoke. "If you are

89

not there and a tree falls down, it won't fall on you."

Nyogokuru had always used this saying when anyone came too late to a meal and there was nothing left over for him.

Teya, who knew most of Grandmother's sayings by heart, used them when she wanted to win respect and to lend special weight to her wishes. Very much to the amusement of the grown-ups, whereas Jeanne and Jando just found her mannerism silly and were sometimes irritated by it.

Jeanne was irked now, too, but she felt much too tired to quarrel. Besides, she'd had no intention of playing with them, for she was still dizzy.

"You're dumb, don't bother me!" she said scornfully. And before Teya could say anything back, Jeanne turned and meandered over to the lawn, where she withdrew into the circle of shade of the big tree, whose densely leaved, deeply weeping branches spread way over the center of the lawn and a part of the cypress hedge. It stayed dark and cool under there, like a cave.

"Wait, Dédé!" Jando called. "You can so play with us!"

"Don't want to," she retorted.

She crept under the tree, searched out a soft place in the grass, stretched out full length, and crossed her arms under her head. Her face was turned straight up, but out of the corner of her eye she observed Jando and Teya, who had meanwhile ended their game and were sitting down at the edge of the path to count their marbles.

Without Teya's cries the yard suddenly sounded very

much quieter. There were only the muffled sounds from the cookhouse, mixed with a few birds' voices and the buzzing of the insects that whizzed among the grasses and the meadow flowers beyond the shade. The rising and falling of the sounds rolled over Jeanne in gentle waves and made her sleepy.

Shortly before her eyes closed, she squinted thirstily at a *maracuja* that was climbing up the cypress hedge. Too high for her to be able to reach it lying down.

Jeanne ran the tip of her tongue over her hot lips and let her head drop to one side. A few minutes later she was asleep.

Although there was rice with mixed vegetables, Jeanne's favorite dish, her plate sat untouched before her when all the others were long emptied. No one noticed, for Jeanne was usually the last one finished. She often was just beginning to eat when the others had long left the table. But though usually during the meals they ate together her mouth was in motion with tireless chatter instead of chewing, today it had been completely still.

No complaints about unpopular neighboring children, no disparaging remarks about Zingiro. She had neither chewed nor chattered, and except for Jando, who once sent a searching side glance her way, none of those present seemed to have taken any notice of it. Florence and Ananie had been animatedly discussing what to do with the washing area, in whose mire the mosquitoes had multiplied so much that you could hardly defend yourself against them.

Florence, whom the mosquito plague caused great concern, finally suggested having the muddy surface paved, and Ananie promised to get it taken care of during vacation, even if it wouldn't be easy at the moment to find someone to do the job.

While Jeanne sat there and moved the rice grains from one side of the plate to the other with the tip of her spoon, her parents' lively exchange of words whirred around her drooping head like the swarm of mosquitoes that was the subject of the talk. It was an enormous effort to sit up straight at the table, for the painful throbbing behind her forehead was almost unbearable. But she bravely suppressed the desire to lay her head on the table.

When Zingiro appeared to clear away, Ananie, Teya, and Jando stood up.

Florence, however, remained seated opposite Jeanne and now looked directly at her. "Now, go ahead and eat, Dédé!" she demanded a little impatiently.

Jeanne scooped a few grains of rice up in her spoon and put them in her mouth. But they remained stuck between tongue and gums like boulders that jammed her jaws. In vain she tried to swallow a few times. A lump blocked her throat.

Florence inspected her keenly. "Déde, what's the matter with you? Why aren't you eating anything? Is something hurting you?"

"No," Jeanne mumbled into her plate. "I'm just not hungry."

Florence leaned across the table, reached under

Jeanne's chin, and forced her to lift her head.

"*Mon dieu*! You have a fever!"

She leaped up, hurried to Jeanne's side, laid the back of her hand on her forehead, then on her neck, on her own for comparison, then back on Jeanne's forehead again.

"You have a very high fever, even. *Mon dieu*, why didn't you say anything? Open your mouth wide!"

She took the spoon, pressed Jeanne's tongue down with the back of the handle, and stared in horror down her throat as if she were looking into the gates of Hell.

Again the lump rose in Jeanne's throat. Her eyes filled with tears, and her throat scratched as if she'd swallowed a brush.

"It's not so bad," she croaked after her mother had finally withdrawn the spoon.

But a swaying and the helpless shivering that now suddenly took possession of her belied her. It was as if Florence's touch, of that cool hand on her hot skin, had given Jeanne's body a push under which her composure, maintained until then with difficulty, had fallen in on itself. Like a pile of burned out pieces of wood.

"Oh, it's bad all right! You're glowing like fire. We're going to the hospital, right now, as fast as possible."

"Mama . . . ," Jeanne tried to resist. But the shivering had already reached her mouth and her teeth were clacking together so the rest of the words, distorted beyond recognition, only chattered out of her.

Without replying, Florence lifted her up, carried her to her bed, wrapped the blanket around her shuddering body, called excitedly and breathlessly out the window to Zingiro and Ananie, and left the room. In a short time she came with a glass of water and a little package of powder, whose contents she mixed with the water to make a cloudy, milky fluid.

Jeanne saw it through a haze, much too weak now to fight against any further measures. Her resistance was wiped away by the ceaseless shivering. She knew the fever medicine would taste horrible, but nevertheless obediently raised her head off the pillow, supported by Florence, swallowed the bitter drink, and let herself fall back. Florence stroked her cheek and left again.

Afterward Jeanne lay there with eyes closed. She followed the sounds in the house, which seemed strangely removed from her, suddenly weird and disconnected. After a while the fever medicine began to work. The stabbing in her head vanished, gradually the trembling of her limbs eased, everything inched away from her, and finally a light slumber superficially covered her consciousness.

You on horseback.

Again and again there are pictures like this one; they imprint themselves on me as if my brain had photographed them.

Your swayback gives the illusion of a secure, proud seat. As if the back of a horse were where you belonged. Or is it the way you carry your head? With your neck ramrod straight.

And yet, until now you've never encountered any horses, at least not close up. You've been with us for just two weeks and there are no horses where you came from.

When you keep your face completely still, as it is at this moment, it could belong to a statue: your round, very high forehead, the broad cheekbones, the strong chin under the full-lipped curve of the mouth—they could have been modeled by a sculptor.

I ask myself what is going on inside you while you trot through the forest with the others, at the head of a line of riders, followed by the ponies carrying the children who must still be led by their parents. A little later I lose sight of you because I'm needed at the back to hold the reins for one of our little ones.

We're spending the weekend with some other families at the pony farm and are on an excursion into the mountains. The farmer is up front, driving the tractor and the covered wagon for the lazy and the tired.

It's a typical April day. Cool and changeable. Now and again the sun breaks through from behind a cloud, drenching the wet leaves with its light and making the damp forest and earth smells rise to my nose. I'd like to take my jacket off. The trail rises steeply. We make a stop every half hour. A pause for catching breath. The ponies change their riders.

I'm standing at a respectful distance beside the pony that I've led behind me the entire time. Then someone runs back to me from the front. I have to come. You're in the wagon and you aren't feeling well.

I quickly hand over the reins and run past the line of ponies grazing and pulling down leaves to get to you. I climb into the wagon and find you crouching on a side bench. Small. A little crooked. A completely different girl now from the one on the horse a few minutes ago.

I sit beside you. "What's the matter?"

"My belly...," you make me understand with your hands.

The wagon begins moving again, shaking and rattling. The chugging of the tractor is deafening. Our youngest is sitting beside the farmer, beaming.

I put my arm around you and you lean your head against my shoulder. The naturalness with which you do

that touches me and amazes me. As does the unembar-
rassed way you say "Mama" to me. From the very begin-
ning.

When we're back, I take you to your room.

"Get into bed. I'll get some tea from the kitchen for
you," I say. You nod. You know the words "tea" and "bed."

When I come back after a while with a mug of hot pep-
permint tea, you're already lying in the wide double bed
that you're sharing with one of your sisters. You look over
toward me, silent and serious, with the covers drawn up to
your neck. When I put the tea down on your nightstand
and sit on the edge of the bed, you suddenly reach under
the covers and pull out your underpants, on which there is
a bright spot of blood.

I'm dismayed.

I haven't figured on this. You're only just ten.

What shall I do?

We don't either of us have enough words yet to be able
to speak about it. We've been relying on gestures.

Perhaps it's just as well. I put my arm around you once
more and nevertheless begin to talk to you. At least the
sound of my voice should give you security. And I can't
very well do without words entirely.

I forget what I said.

After I've provided everything necessary and gone out
so that you can sleep, I remain standing by the door for a
moment. Leaning my back against the wall, I examine my
own feelings.

The unquestioning trust that you show me makes me

happy.

Only very much later, when I knew you better, did the thought suddenly occur to me that perhaps it was pure desperation that drove you so unreservedly into our arms.

Jeanne didn't feel sick at all anymore. Her lively spirits were reawakened.

Warmly wrapped in long trousers, pullover, and wool poncho, she sat with her mother's arm around her on the backseat of the car, which, driven by Eugène, was approaching the hospital much too quickly, to her mind. Her opposition to what lay ahead of her grew with every yard that the car rolled pitilessly on: endless waiting, embarrassing examinations, and perhaps even a shot. Don't let there be any shots!

In the past she had sometimes succeeded in putting off the moment when they tried to shift her into a white hospital gown, that horrible thing, or even completely avoiding it by insisting shortly beforehand that she was hungry or had to go to the bathroom so badly that she couldn't wait any longer. As a rule, both declarations would lead to Florence's leaving the hospital with her to go visit a friend who lived in the center of Kibungo. For it was out of the question that one of her children should eat anything in the hospital or possibly have to use the toilet. Hospitals were breeding grounds for dangerous bacteria and viruses. While there you sat up straight on a chair until your name was called and you didn't touch anything.

Over the course of time, however, she had used up the various tricks to lure Florence out of the hospital, so that now all her pleas and requests had no effect and always received the same imperturbable answer: "Yes, after we're finished here. You'll just have to hold out till then."

At the thought of a shot, Jeanne began to sweat. She would have liked to loosen herself from her mother's embrace and slide a couple of feet away from her. But it wasn't only Florence's arm that fastened her, but also her wool poncho, a brilliantly striped, crocheted piece of clothing, apparently produced for an armless person, for it had no armholes. It stretched so tightly across the shoulders that you were forced to keep your arms at your sides, as if you had to stand at attention.

Jeanne had never seen anything like it anywhere, but the strange item had been in the family's possession for a long time. It was called into service now and again, like today, when one of the children was sick and needed to be kept especially warm. Jeanne suspected that it had come with other oddities in a package from Europe at some time.

Her eyes fixed on Eugène's neck over the light-yellow collar of his shirt, she thought feverishly of another excuse she could use to prevent the dreaded shot this time. She noticed that with each motion of the chauffeur's head, the fissured neck skin made a network of dark folds. The sight reminded her of a muddy spot beginning to dry out again after a heavy rainfall.

She lifted her shoulders and carefully turned herself out of her mother's arm. If necessary she would swear that the fever medicine had helped long ago, so any further treatment was foolish, a pure waste of time.

"*Saligoma*! Lazy bunch!" Eugène grumbled crossly. They were just passing the water place, where a few street boys had clumped together in a knot. As he steered the car past them closer than necessary, some of them gestured angrily and made faces behind him.

The stack of the power plant now appeared beyond the windshield, next to it the points of the small iron pylons, from which thick wires spread out over the town. Lots of little Eiffel Towers, as Jeanne termed them, since once she'd seen a picture postcard with a gigantic tower of that name from Aunt Colette from Paris.

The power plant was right beside the hospital. So was the jail, a somber, two-story brick building with barred windows whose entrance was secured against the outer world by high walls and armed guards.

Even though Jeanne did not find the power station and its tangle of big iron structures, masts, and wires the least bit creepy, she thought that, all in all, they were approaching an especially uncomfortable part of Kibungo.

Of course, considered from the outside, with its low, flat-roofed, pastel-colored buildings—pale yellow for Admitting, pink for the lab section, and sky-blue for Pediatrics, the hospital looked nice and friendly as opposed to the threatening aspects of its neighbors, but Jeanne, who knew the inside well enough, knew better. The outer appearance lied. It was merely a deception, which the people inside played along with by wearing smocks in the colors of their departments.

Eugène drove through the big gate into the inner court-yard of the hospital.

With a sigh Jeanne took in the long line of people in front of the Admitting Department. There were already many patients standing and sitting on the roofed terrace: mainly mothers with their babies and children, a few young people, a few old people, and between them a soldier with a bandaged arm. Again it would probably take until evening before they could be on the way home.

When Eugène came to a stop, Florence looked at her watch.

"Come back toward six and wait here for us," she requested.

Eugène turned around to her and nodded politely. "I'll get the car washed in the meantime," he answered.

Florence got out, but Jeanne was glued to her seat.

"It won't be so bad!" Eugène whispered encouragingly to her.

But at that moment she was insensitive to reassurances. For her head was filled with thoughts of white-robed figures in front of whom she must undress, who took hold of her with strangers' hands and poked her all over, peered into her eyes, mouth, and ears, and perhaps stuck her with a needle.

She intended to remain where she was. To drive with Eugène to the car-washing place, where eager street boys splashed about while they waited hungrily for jobs. She'd been there several times with her father when he'd had his motorcycle washed, and she enjoyed it very much.

Afterward she'd gone with him to the big snack bar on the main street and sat in one of the open, straw-thatched pavilions and had refreshments, a beer for Ananie and lemonade for Jeanne. While she drank she looked over toward the neighboring field and turned her eyes to the sky to watch the kites made of old paper bags hanging motionless in the air or pitching about with fluttering tails, depending on the strength of the wind. She'd seen some of them crash, get caught in the branches of a tree, or get tangled in the string of another one. In such cases, the owners went into action. Not uncommonly, when it was a matter of enemy kites, a minor riot also ensued.

"Come on, Dédé, you have to get out!" Florence demanded gently.

"I'm not sick at all anymore. Really, I'm not!" Jeanne made a last attempt to deflect the unavoidable.

"Now come along!" Florence pulled her out of the car. "We're going to find out what's wrong with you right now."

What Jeanne had been afraid of all along did in fact happen. She was sitting in the laboratory, waiting for the shot. As usual her mother had temporarily left her with Mathilde, a laboratory doctor friend, while she went to buy the injection.

Florence always bought them herself because she didn't want to take the slightest risk that a perhaps dirty hospital hypodermic might be used on one of her children.

On the one hand, Jeanne was glad to gain a little delay this way; on the other, a tormenting unease was growing in her from minute to minute and making her legs fidget.

Trying to distract her, Mathilde chatted with her a little, but when she only got monosyllabic replies, she finally gave up and returned to her microscope and the test tubes filled with blood that were in a stand awaiting her examination.

Jeanne stared at the open window, before which Philippe, a second laboratory doctor, was taking blood from a line of patients in high-speed processing.

Down the row, hands with pastel-colored slips were reached through the window. Philippe took the slip from them; there followed a brief stick in the fingertip, which let out a fat drop of blood; the drop was transferred with the aid of a pipette to a tiny glass slide and laid aside, together with the slip, arranged according to color. Later it would be looked at under the microscope and Mathilde's watchful eye. A smooth process, which was completed in great silence. Hardly a word was exchanged.

The thought popped into Jeanne's head of how at school she sometimes had to come forward with outstretched hands to take the ruler blows of a teacher. Often she had no idea why she deserved them.

Near the lab section some patients were keeping within the shade of a great leafy tree. They gave the impression of complete stillness, withdrawn into themselves and sunk in silence. As if there were something paralyzing emanating from this place that stopped all speech.

Then, suddenly, the silence was broken.

Jeanne wasn't the only one surprised. The heads of

those waiting at the window whipped around and stared at a few small figures heading for the laboratory in a great hurry and chattering to each other in high-pitched voices.

They all looked the same: garbed from head to toe in white, in caps, masks, and long gowns.

They approached the window purposefully, stopped, and stuck their heads curiously through the opening. The skin around their noses and eyes was also very light. Like milk, tinted with just a few drops of tea. They didn't stop chattering, and when they discovered Jeanne on her stool, they waved to her vivaciously.

From the slanting shape of their eyes, which gleamed dark in their pale faces, Jeanne knew that they were Chinese. She even knew where they lived. Florence had showed her the Chinese House, which was very close to the Post Office.

The group left the window and now crowded through the door into the laboratory.

To Jeanne's dismay, the Chinese seem to have focused on her. She was already encircled by them.

Her ears rang with an incomprehensible singsong of words, always with a little laughter lurking in its swoops. Nose tips sank sniffing over her, a hand with sharp fingers pulled at her poncho, another raised its zigzag hem as if there were a secret buried under it. And someone took her hands.

Help, thought Jeanne, they're going to undress me! She cast a despairing glance toward Mathilde, but she sat calmly at her microscope, observing the goings-on but not moving and clearly very amused. A broad grin spread across her face.

Jeanne was upset. This was anything but funny.

The Chinese also acted highly amused. True, their laughing mouths were hidden behind the white rectangles, but their eyelids, so scrunched up with laughter that their eyes disappeared completely under them, betrayed them. Besides, you could hear them giggling.

That was too much.

Jeanne burst into tears.

Immediately the giggling stopped and yielded to sympathetic clucking. Someone stroked her shoulder, lovingly patted her cheek. The others drew away from her and took a step backward.

Mathilde, now attentive, left her microscope and came over.

"What's the matter, Dédé? Nothing's going to happen to you!"

Jeanne sobbed.

"What are you afraid of?"

Rebuffing her, Jeanne drew up her knees and buried her face in them.

Mathilde shook her head in puzzlement. Then she explained something to the Chinese in a strange language, and they, still smiling, took off their masks, one after the other. One of them answered in the same language, pulled again at Jeanne's poncho, beaming broadly as she did so.

"See, Dédé, no need to get upset. They were admiring

105

your beautiful wrap. Wherever did you get it?" Mathilde asked.

Jeanne clenched her teeth. She wasn't going to answer, for she was ashamed. She wanted the Chinese to go away right now and leave her alone. And Mathilde too!

When the door opened and her mother finally came back, she was so relieved to be released from her undignified situation that she rushed over to her. Even though Florence's arrival meant that the moment of the shot was shifted to unavoidable imminence.

On the journey home, consoled by a big bag of candies that Eugène had picked up at a kiosk on the way, Jeanne found her tongue again. Bubbling over, she told of her adventure with the Chinese, ranted in the same breath about Mathilde's deserting her in her hour of need, and plagued Florence with questions. She wanted to know how far it was to China. What were the Chinese doing in Kibungo anyhow, and how they could see out of such narrow eyes. Her cheeks burned with excitement. Perhaps also from the fever, which was climbing again. Still, she felt much better than this morning. As soon as they got home, she jumped out of the car and ran to the front door, ignoring her mother's warning look.

In the hall, however, she was met with loud, unfamiliar voices coming from the dining room. Surprised, she stopped in her tracks. There had been no one invited for a visit. She turned around to Florence.

At the same time, but from opposite directions, both

parents appeared in the hall. Ananie, followed by his sister-in-law Joséphine and her small daughter Marthe. In addition, the faces of Ernestine and Charles, Joséphine's almost grown-up children, appeared beside Jando in the opening of the dining room door. Teya squeezed past them and ran to her mother.

If Florence was nonplussed by the unexpected visit, she didn't let it show. She greeted Joséphine with a hearty embrace and lifted Marthe, who was hanging onto her mother's dress, to give her a loving kiss.

"There you are," said Ananie. "What's wrong with Dédé?"

"As I feared . . . ," answered Florence. "Pierre says it's malaria. We really, finally, have to do something about the mosquitoes!"

Jeanne, only now learning what was wrong with her, was alarmed. Teya had had malaria some time ago, and it had been a long time before the recurring attacks of fever were entirely gone.

"Get back to bed quickly, Dédé," Florence told her. "You have to rest."

But Jeanne didn't want to go to bed.

"I want something to drink first!" she parried, and she slipped into the dining room. The others followed her, and Florence, with Marthe still on her arm, poured her a mug of tea.

During the general confusion of greetings, Jeanne and her illness slipped into oblivion. Jeanne used the opportunity to withdraw quietly into a corner. If she were lucky, it could be a while before anyone noticed her again. She gnawed at the edge of the mug and pricked up her ears.

Florence complained bitterly about the long wait at the hospital and then reported on her talk with the pediatrician.

"*Dieu soit loué*, it isn't a bad form of malaria," she finished. "We can treat her at home. By the time school begins, Dédé is sure to be over it."

"*Très bien*," Ananie replied. "I promise you, I'll take care of the washing area tomorrow. And afterwards I'll hang up mosquito netting. I should have thought of that before." He fell silent. Then he added casually, "Ernestine and Charles would like to spend a few days with us. *D'accord?*"

"Alphonse is abroad right now. He's coming home at the end of the week," Joséphine explained. She looked uncertainly around the circle. And when she spoke again after a pause, she lowered her voice to a whisper: "I don't know what it means . . . a little while ago the militia appeared all over in our area . . . raiding our houses. They haven't been to us yet, but the whole thing scares me. . . . Marthe and I will take a taxi back to Zaza afterwards. We can stay with my mother until Alphonse is home again. I think Ernestine and Charles are safer with you for the time being. Just for a few days!"

Florence set Marthe down with a bump.

"When did you arrive?" she asked abruptly. "Certainly you all must be hungry." Energetically she pushed Jando toward the door. "Run to the kitchen, tell Zingiro that we have guests this evening! Teya, you can go with him. See whether supper is ready. And you, Dédé, go to bed at once, didn't you hear me? I'll come to you later."

Grabbing Teya's hand, Jando left without any back talk.

"Don't you want to stay here overnight?" Florence suggested to Joséphine. "You and Marthe could take the bus early in the morning."

Joséphine didn't answer right away.

"Let's eat quietly first and you can think it over," said Florence. She cast a threatening side glance at Jeanne. "Well, Déde, what are you waiting for?"

Resentfully, and with a bad feeling in her stomach, Jeanne slipped off to her room, where she sat for a long time on the edge of her bed, brooding, before she finally crept under the covers. She couldn't go to sleep for a long time.

And hours later she was tossing from side to side, trapped in a confused fever dream.

Small figures with slanting eyes raged around her. Faces concealed behind surgical masks. With extra long hypodermics, whose needles were aimed at Jeanne like rifle barrels, they kept moving toward her, ever closer. She wanted to scream, but she had no voice.

Instead of white uniforms, the Chinese were wearing green-and-brown-spotted camouflage.

The bell rang for the first time.

As always, the children stood still for a moment, waiting patiently for the second ring.

That sounded a little later.

Jeanne bent and picked up the ball, which had fallen to the ground in the game of dodgeball a few seconds before, luckily without hitting her. Too bad they had to stop now. The end of recess robbed her team of victory.

The groups of playing children slowly dissolved and everyone streamed toward the entrances, heading for the section of the brick building holding their own classrooms. Here they formed long lines. Two by two, arranged by size, boys and girls separated.

Teya approached from another corner of the playground, where she'd spent recess jumping rope. She attached herself to Jeanne and Prudence, who had already taken places next to each other. Because Teya still wasn't a regular pupil, usually it was leniently overlooked when she broke into the two-by-two order. In her case, people chose to wink at minor offenses, although she had to adapt at times too.

Maîtresse Béatrice, Jeanne's teacher, was waiting for the children in the small yard at the entrance to the classroom. During recess she'd been working around the flower bed, which, at the beginning of October, was in especially brilliant, luxuriant bloom. After the hot, dry days, the rainy season had begun and now it was again providing the plants with regular nourishment and moisture.

Maîtresse Béatrice's eyes glided over the flowers once more with satisfaction, before she turned her remarkably cooler look to the double row of short-shorn, curly heads to her right and let it travel deliberately over them, appearing to be counting them silently. When she came to the end of the line, she frowned. Perhaps someone was still missing.

Jeanne stole a look around and discovered Adolphe,

her seat mate, who was stumbling across the schoolyard more than thirty feet away. She hoped the poor thing wouldn't have to kneel behind the row of seats for a whole hour in punishment again. She liked Adolphe. He was a nice boy, always friendly to her, although she was a girl.

The bell rang a third time.

Maîtresse Béatrice walked forward. With each step she took, the slit in her long, narrow dress opened a little and revealed her sturdy calves. She had gathered her straightened, shoulder-length hair at the neck with a large barrette.

The children walked into the classroom and silently took their places. Boys and girls—now mixed for the sake of general peace—stood right and left beside the double-seated school benches, which were placed in three long rows, one behind the other, in front of the board and the teacher's desk. There were more than thirty children here.

The room was without decoration except for a crucifix and a picture of the Virgin Mary just beside the door. And a few already yellowing signs with word examples, in which letters were emphasized in color.

It was the last hour of the afternoon. Prayers and greetings lay behind them. So now they waited for the command to take their seats.

Art was on the schedule for today. Jeanne hoped to be allowed to go out into the schoolyard now with her drawing pad and pencil. In good weather they usually drew outside.

Trees, houses, the church beside the school, plants. In short, everything there was to see in the immediate neighborhood.

Just as Maîtresse Béatrice was opening her mouth to give the command in a strong voice, Adolphe, out of breath, arrived at his place.

Jeanne didn't dare look at him. Virtuously facing forward, she waited tensely for the teacher's reaction.

Adolphe frequently failed to hear the bell, and since each repeat offense was more severely punished than the last, this time there was the possibility that Maîtresse Béatrice would send someone out to get the stick.

But, unexpectedly, the teacher kept her mouth shut and merely reprimanded the culprit with a crushing look. For so long that he dropped his head. When she opened her lips again, her words hissed sharply through the broad space between her prominent incisors.

"Sssit down!" she commanded.

By some miracle, Adolphe had escaped his punishment.

The children slipped into their seats and placed their hands in front of them on the slanting writing surface. Teya was sitting on Jeanne's left, separated from her only by the narrow passage between the rows. She opened her eyes wide and stared rudely over at Adolphe, whose chin was still down on his chest.

"So, children, now listen carefully! We are not going outside, at least not right away. That is to say, I must ask you something!" The teacher paused for a moment before she went on: "You all certainly know what tribe you belong to.

I must enter your tribal affiliations in my list."

She took up an already prepared piece of paper and a pencil. "Now, then! All Hutus stand up!"

Most of the children in the class got to their feet and stood beside their desks. However, some hesitated at first. Like Prudence, whose parents belonged to different tribes, Jeanne knew. Her mother was a Tutsi, her father a Hutu. But the father's tribe was what counted.

Only seven children, among them Jeanne, were still sitting in their places.

Teya was standing too. When Jeanne noticed it, she reached over to her.

"Teya! What are you doing? Sit down! That's not right at all!"

Teya hit out with her elbow. "It is so right!" she hissed. "You just weren't paying attention."

Jeanne glared angrily at her. "Stop it! I know very well that we aren't Hutus!"

"I'm going to tell Mama!" Teya threatened.

"Go ahead! Then you'll see where you get with that." Jeanne turned away. She was fed up. Teya was really impossible.

The teacher, who'd been making big checkmarks on the list of names, looked up in annoyance. "Teya! Dédé! What's going on? You can both stay sitting. I know anyway."

Teya remained stubbornly standing beside her desk.

"Very well, Teya." Maîtresse Béatrice sighed and went on making notes. "So, you can all sit down again. And all Tutsis stand up!"

Jeanne could have remained sitting after the teacher's remark. Nevertheless she stood up. Just to show Teya.

Teya pinched her on the arm. "Why are you standing up?" she demanded furiously.

Jeanne didn't even look at her. She looked over Adolphe's head to watch Hélène, who got up with exaggerated slowness. Raissa, on the other hand, made no motion to follow. She wept.

Jeanne could understand her. It was a terrible feeling to be one of the few whose tribe was looked down on. Of course that mostly wasn't very noticeable in school, but at occasions like this, it became all too public that you didn't quite belong.

Five of them were standing.

Besides Raissa, only Jean d'Amour hadn't moved. But he looked anything but distressed. Jeanne couldn't help feeling that he was even secretly grinning.

He was the best in the class, a clever, self-confident boy, who usually went his own way and did what he wanted. No one knew whether he was Hutu, Tutsi, or Twa.

Twa! That was the lowest you could think of.

Some who gossiped about Jean d'Amour maintained that he was a Twa. But there was not one bit of evidence for that.

The teacher surveyed him wordlessly and then made her last checkmark on the list.

"Sit down, children!" she said. "We will not go outside, there isn't enough time for it now. Take out your coloring books and your crayons. Today you may draw our flag."

Like all the others, Jeanne obediently took out her coloring things and laid out the red, yellow, green, and black crayons. Drawing the flag out of her head was simple.

She saw it around 7:30, every morning, after all, when all the boys and girls had to gather at a central spot in the schoolyard in front of the tall flagpole, where the national flag was raised. And while it was being raised, they sang the national anthem:

Rwanda rwacu Rwanda Gihugu cyambyaye.
Ndakuratana ishyaka n'ubutwari
Iyo nibutse ibigwi wagze kugeza ubu
Nshimira abarwanashyaka
Bavandimwe, b'uru Rwanda rwacu twese
Nimuhaguruke
Turubumbatire mu mahoro, mu kuli
Mu bwigenge no mu mu bwumvikane

Our Rwanda,
Rwanda, the land of my birth,
I show you my reverence by service
and diligence.
When I think of your achievements,
I thank the party that formed this country....

While Jeanne drew the outline of the flag and divided the rectangle into three fields, the third verse of the anthem went through her head:

All the children of Rwanda should rejoice,
Our democracy is great, we have all striven for it,
Little Tutsi, little Twa, and little Hutu
And all Rwandans who are for it.
We have all won the independence. . . .

She wondered why it was so important to always label the people in Rwanda by their tribes. That was never the subject at their house. Just the opposite. Jeanne felt clearly that talk that led in this direction was quite consciously avoided. And she herself could not have even said what the differences were. Without lists, she would never have known who belonged to what tribe.

Shortly before the end of the vacation, on a Saturday morning, two town officials had come to their house to register the inhabitants of the house. Not for the first time. Ananie had to show his papers. Also his passport, in which "Tutsi" was entered.

Jeanne and Teya were thoroughly interrogated by one of the men. About their age and about their abilities. They had to place their right arms over their heads and grasp the left ear with their hand. Then the right ear with the left hand. That had seemed quite silly to them, and they had been giggling the entire time. Their parents had laughed too, but it was somewhat strained, and Jeanne had had the feeling that the salon was loaded with tension.

Meanwhile she'd filled in the red and the yellow fields of her flag with color without any bare spaces and now picked up her green crayon.

"Done! Look, Dédé!" trilled from her left. Teya held up her drawing, unmistakably proud that she had once again run rings around her big sister.

Scribbles, Jeanne thought, unimpressed, but she bit back the remark. With the greatest possible care she filled in the green area of her flag. Finally she put a fat black R in the middle of the yellow rectangle.

"There!" she said, regarding her work.

At that very moment the bell rang for the last time that day. Maîtresse Béatrice slowly stood up behind her desk.

Now came putting things away, standing, the closing prayer.

School was out.

After Jeanne had said good-bye to her friends, she and Teya ran to their mother's classroom to pick her up.

Teya, bursting with impatience to bombard Florence with the news of the day, was hopping around the teacher's desk.

"Mama!" she started right in, paying no attention to the fact that Florence was still busy with her class book entries. "I have to tell you something. . . ."

But Florence stopped her. "Later, Teya!" she said firmly. "I have to finish here first. You can wait outside for me until then."

On the way home soon afterward, as they were crossing the church plaza, Teya could be restrained no longer. "Mama, Maîtresse Béatrice asked us what tribes we belonged to. Dédé stood up with the wrong one and wouldn't listen to me at all! Although the teacher said—"

"That's not right at all!" Jeanne interrupted her angrily. "We aren't Hutus, Mama, are we?"

They were passing the military grounds, where soldiers were patrolling.

"What did you do at recess?" Florence asked more loudly than necessary. "I missed you this afternoon."

"We are so Hutus!" Teya protested.

"We are not!" Jeanne snapped back.

Florence winced. "Why didn't you come to me? I'd packed cookies and *maracujas,* too. Weren't you hungry, then?"

"We are so!" bellowed Teya.

Florence nudged Jeanne in the side and gave her a conspiratorial wink, whereupon Jeanne swallowed her vigorous contradiction. It wasn't easy for her, but her mother's making her an ally placated her.

She winked too and said, "I wasn't hungry today. We played dodgeball during recess and would have won by a hair. But then the bell rang and so we had to stop before it was over."

"Mama!" Teya impatiently demanded the floor again. "Now, what are we, then, Hutu or Tutsi?"

"Be still, Teya! We don't need to talk about it here on the street," Florence replied. "I'll explain it to you at home."

She headed for a kiosk, stopped there, and to Jeanne's boundless astonishment bought a bag of fruit candies.

"Maybe you're hungry now. Your cookies were eaten up in the meantime," she said, holding the opened bag out to the girls.

Teya's hand shot out and began to root around in the bag. She liked the red ones best.

And for the rest of the way her big mouth, stuffed full of candy, was silent for once.

The telephone rings.

It's for you, as it so often is.

"Jeanne Jansen.—Hello, Manuela," I hear you say.

You have a special telephone voice. It seems to me some-how rasping. As if you wanted to mold your words soft or pare them down so that they would pass through the tele-phone. But perhaps it's only that way when I'm within hear-ing distance?

"Yes, I know that film is going to be on.—Yes, thanks.—Yes, I'm going to be allowed to watch it. Even on a Monday night, for once."

Now I know what it's about. They're showing the story of Joan of Arc on television. A monumental two-part series.

Of course you're allowed to see it. For a long time now we've been hot on the trail of the maid whose name you've borne since your baptism.

Last summer in Bordeaux—on an excursion from the Atlantic coast—we photographed you beneath her statue. Your hair, braided into hundreds of long, thin braids gathered to the top of your head, a helmet. Just like the Maid's metal one. As is the way you are looking forward.

I think about Jeanne d'Arc of Orleans, who has always impressed me very much but who also remains a puzzle to me. Think about her unshakable courage.

Now I hear you laugh.

"Yes, so now you know! I won't be at school on Tuesday. Because tomorrow night I'm going to be burned at the stake."

You say. And laugh. Blithely unthinking. Child of our time.

But yet, not you!

I get goose bumps.

PART II

turi abatabazi
we are mourners

As long as the dead are not buried,
we will keep watch by the fire for them

Jeanne started up out of sleep when someone touched her lightly on the shoulder.

She opened her eyes, only to close them again immediately. Her room was filled with the dim light of early morning, and her time sense also told her that it was still much too early to get up.

There had been a tremendous thunderstorm raging around the house during the night. She'd been torn from her dreams several times by the crashes of thunder, and not until long after midnight had the storm gradually died away. Now, after quiet had finally returned, she only wanted to sleep on. After all, it was Easter vacation.

She curled up and pulled the covers up to her nose.

"Dédé, you have to get up, something terrible has happened!" Jando's voice was whispering close to her ear.

Not ready to listen to it yet, she made a few reluctant noises and snatched the covers a bit higher.

"Dédé, listen to me, now! You have to get up!"

The voice still sounded restrained, but it held an undertone of urgency that alarmed Jeanne. She snapped open her eyes and lifted her head.

"What's the matter?" she murmured confusedly.

Jando was sitting on the edge of her bed. His features blurred and his expression was not readable. But his posture showed how downhearted he was.

"The president's been in a plane crash. Over his palace. And the president of Burundi, too. The plane was shot down. Both dead. Along with all the others on the plane. It was on the news last night, after you'd already gone to bed."

Slowly Jeanne sat up. She refused to believe Jando's words. Surely he was just trying to scare her. So many dead . . . that just couldn't be!

"You're lying. Cut it out!" she said bluntly. "You're just trying to fool me again!"

He gasped. "Shut up!" he ordered. "I wouldn't think of fooling about a thing like that! If you'll just get out of bed, you'll find out for yourself."

Abruptly he stood up and left, slamming the door behind him.

She looked after him uneasily. It wasn't like him at all to get so angry at her right away, but maybe that was part of the game. In the stillness he left behind him, she thought she could hear the irregular beating of her heart. In any case, she intended to find out for certain whether the news was true.

She swung out of bed, reached for the dress she had laid out the night before, wriggled herself through the neck and arm holes, and pushed the window curtain aside slightly. A dark-gray cloud cover hung over the yard, and the black crowns of the trees were dripping wet. The sky, completely covered over, revealed no time of day. And there was no sign of the usual life to be seen anywhere outside. Day probably hadn't really quite arrived yet. Jeanne yawned. Weariness and perplexity made her tremble. She longed to go back to bed.

But she pulled herself together. She opened the dresser drawer and took out a sweater. The light blue with the gray sleeves, which she especially liked. She pulled it on over her dress and stuck her feet into her shoes.

She hesitated a moment longer before she opened the door and listened into the dark hallway.

Nothing.

Nothing but silence.

She didn't understand it and wondered if Jando had only wanted to annoy her.

She resolutely crossed the hall and in a few steps reached her father's study, where the radio was. If she turned it on, maybe she could hear news, and then she'd know what was going on. The door to the study was ajar. She pressed against it with the palm of her hand, opened it and turned left to the small corner table between the book-shelves on which the radio stood, felt blindly for the knob, and turned it on.

At once, strange music poured out at her, dark, woeful sounds, much too ponderous to permit a rhythm to be heard. They dragged through the room and enveloped her as gloomily as the morning. It was a strange mixture of instrumental voices, a lamentation without words. She had never heard anything like it before. The long drawn-out sounds penetrated not only her ears but into her pores, cutting like a pain that took hold of Jeanne and made her shudder. Sounds to which she did not intend to surrender herself!

Hastily she turned the dial. But always, whenever she finally found another station among static and noise, she again fell into the trap of the music that dominated the radio. It was creepy.

"What are you doing there, Dédé? Stop playing with the knob!"

Her father's quiet command from the opposite corner of the room took her completely by surprise. But it hardly frightened her. Just the opposite! She was relieved. The familiar voice broke the bad spell and rescued her before anxiety overpowered her.

She had been so focused on the radio when she came in that she hadn't noticed Ananie's presence at all. He was sitting at his desk in front of the window, half turned in her direction. He hadn't turned on a light, but that part of the room was weakly illuminated by the gray gleam of the morning. Papers lay spread out in front of him on the desk. His arm was resting on the back of the chair.

She obediently turned off the radio and took a few steps toward her father. And in spite of the shyness she always felt in his presence, she asked him straight out, "What's going on, Papa? Why are they playing such funny music on the radio?"

He spread his thumb and forefinger and pushed his

glasses up, a gesture Jeanne had seen him make many hundreds of times. He looked thoughtfully through the round lenses into her face. As if he was going to prepare one of his exhaustive explanations.

But finally he answered only: "Our president is dead. It may be that soon the war will come here to us. Go to the others, Dédé! You should drink something."

"Papa . . . ," she began hesitantly, still so many questions on her tongue. She wanted to know what it would mean if the war came to them.

But he had already turned away from her and bent over his papers again.

Quietly she left the room.

The dining room was empty. Frighteningly empty, as the whole house seemed to her to be. Where was Florence? And where was Teya? Where was Jando? Not only were they nowhere to be seen, their voices were missing!

Nothing was as usual. And suddenly she was seized by the terrible certainty that nothing would ever be the same again, either. Her heart stopped, as if it could no longer keep on beating with this thought. An aching recollection of the music, which had stuck in her ears, brought tears to her eyes.

With nervous fingers she grasped the thermos and poured some hot, runny *amasaka* gruel into a mug, sweetened the drink, and acting on an impulse, went to the back door, which someone had left open.

She stopped on the doorstep. Rubbed at her eyes and let them search the yard. Meanwhile the sky had brightened a little. The cloud cover had lifted a bit, was even gradually breaking up. There was mist rising from the lawn. Jeanne heard the droplets falling from the trees. And the songs of a few birds. Then there were voices from the storehouse.

She pricked up her ears.

It was Ndayambaje, the houseboy Florence had hired after letting Zingiro go, and Julienne.

What were the two of them doing there at this hour?

The window of the storehouse was wide open. Carrying the mug of hot gruel in front of her, Jeanne carefully approached the voices. The mug warmed her fingers. She sat down on the little wall not far from the window, blew on her drink, sipped at its surface, and tried hard to follow the excited discussion inside.

It wasn't easy, for Julienne and Ndayambaje were trying to speak as softly as possible. Obviously it was about the news.

"Do you think it was the Rebels who shot down the plane?"

"Who else?"

"I don't know . . . after all, they're all dead . . . Burundi's president, two ministers of Burundi, Rwandan politicians who wanted to make peace with the Rebels . . . and the French crew. . . ."

"And if it wasn't the Rebels . . . ?"

"What does it mean: no one's allowed to leave their houses?"

"How long is this supposed to last? How's it supposed

to work if you can't even go get water!"

"And what if there's war? What are we doing here? I want to go home! Now! To my family!"

After this outburst from Julienne it was quiet again for a moment. Soon, however, there came the voice of a radio announcer.

". . . since the early morning hours the government troops have regained control. No one is permitted to leave their houses for the time being. . . ."

While she listened to the words, Jeanne drank the warm amasaka gruel a swallow at a time.

Then again they broke the news of the death of the president, named all those who had died with him, and said that the peace conference was wrecked. After a short pause the funeral music began again.

Jeanne pressed her hands over her ears. She was on her way to run into the storehouse to turn off the servants' radio when she was deflected by Jando, who had just left the cookhouse and came over to her.

With a fleeting glance at the window he sat down beside Jeanne on the wall.

"Now you know it," he said seriously.

He sat there sunk in his own thoughts. Bent under an invisible weight that pressed his narrow shoulders forward. His long, bony fingers hung limply over his knees, his dark eyes roamed about, resting nowhere, and the silence that followed his words was such that it prohibited Jeanne from saying a word, although she could hardly bear it.

To see Jando that way was worse than everything else

she had learned this morning. Although she had experienced similar moments with him, which all had passed again, it made her terribly afraid.

Now and then he would be overcome with dark forebodings. A few times, when something happened that he interpreted as a bad omen, he had sunk into a deep depression that Jeanne could not find an explanation for.

Not long ago, only a few days after her birthday, when she turned eight, they had been sitting together on the little wall, just like today. It had already grown dark, time to go to bed, but they were still washing their feet in a big tub and having a fight in the tub by stamping on each other's feet. As they did so they stared at the only dark corner of the house, a place that wasn't reached by the outside lighting.

If anything bad ever came, it would make its way from that corner, they were agreed on that. And as so often, they considered what they could do if it ever were to happen.

"You should call loud for help. And run away as fast as possible. I would fight," Jando had said.

"Pooh!" she'd answered. "I'm not anywhere near as afraid as you!" Convinced unshakably that she was the bravest of all.

At Grandmother's, when they had to cross an especially dark and indistinct part of the farm to get to the bedrooms, the others always hurried as if the devil were after them. Even Jando. She, on the other hand, took her time. Loudly whistling or singing, she outplayed the fear, and when, last of all, she finally came walking up with exaggerated slowness, she felt very superior.

No. She would under no circumstances run away and leave Jando to his fate.

"I would stay. Protect you!" she had insisted. "I'd put myself in the middle between you and the wall. Then I would be caught first and you could flee."

That the best was always in the middle and would be taken first was another piece of old wisdom that came from Nyogokuru. If you were strong enough you could stand in the middle to protect the others.

Usually Jando strongly protested against Jeanne's claim of being stronger than he. But he wasn't really listening to her anymore.

"Pst! There was something!" he'd whispered.

"Nonsense. You're imagining it."

"Yes! I just heard it. There were steps. Come on, let's check it out!"

They had sneaked over to the fence and seen a strange figure, who darted along the path and soon vanished into the darkness. A street boy, probably. With a remarkable hat on his head with a long feather sticking out of it.

Jando had looked at her with a petrified expression and then declared tonelessly: "That was a sign. I feel very certain, Dédé, something terrible is going to happen!"

There were cooked bananas with peas for lunch. Jeanne hardly touched it, and the others also pushed the food around on their plates. They all acted numb. From time to time something started moving outside. There were shadows that hurried past in their front yard, excited calls, snatched away with the clatter of quick feet. At such moments the tension in the small group around the table heightened, but not one of them said a word.

Once someone hammered a hard object against the front door, which Ananie had carefully locked before the meal. The thumping blow, repeated several times, thrust into Jeanne's bones as if they had been struck, while she clutched involuntarily at the edge of the table and saw that Teya was doing the same.

The children's eyes clung fearfully to their parents and asked silently what they were going to do. The parents did nothing, however, but carried on with unnatural calm. Florence, her lips pressed firmly together, as if she had to keep back any utterance behind them. Ananie with a still, absent gaze, expressing nothing.

Jeanne would have liked to scream, "What's it all mean? What's going to happen to us now?"

For that something was going to happen was now beyond any doubt. They just didn't know what, and this uncertainty tormented them.

When Florence picked up the plates despite their still being half full and began to clear the table, Jeanne knew with final clarity that all the rules that used to be in force were valid no longer.

"You go take your naps now!" Ananie commanded. "We're going over to the neighbors for a little while."

Going to the neighbors during the noonday? That had never happened before. But they were supposed to sleep all the same? Who could think of sleeping now?

The children looked blankly at their father and made no move at all to stand up.

"Dédé! Jando! Teya!" Florence admonished with strained patience. "Go sleep!"

One after the other they stood up. First Jando, who, as always, set a good example, followed by Teya, and finally Jeanne. Wordlessly they withdrew and disappeared into their own rooms. To Jeanne it felt as though she had been placed under arrest and someone had issued them a ban on speaking.

She took off her clothes, climbed into bed, and wrapped the blanket around her. So tightly that she could hardly move. The very next minute she was asleep. She fled into a sleep so unfathomably deep that hours later she had to be awakened to this day a second time.

Again it was Jando.

He was shaking her shoulders as hard as he could. She started up, already intending to fly angrily at him, but his face, very close to her own, kept her from it.

He was trying to saying something but could only get out a strangled sound. His fingers, still holding onto her shoulders, were digging into her skin.

"What's the matter?" she asked in distress.

"Gatori . . . ," he stammered finally, ". . . he's outside in the courtyard . . . he ran here from Zaza . . . he insisted on speaking to Mama or Papa, but they still aren't back.

"Dédé . . . he said—" Here he broke off and gulped, fighting for composure. "He said that Uncle Alphonse is dead. He said they murdered him . . . looted his house and set it on fire . . . it was neighbors, he said . . . and that they—"

He could say no more. A groan forced itself from his throat.

With a quick movement he freed Jeanne from his despairing grip, jumped off the bed, and pulled up the shade.

There was Gatori! He was walking back and forth on the terrace, head down. The herdboy seemed to have become considerably taller since she'd seen him in the last summer vacation before Grandmother's death. Suddenly she realized that today she was seeing him for the first time with proper shoes on.

Now he looked up and saw her at the window. He showed no sign that he recognized her, however. At that very moment Florence and Ananie ran through the back gate, and Jando, who'd just left the room, appeared in the courtyard again. Julienne hurried from another part of the yard, holding Teya by the hand.

And as if called, Ndayambaje joined the small group that had collected around Grandmother's former herdboy.

Now Jeanne couldn't stay in her room a second longer. In her hurry she put her dress on inside out. She left it that way and stormed out.

Again an uncertain feeling held her back on the doorstep. As she hesitated, she watched Gatori talking excitedly to his audience. They were standing close together next to a large puddle, its shining surface reflecting their bodies.

135

Jeanne still did not move from the spot. She could understand what Gatori was saying from where she stood.

"You have to get away from here!" he was warning. "They're going to kill all the Tutsis. I know it! I was there when they got the weapons. . . ."

And there followed a confused report of what had happened very early in the morning in his village of Zaza. Gatori kept interrupting himself, as if he had to struggle for words. What he was saying was inconceivable. So inconceivable it seemed to be beyond reality.

Before they'd also murdered others, the men of the village, armed with machetes, clubs, and farm tools, went first to the house of Alphonse, the supposed leader of the Tutsis.

They had pulled him out and marched him away. They mocked him and beat out their hatred on him. Accused him of snobbishness and illicit wealth. Then they had all started battering him until he no longer moved. One of them got the idea of setting up a memorial. With his head. They separated his head from his body, put it on a pole, and set it up on the street for all to see.

Later someone put a sign under it saying: *I am the king of the Cockroaches. Let me be an example to you.*

At this point in his report, Gatori broke off because his voice failed him.

His listeners stood looking at the ground the whole time. Even now no one looked up. And although Jeanne was not among them, she felt to her fingertips the shock that made them all incapable of doing or saying anything. She herself felt like a doll that someone had slung away with force.

Finally Ananie raised his hand helplessly.

"What's happened to Joséphine and the children? Have you seen them?" he finally managed almost inaudibly.

Gatori looked at him as if he hadn't understood the question. "They killed all the Tutsis, women, children. . . ."

Now Florence came to life. She grasped Gatori by the arm and kept him from saying anything more. "Thank you, Gatori! I think it's better for you to go. Otherwise you're going to be in even more danger yourself. We'll consider what to do."

He looked doubtfully around him. His eyes brushed over Jando, his friend from earlier vacations.

"Now run, before anyone sees you with us!" she repeated with emphasis.

Then he nodded. Without another word or a gesture of farewell he left their circle and quickly vanished through the courtyard gate.

"Do you know him well enough?" asked Ananie. "He's Hutu, isn't he? So can he be trusted?"

"I think so, yes," Florence said, answering the last part of his question first. "He was with my mother a long time as herdboy. Why should he have come all this way if he didn't mean us well? He risked a great deal."

And with the same decisiveness with which she had just sent Gatori away, she now linked arms with Ananie and drew him past Jeanne into the house. Jeanne looked after her parents, who withdrew into their bedroom where they could talk undisturbed.

Jeanne left the doorway and joined the others, among whom, as soon as Ananie and Florence had left the courtyard, an excited discussion had sprung up.

Julienne was completely beside herself. "How is such a thing possible? Who would do such a thing?"

"I don't believe it! Surely the boy was exaggerating. None of it makes any sense!" cried Ndayambaje.

"It's madness! Have the people just gone crazy?" Julienne's eyes were full of disgust.

"Our prime minister was also murdered this morning. In her own house. And the Belgian soldiers who were supposed to protect her along with her. I heard that on the radio just now. The devil is loose in Kigali!" Ndayambaje reported.

"No wonder . . . a woman prime minister . . ."

Teya inserted herself into the discussion. "How can they remove someone's head, anyhow?"

"Be quiet, Teya!" hissed Julienne, her face disgusted.

Jando clapped his hands over his mouth and turned away.

"But I want to know how they did it!"

While the others, ignoring Teya, continued talking, Jeanne thought it over. She had just asked in silence the same question that Teya asked aloud. And something else was on her mind. Shortly before Easter they'd heard in church the story of the crucifixion of Jesus.

When Gatori was telling of the death of her uncle, it unavoidably called up the picture of Jesus as he hung on the cross. But Jesus's head had stayed on, of that she was

certain. Only the business about the sign had been so similar to that with her uncle. Jesus had also gotten a sign with
something about a king written on it.

"They must have used a machete," Jeanne said, joining
in the others' conversation.

"Be quiet and come into the house!" Florence called
over from the doorway. "You shouldn't be making such a
commotion here outside."

They obeyed at once, for they felt caught in the act.
They found Ananie in the front room, sitting there waiting
for them and now much more collected than before.

"*Alors*, go to your rooms and put on warm clothes!" he
dictated. "Ndayambaje, pack us something to eat, please,
and something to drink! We're going to leave the house
together to find out what the situation is like outside. Zaza
belongs to a different commune. What happens there may
not necessarily happen here. I don't believe anyone would
do such a thing to us. *Jamais*!"

"But on the radio it said that it's forbidden to leave the
house—" Ndayambaje objected.

Ananie interrupted him: "*Bon*, I know it," he said. "We'll
probably already be back this evening."

How could that happen?

Almost a million dead in only a hundred days. Murdered. Not killed in war.

And the world looked on. Or looked away.

"But that's obvious," you say. "Who was interested? What's Rwanda, after all? A little speck in Africa that nobody knows about. A nothing."

I have to fiercely contradict you. You must not think of it that way under any circumstances. Not ever.

Nothing is everything. Everything nothing.

I can also ask you: What is Earth, then, measured against the size of the universe? A flyspeck. A nothing. But it's all we have. And we are all that we have. Every one, you understand, every one of us is all.

We are approaching the days of the genocide and it lies before me, a thicket whose end I cannot see. Sometimes I find us at the edge of an abyss. Each step along it is a balancing act. I am holding you and you are holding me. Four-legged, we're more secure.

Over a thousand hills I walk with you. Uphill, downhill.

Dimensions open. And slowly I am also approaching the vastness of your grief, which sometimes is all and yet sometimes melts into nothing.

Yesterday evening, for example:

We're on vacation in Majorca. We're sitting in a restaurant. In our great circle. We're very relaxed, sharing what's on our plates.

"Let me see how that tastes!"

We pass the time with games while we wait for the food.

Pack a suitcase. We pack endlessly, each his own things and those of the others. It gets to be more, round after round. Whoever leaves out something is out of the game.

You win in the end. Your memory for detail makes you unbeatable.

"Which of you can say the fastest: 'Blue brew browns blue rue, but brown brew brews rue blues.'?" I change the game with an eye toward your trouble with Rs and Ls. You ought not to win all the time.

But this tongue twister is familiar to you. You master it with ease, while we others get stuck in a hash of word patterns, one more contorted than the other, and finally drown in shrieks of laughter.

Our youngest one rolls under the table. We others gurgle, bleat, bellow, exult, disturb the other guests, gasp for breath, keep goading each other to expose our inability, and carry on into a laughter that will not end.

"Shh! We're in a restaurant here!" I halfheartedly try to rein us in under the mistrustful glance of the waitress.

"Mama, your makeup is smeared!"

What does that matter! The moment is precious. Priceless. Utterly filled with laughter.

Sometime later, a woman comes over to our table. She's in the process of leaving. An Englishwoman who speaks to me and asks if I understand her language.

In order to tell me how happy it has made her to see us all that way.

Ndayambaje and Julienne stayed behind in the house.

Jeanne and her parents and siblings had barely walked out through the gate when they joined a stream of people who had left their houses and were hurrying forward, as if they didn't want to be late to some event that was going on in the area.

It had been like that sometimes when a special ceremony or a presidential appearance was taking place in the Kibungo stadium and all the inhabitants of the town were making their way there. Events of that sort always put Jeanne's patience to a hard test, for she and her brother and sister had to endure quietly on the benches with their parents, who occupied places on the platform as privileged guests, and suffer through the often endless and boring program, while many families romped about uncaring on the grass at the edge of the stadium. Jeanne had envied the other children their freedom.

As always, Ananie went in front, Jando at his side. Florence was holding Teya firmly by the hand. Jeanne would have been only too glad to take her mother's free hand, but the age of hand-holding was past for her. Long since. She was a big girl. And she intended to act like one, too.

The sun cast its late afternoon beams on the hurrying people. It would most certainly begin to rain again sometime. However, probably not before nightfall or the next morning.

They were going in the direction of the school. After they rounded the little eucalyptus wood, the landscape opened out and hills and fields lay before them.

Jeanne stopped short.

She had come along this path almost daily, but now it seemed to her as if, without intending to, they had suddenly gotten to someplace entirely different. Nothing seemed familiar anymore.

Yellow-gray clouds were rising from the surface of the earth like oversized mushrooms. Pushing in front of the view of church and school. Not rain clouds. Swelling clouds of smoke that rose to the hills from burning houses.

People were running. Following the course of the street, ducking down behind bushes and banana palms. Again and again Jeanne saw individual figures break out somewhere and immediately disappear again. Men's cries, echoing from hill to hill, chased after them. From somewhere there arose a continuous wailing; in between there were screams audible.

A little later they approached the playing field, where a crowd of people was already assembled. And fleeing people kept streaming in from all sides.

Jeanne heard gasping behind her. Then a boy, not much older than Jando, fled past them. Her gaze remained fastened on his back. Between his shoulders, where his blood-soaked shirt was hanging in shreds.

How did he manage to keep running in spite of that?

The playing field, a wide, flat lawn bordered by low bushes, with two soccer goals, usually held several school classes. Now and then competitions between neighboring schools took place there. Jeanne had also been there a few times with her class for gym. It was only a few minutes on foot from her school.

Now the field was filled with people, who formed little groups everywhere and whispered together. There was a constant coming and going, a terrible confusion of figures running zigzag. It seemed to Jeanne as if the entire field was set into vigorous motion, like a wheat field through which a storm was sweeping.

Ananie looked searchingly around him. Jean discovered a few children from her school standing by their families. The children looked at her like a stranger. This was no longer a place where people ran up and greeted one another.

Ananie now steered to the center of the field, where he had discovered their neighbors Murayire and Bavakure with their two daughters, Claudine and Angélique. Claudine and Teya were friends. Claudine caught Jeanne's eye immediately because today she was wearing a brilliant red pullover. Two-year-old Angélique perched on Murayire's hip and clung fast to her, her head buried on her mother's breast.

When they reached the little group, Ananie and

Bavakura stepped to one side in wordless agreement and went over to talk with some other men.

Women and children huddled silently together.

Faces frozen into expressionless masks, they observed what was happening around them. Jeanne felt Florence's hand on her shoulder, felt the firm, unceasing pressure that betrayed her mother's enormous tension and at the same time commanded her to stay still.

This silent command was unnecessary, for Jeanne was incapable of doing anything. Her emotions were cowering in a deep, dark corner and did not move. Outside herself she heard the desperate, warning calls of the people running past.

"What are you still doing here? You must get away. Aren't you listening? Hide!"

"The murderers are on their way, they'll be here soon!"

"The Interahamwe is hunting us all down! They have dogs with them. . . ."

"Run away, they're coming with machetes! They'll kill us all. . . ."

Many of the fugitives were badly injured. Some of them stopped briefly to talk. They spoke breathlessly of burning houses, of masked murderers who had fallen on them with machetes, of neighbors who massacred neighbors, of families who no longer existed. . . .

Jeanne heard their words and saw their wounds, but something in her blocked out the horror that gushed over the field and threatened to engulf all. She kept aloof so that it could not fall upon her, stiffened herself under the ever harder and firmer grip of her mother—the only reality in this moment—and persuaded herself that they would leave here again. And then it would all be over.

Ananie and Bavakure came back. Ananie was just starting to speak when someone rushed up to him and sank down in front of him on her knees. A young girl, with a gaping wound across her skull. Her face was gray and beaded with sweat. When she moved her lips to speak, hardly a sound came out.

Ananie bent over her and carefully raised her. "Immaculée!" he cried in consternation. *"Mon dieu,* what have they done to you!"

Instead of answering she bowed her head. Her entire body was trembling.

Jeanne stared at the bloody fissure in the black hair. The sight struck her to the core. Immaculée! A pupil of her father's. She knew her well: always bubbling, smiling. Full of high spirits. When she laughed, she showed two dimples. And now . . . suddenly the horror had a face.

"Who injured her so badly? Who would do that to her?" Ananie whispered to Florence. He turned to Jando. "Find out if there's anyone on the way to the hospital! Hurry! She needs help right away. And probably she'll be safe there."

Jando rushed away. Jeanne heard "hospital" and "safe." The world was upside down.

Florence put her arm around Immaculée's waist and supported her. Said something to reassure her. And for the first time since they'd come to the playing fields, the rigidity left her face. Life seemed to have returned to her with the gentle words she had to use to encourage the girl.

Soon Jando came back with two teenagers, who took Immaculée between them and hurriedly led her away. A passing car stopped. The doors were opened. The three climbed in and drove away.

Meanwhile four men had sauntered up to Ananie and stopped a few yards away from him. Jeanne recognized among them the officials who had examined the family a short time ago. This man waved Ananie over to him and began to speak to him, gesturing vigorously. As if he had something to offer or wanted to bargain. Jeanne watched her father reach into his trousers pocket and hand the men something before he turned away and returned to them.

"*Alors*, I paid them," he declared brusquely. "For that they'll protect us. We'll go back now, eat something, and after that we'll pack a few things."

He nodded to Bavakure. "*A bientôt, mon ami!*" he said.

During the fast-paced walk back in the approaching dark, the blood suddenly began to flow in Jeanne's arteries again. It spread out almost painfully, to the very tips of her hands and feet, sweeping with it her heart, which began to pound madly and stumbled over the even rhythm of her feet. The picture of the burning houses before her eyes, she wondered fearfully how they would find their own house after their absence.

It lay at the end of the path, quiet and unharmed.

The sturdy yellow of fully opened roses glowed in the

dusk. Small, friendly lights in the hedge. Nowhere was there the least sign of impending danger. The house presented such a friendly aspect that it seemed to Jeanne as unreal as all the recent sights and experiences.

Ananie closed the gate. He waited and listened before he resolutely crossed the front yard and opened the front door.

"Julienne! Ndayambaje!" Florence called when she came in.

The house was silent.

Florence stroked Teya's head. "Dédé, Jando, go to your rooms and lay out your things for a few days and nights," she commanded. Her voice sounded exhausted. "Long pants, pullovers, underwear, you know what. Then you must put on warm clothes. I'll send Julienne along to help you."

She repeated her call to the servants, somewhat louder than before. Soon hurrying steps approached from the rear courtyard. Ndayambaje, who had obviously been in the kitchen, came into the house.

"Is supper ready?" Florence asked.

He nodded.

"Where is Julienne? She should help the children!"

"She left," he said softly and looked awkwardly to one side. "Shortly after you were gone."

An expression of surprise appeared on Florence's face and then slowly gave way to annoyance.

Now she's going to let go, thought Jeanne.

But her mother said only, "Oh, indeed." And then: "Very

well—Jando, Dédé, go to your rooms! Get started until I call you. I'll help you afterwards. Ndayambaje, we want to have supper quickly! I'll set the table."

"Yes, Mamam-Jando," the houseboy answered. "I understand. I'll hurry."

It was already dark when they left the house for the second time that day.

During supper Ananie had explained to the children that they were going to meet at Bavakure's and Murayire's with some of the other families and spend the night there. Ndayambaje was supposed to stay behind and mind the house. The next morning they'd see how things looked.

Shortly before they left, some Hutu neighbors knocked and called loudly for them. Florence had flinched and tried, with energetic shaking of her head, to keep Ananie from opening the door. He, too, had clearly hesitated. But when the voices outside didn't stop, he finally went outside.

"They wanted to know if we needed their help," he explained afterwards. "*Donc*, I gave them money to watch our house while we are not here."

Jeanne realized then that Hutus were allowed to stay in their houses. Or might go where they wanted, like Julienne. Without being attacked.

Only Tutsis were in danger. She didn't understand why it was so, yet there was no point in asking. A grave silence prevailed among them as they hurried along. No one would explain anything to her now.

Meanwhile Jeanne also guessed why the choice for the overnight stay had fallen on Bavakure's house. It lay somewhat set back, sheltered from view by banana fields.

When she had trudged out of the house behind the others, she felt like a barrel. She was wearing a pair of long pants over shorts and two pullovers on top of a T-shirt. Not because it was cold but because each of them was supposed to take as much as possible.

Jando and Teya had also visibly increased in girth. Bent slightly forward, Jando carried his sports bag on his back like a hump, both arms stuck through its straps. On any other occasion, the sight of the misshapen, clumsy figures would have made Jeanne laugh, but now she felt miserable.

As she went down the cement walk behind them with her little suitcase, she turned her head and looked back.

There stood the house. Without any glimmer of light behind its windows it looked unseeing and somber. But the roses, small, bright hedge eyes, gazed after them.

The countless stars overflowing the sky provided them with lighting enough. However, Ananie and Jando were holding flashlights in front of them, regularly sending their beams in all directions, letting them travel between the bushes along the side of the road and sink to the ground again.

The evening sounded the same as always: there was the croaking of frogs, accompanied by the rattle of the locusts from the adjoining wheat field and by the wailing howl of a farmyard dog, who received no answer.

There were no more screams. Only the crunching their

feet made on the tiny stones of the sandy lane. Even Teya made no sound. Jeanne had not heard Teya the whole day long.

Ananie and Jando turned off their flashlights as they approached the house of their friends. They walked into the front yard. Shadowy figures of men who were posted around the house detached themselves from the darkness and raised a hand in greeting. Ananie returned it. He guided them toward the front door. There he gave a soft knocking signal. Someone immediately opened the door to admit him and his family and closed it promptly behind them.

Many people had already gathered. A subdued babble of voices filled the house. The air was warm and stuffy. Murayire led Florence and the children to the salon. Ananie stayed with the men, who were crowded into the foyer.

The salon, weakly illumined with only candles and kerosene lamps, was even warmer and stuffier than the foyer.

Some women and children were already busy using mattresses, blankets, and cushions to set up a big sleeping area, covering the entire floor surface. Young children crawled around among them, some of them crying because they were overtired. A few of the bigger girls had sat down on the floor in a corner so as not to be in the way. Sitting opposite each other in pairs, they were singing a nonsense counting song in French:

Un indépendant,

deux députés,
trois, trois butons,
quatre à l'arrière . . .

Palms raised, they crossed and clapped with each other in the rhythm of the verse. Faster and faster, until a hand was pulled back and the clapping one hung in empty air. A giggle followed. It was smothered, as if it were not allowed.

Florence and Jando helped with the setting up, and Teya crept over to Claudine, who had lain down on one of the mattresses, ready to sleep. But Jeanne stood in the doorway, waiting. Filled with uneasiness, she observed the activity of the others. She would certainly not be able to sleep here. She couldn't sleep when strangers watched her doing it.

Again a knocking outside. The front door opening. Voices. Murayire ushered a young woman with a baby into the salon.

Barely an hour later, when Jeanne was sharing the mattress dormitory with the other children and some of the mothers, she lay on her back, wide awake, and sought to pick up scraps of words from the murmur around her. She was suffering from the heat, which radiated toward her from the bodies of the others, and stared alternately at the ceiling and at Jando, who sat on the edge of the mattress encampment with his knees drawn up. Incapable of falling asleep herself, she was grateful for any interruption: for instance, when the door opened and one of the women peered in to look for someone, or when someone came in late and lay down among them. At least the open door let some air into the room and allowed a view of the women who were sitting on chairs or the floor in the foyer. Florence was among them. Jeanne noticed that she wasn't sleeping either. At the sight of her mother's small profile, her upright posture, she didn't feel quite so forlorn. She clung to that view every time the door opened.

Angélique was rolling back and forth. She groaned in her sleep. Her mother had bedded her down beside Jeanne after Teya and Claudine had insisted on sharing a sleeping place. Now and again a slight shudder ran through the little girl's body. She appeared to be running in a dream and kicked Jeanne.

"We have to get away from here before they can do anything to us," someone behind them whispered.

As Jeanne thought over the words, she wondered if her family would also have to leave home. Perhaps for a long time, or even forever. Then they would be refugees.

She had long been familiar with the images of refugees, who streamed from the part of the country where the war with the Rebels had been going on for years. She'd often seen them passing in the distance. Loaded down from head to foot with sleeping mats, baskets, cooking pots, and countless shopping bags with their possessions. Some of them had a handcart or animals with them, and Jeanne had wondered where they were going. Or if they even had any destination. At her grandmother's she had a few times seen refugees come to the door to ask for food or water.

She didn't want to become a refugee and have to go begging!

Maybe it would help if she prayed for an especially long time today.

She began with the Our Father. She couldn't think of any sins she had to confess. But there were many things she wanted to plead earnestly for! Only it wasn't easy to find the right words. The events of this day still lay beyond what she could imagine or put into words. And so her thoughts only circled around a single sentence that she murmured to herself in the silence until finally it wrapped around her like a blanket and at last, long after midnight, let her fall asleep.

"Protect our house and the family."

"Jeanne, wake up, we have to leave. Go sleep somewhere else."

Florence's voice, coming from a long way off, drilled its way through the layers of sleep to Jeanne, who heard it but without coming awake. She didn't even wake up when she was seized and picked up. When she felt someone put on her shoes, lay something around her shoulders, and then carry her outside. Even when she felt the ground under her feet and the fresh night air struck her, she remained in a condition of sleep-protected peace.

Supported on each side between Ananie and Jando, she stumbled through the darkness. Part of a crowd that moved forward like a single large body and carried her with it. Somewhere.

Sometimes, when the sound of someone crying reached her, it dragged her consciousness upward. She tried to open her eyes, but sleep pressed her eyelids down and pulled her back into its depths.

Hard ground under her back, cold that came through the blanket. Crying again.

Teya's voice. Whining. "I don't want to sleep under a blanket with Dédé."

"Then don't. We have only the one." Florence. Softly. Tired. Sad?

A lifting of the blanket. Cold draft of air. But now Teya warm at her side. All only part of the dream.

And then they were there again. The screams!

Jeanne opened her eyes and saw the faces of Florence, Ananie, and Jando over her. Jando's eyes were too large, as if he had to widen them to keep them from closing with weariness.

They were lying in a coffee field among people and bushes.

The night had already vanished. Dust-fine drizzle was falling from a leaden sky and collecting into fat drops on the dark-green leaves of the coffee plants. Silvery beads among the red beans. The dampness penetrated the thin blanket around Jeanne and Teya. Teya was asleep.

There was great unrest everywhere. People were jumping up and leaving their places in a great hurry.

Florence, Ananie, and Jando were also ready to leave. Ananie bent down. "We're going to Birenga," he said. "We're not safe at home anymore."

Jeanne poked Teya. Her limp body did not react. A second time. Teya growled, reached out, and struck at Jeanne.

"Teya, come, we have to go. Do you hear?"

Ananie picked Teya up in his arms, and Florence helped Jeanne onto her feet.

"Hurry! It's already much too late!" she demanded urgently, as she bundled up the blanket, each of her movements making her anxiety palpable. After the wakeful night, she no longer had the strength to conceal it.

Jeanne rubbed her stiff, aching limbs. In vain she tried to resist the numbing fear that spread from her mother and slowly seeped into her the way the rain was seeping into the fabric of her clothes.

"Allons, enfants!" Ananie said, turning to go.

They followed him.

You interrupt me.

I've just read to you all from the first part of the book. You've all listened to me. You on the sofa, curled up like a cat. Both eyes half closed.

Afterwards we talk for a long time with one another:

About human beings. About their capacity to rise above themselves. About their depths.

You act relaxed at this moment. The tension of the recent days seems to have fallen away from you.

I try to explain to you why I feel so compelled to write the book.

You interrupt me.

"I'm thinking of a story, I think I've already told it to you . . . ," you say.

Eagerly I take the bait.

"What story?" I ask.

"The one about God and Death and the Devil and the old woman."

"No, I don't know that one at all. I want to hear it. Absolutely. But not now. Now I'm much too tired. Tell it to me tomorrow, okay?"

"I'll be sure to have forgotten it again by tomorrow," you say, smiling your smile.

I hesitate. It's grown late. But the faces are turned toward you.

"All right," I say.

And you tell.

God and Death and the Devil were brothers. They argued with each other over who should be master of the earth, and they couldn't agree. Then they decided to resolve the question another way. With a race to the earth. It would belong to the winner.

They all arrived there at the same time.

Death discovered an old farm woman who had already lived on the earth for many years. He entered her body and took possession of it.

But God and the Devil, trying to clasp the entire world, each received only half of it. They are still fighting for the whole.

And only Death has incontestably what belongs to him.

The commune center of Birenga was barely an hour away in a very small suburb on the outskirts of Kibungo. In a valley between two hills.

Except for the administrative buildings, the office of the mayor, a police station, the registration office, the school board, the community center where the young people got together sometimes, and finally the jail room for petty offenses, there were only a few houses, nestled in fields and banana groves. The mayor also lived here.

They made slow progress, for the narrow path that snaked between coffee and vegetable fields to the main road was softened by the rain torrents and the steps of countless feet. They had to step over puddles, and sometimes the ground threatened to slide out from under them. And with the burden of their packs and the imprisoning layers of clothing, it was hard to keep their balance.

Jeanne was sweating. She felt the dampness on her back. And on her forehead. And mud was sticking to the thin soles of her sandals.

Close behind and ahead of them were others, also laden with everything they could carry. Wrapped in clothing, fear, and silence.

They made one more stop at the playing field on the way. But after Ananie had spoken with a few men there, he urged them on.

When they reached Birenga, the small plaza in front of the buildings was already overflowing with people. Jeanne recognized Aunt Pascasia, Saphina, and Lionson. She didn't see Claire, Aunt Pascasia's eldest. Jeanne knew a few of the families there with all their belongings by sight.

The women waited patiently with the children, while their menfolk spoke with one another. Two policemen had positioned themselves a little to one side. Legs widespread, arms crossed on their chests, they stood there impassively watching the goings-on. But Jeanne felt that they were carefully taking note of all new arrivals.

After Ananie had spoken with the other men for a while, he gave Florence and the children a sign to follow him. He headed straight for the small house of the mayor, which was set back behind other houses only a few hundred yards from his office.

They met the mayor at his front door, where he was pacing back and forth. In tie and collar, as if he were dressed for a reception. He was a tall, portly man, who bore his great belly proudly before him. And thus he approached them. With a broad smile of greeting on his round, shining face, as usual, and a jovial, nasal hello that crossed his lips with notable ease. As if this were a day like any other.

Ananie and Florence walked up to him without hesitation.

"*Bonjour*, Innocent!" Ananie greeted the mayor. He knew him well and therefore had no inhibitions about speaking candidly to him. The children remained a few steps away. While the grown-ups were greeting each other and exchanging some courtesies, Jeanne carefully studied, as she had before, the strange, light-gray spot in the mayor's pitch-black hair, which stood out as if someone had dabbed him there with a paintbrush.

Ananie inquired what he and his family should do in view of the events, but Jeanne stopped listening and instead turned to the street, where there was much to see. People constantly arriving with luggage. Clearly firmly determined to stay. She looked for familiar faces and wondered where so many people could be housed.

After the conversation was ended, the mayor smilingly waved good-bye to the children.

"*Alors*, we can stay," said Ananie. But he didn't sound

very relieved. "They've made the community center and a few other rooms available, so that we can sleep there. I'm going to go back quickly and get blankets."

"No, that's much too dangerous!" Florence said, trying to dissuade him. "Didn't you hear what Innocent said? We shouldn't leave the commune anymore now!"

"*Oui, je sais,*" replied Ananie. "Only a few blankets. We need them. I'll hurry."

In fact, he wasn't gone long. In less than half an hour he appeared in the plaza again, but without the blankets. Completely out of breath and distraught.

"Our house—" he began. At Florence's despairing look he broke off.

She wrapped her arms around herself. And when he made no other attempt to continue speaking, she asked: "What's wrong with our house?" It sounded oddly detached.

"I never got there," he answered. "I ran into Ndayambaje at the playing field. He called to me I should flee. . . . They were there. . . . They're looking for me. . . . since yesterday already . . . They've destroyed our house. . . . looted it . . . I couldn't believe it. . . . Then I saw it from a distance . . . over the trees . . . nothing left . . . There was no roof there anymore!"

Everything began to spin inside Jeanne. Her father's voice reached her from far off, but his words stuck into her like tiny splinters of shattered wood. Through a haze she saw Florence's face twist in pain as if someone had struck her. Jando's shoulders sagged. And Teya began to sob.

Florence stroked her head, an absent gesture that seemed aimless. The sobbing stopped.

Jeanne was so filled with fear that she couldn't move. Her thoughts tumbled over each other.

The roof . . . what had happened to the roof? Who had done that? . . . The beautiful red tile roof . . . You could see it from a long way off when you came home. . . . Was it war now? . . . The war her father had said would be coming to them soon? . . . Without a roof, that was impossible . . . It was the rainy season. . . . In a war there were soldiers. . . . Where were the soldiers? . . . They had only seen the ones who were always there. . . . Her bed would get all wet in the next rain, the mattress . . . everything . . . Who would want to fight against her father? . . . He didn't even have a weapon. . . .

Since the morning when the frightening music on the radio had announced the calamity, something was approaching them that was much worse than war. And she sensed that no one could do anything against it.

Ananie bent down to Teya, who was still weeping, but soundlessly now.

"*Doucement, ma petite*, don't cry!" he murmured. Then he lifted his head. He looked at Florence and clung to her gaze. "We'll see where we can find a place."

In the following days, time lost all measure.

Had it not become dark sometimes and then light again sometimes, Jeanne would have lost any orientation to time. Without the usual rhythm of the divided days, life appeared to stand still. Imprisoned in an endless moment of waiting. Without purpose. Without prospects. You ate sometimes, you slept sometimes. In the meantime there was nothing that you had to do. And also nothing you could undertake on your own.

Everything was in the process of complete disintegration, everything seemed sunk into permissiveness. No demands from the grown-ups. No reprimands. For hours Jeanne saw her parents or her siblings only at a distance, the families were no longer together. They lost themselves in a crowd of people in which they all looked out for themselves. Jeanne resigned herself to it. She had shared another life with her parents and siblings. And the breakdown was easier to bear if you weren't being reminded of it all the time.

You became one of many. Turned to those who were right next to you. Sat silently in the shadows of the houses. At a place of confinement where you must share all. Where you could not be your own self anymore. In which there were no secrets anymore. And once you were there, you had to stay there.

"It's for your own protection!" the mayor had said when he gave the order not to leave the commune anymore.

Under the supervision of the militia, an emergency camp was set up in short order. The men laid out sleeping areas with mattresses and blankets. You slept where you found a place. Or if you found a place. For there wasn't enough space for all. Children, old people, women with babies or who were pregnant received preference. Some grown-ups apparently didn't sleep at all.

There were also sacks with flour, corn, rice, millet, sugar, and salt provided. And cooking pots.

Several fireplaces made of stones piled on top of each other were set up on the plaza, in whose centers a fire burned all the time, where women stirred the flour and millet into a broth or dough, neither of which tasted of anything. Now and again someone succeeded in procuring tomatoes or vegetables from former neighbors who were still living in their houses in the immediate neighborhood. Then they would be used to make a sauce that made the whole thing taste a little more enjoyable.

If you were hungry, sometimes you were allotted a small meal. Jeanne almost never felt any hunger, and so she ate scarcely anything. Nevertheless, she often stayed in the vicinity of the fireplaces. At least something was happening there. Now and again, when the women forgot the circumstances in which they found themselves as they worked, the give and take among them sounded almost ordinary.

The older children collected sticks, branches, and small logs along the edge of an adjoining eucalyptus wood. Jando and Aunt Pascasia's daughters Claire and Saphina were among them. Jeanne would have loved to work along with them! For gathering wood offered a welcome change and the chance of getting away a little. But she wasn't allowed to join them because it was too dangerous. To her annoyance, she was still considered one of the small children.

It hardly rained at all during the day. That made staying in the community center easier because most of the time you could be outside. Sometimes Jeanne wondered how her parents could stand it at all to be in such a small space with so many people day and night. Her father enjoyed solitude. And her mother, with her exaggerated fear of dirt and illness, surely must be suffering torments.

For showers, the grown-ups went to Dativa, an old woman living alone who voluntarily placed her bath at the disposal of the roofless refugees. The small children and the adolescents had to wash at a construction site. In a house without windows or doors. Carrying a basin or a bucket full of water, they would vanish behind one of the walls and try to get clean as well as they could. Often they would be disturbed by someone while they were doing it. In the beginning Jeanne found that painful, but after it had happened several times, she thought nothing more about it. Anyway, she was getting used to a lot of things. To sharing the sleeping area with strange people, and even to the long lines in front of the outhouses of the residents. If you had to go badly, you ran from one to the other. In the hope that somewhere it would be faster. Or that someone would let you go ahead, which also happened sometimes.

It was clear that the residents only reluctantly tolerated the pressure on their toilets. But there was nothing else for them to do but to accept it. Because someone asking could not be refused. That was the custom.

Wide awake, Jeanne sat on the mattress that was assigned to her, Teya, and Jando as a sleeping place. She was already changed for the night, wearing a flowered summer dress that now served her as a nightgown. She could also have just lain down and gone to sleep in her day clothes, for no one paid any attention anymore as to whether she changed her clothes at night. She did it anyway because she was used to doing it. Teya lay beside her, her arms and legs bent, and was already fast asleep. The hideous gray army blanket had already slid down to the end of the mattress. Jeanne regarded the coarse heap with loathing. She wouldn't cover herself with it, either. She was much too warm anyway.

Jando was talking with some boys in the back part of the big office space, which, stuffed full with people and their belongings, betrayed nothing more of its original purpose. Anyone coming late had to step over people already asleep to get to his place. Smaller children were passed over on raised arms.

Jeanne, Teya, and Jando had come inside when darkness fell. Jeanne couldn't say how much time had passed since then. She waited.

She could only fall asleep when she was dropping with weariness. The fluorescent tubes in the white-painted ceiling spread a wan light that made all the faces around her appear gray. The light stayed on all night so that anyone could find his way at any time. Floor-length curtains drawn over the open windows kept enough fresh air from blowing into the warm, stuffy room from outside. But they also kept swarms of mosquitoes from being able to invade. Nevertheless, a few did find their way through the gap between the curtains and whined aggressively around the sleepers' heads. Their whining as they approached was louder than the murmurs of the voices. As were the small, hard drumbeats of the raindrops on the room's roof.

The door to the hallway was opened and closed again. Jeanne listened to the whispered words behind her. Just a few yards away a few girls had gathered, huddled together, and begun complaining. "I can't stand this any longer. If I could only take a real shower..." "I didn't bring enough with me. I have nothing clean left. And you can't wash either...." "I'd love to get a few things from home...."

Jeanne waited.

She waited for the soldiers who came every evening.

Whether it was always at the same time, she wasn't quite sure. But they were certain to come. At least two of them. Sometimes even three. When they threw open the door and planted themselves in the doorway, everyone in the room shrank. The murmuring died. People dropped their eyes. Or looked toward the doorway.

In the same way she was unable to tell how long she'd been there, Jeanne couldn't have said whether it was different soldiers every time. Their voices differed, as did the shades of their skin. However, the spotted combat uniforms, the red forage caps shaped like little ships aslant on the head or pulled down deep over a dark forehead, the long billy clubs on leather thongs dangling at the wrist, the heavy boots whose tips could kick out unexpectedly, and finally, the grenades hanging loosely at the belt as if they were harmless cowbells were what formed their image. Not their faces.

Jeanne awaited them with a mixture of fear and suspense. What would they do today? Sometimes they were clearly irritated and therefore were out to spread fear. Then they would hit out without reason at someone who'd just stopped in the vicinity of the entryway and couldn't pull back in time.

"Out of the way!"

"What're you staring at, stupid!"

Sometimes they tried to push their way into the over-crowded room. "You there, move!"

Their boot tips would bore into a person lying at their feet. But Jeanne didn't believe the soldiers really wanted to come in. They were only looking for an excuse to hurt someone and show their superiority.

They almost always went after the older girls. Especially Madeleine, who was a beauty. "Hey, you over there! What's your name? I know you! Didn't we meet at the barricades in Butare?" Words bawled across the room. To the very far-thest corner of the office space, where Madeleine had anx-iously crept every evening since the first incident of this sort. "C'mere, you! You can come with me. I want to marry you." A commanding beckon. Laughter from his buddies. "Now, c'mon! What do you want here when you can get to be my wife on the spot!"

Their shameless behavior in front of everyone filled Jeanne with indignation. You didn't do things like that! You had to ask the father first. And give him something for the bride. A cow, for instance, or a piece of land, or even money. And a wedding had to be prepared for. That was a family matter. All the relatives and friends had to come and be there when the bride was brought to the bridegroom.

Jeanne had once been to a wedding at neighboring friends'. She still remembered it very well.

Germain, the bridegroom, had waited for his bride, Espérance, in his parents' courtyard in the midst of a large wedding party. Espérance, in a long, white lace dress and half hidden under a white veil that fell to the floor, was led to Germain by two older women and a crowd of festively dressed girls. The ceremony had impressed Jeanne deeply, but it had also confused her. Espérance had cried hard, and the girls who accompanied her had obviously been very sad too, because some of them had been moaning loudly.

"I'm never going to marry," Jeanne had said to her grandmother later, after Nyogokuru told the grandchildren how in earlier times bride and bridegroom had been destined for each other since childhood.

The old woman had looked at her in surprise. "Why don't you want to marry?"

"If you get married you have to go away from home and cry really terribly."

Nyogokuru smiled in amusement. "A bride who doesn't cry is not a happy bride," she answered knowingly. "But you'll only understand that when you're older."

Jeanne was still firmly determined never to marry. And what she was experiencing here in Birenga strengthened her resolve. She wondered what the soldiers wanted from the pretty girls and why they called out to them every evening, though they never got any answer.

The door was thrown open.

This time there were two. They stood there with night-sticks raised, leaning on the door frame and letting their eyes wander over the room. A young man in civilian clothes pushed past them. He also looked around and then toward a small group near the door. There Suzanne, her two brothers, and a few other young people were talking together.

Jeanne noticed how Suzanne recoiled. She knew her slightly because she'd been a pupil of her father's.

The young man moved toward the group, but no one moved aside for him.

"Suzanne, come here! I've been looking for you!" he called then.

She looked at him briefly and dropped her head.

"What do you want here, Gaspard?" asked the older of Suzanne's brothers, his voice raised. It didn't sound unfriendly, though.

"I want to take her with me. This is no place she should stay any longer," Gaspard replied.

"But we're here too." This answer was quiet and firm.

"Let her go with me! I beg you! You know our wedding is supposed to take place a week from now."

"You'll have to wait until all this is over."

Jeanne thought she saw Gaspard's face change. She couldn't read his expression.

"We're engaged. I'll take her to my parents. She can stay there until the wedding," he said, trying again.

Suzanne's brother shook his head firmly. "Our sister stays with us! We won't let her go with you before the wedding."

"Suzanne, please come outside with me! I have to talk to you!" Gaspard demanded urgently once more.

Suzanne looked at her brother inquiringly. He finally nodded. Then she detached herself from the group and walked slowly to the entrance. In contrast to her fiancé, people gave way to her immediately.

Gaspard, clearly relieved, met her and pushed her out ahead of him. The soldiers who had taken up posts at the door and observed the proceedings attentively from there now followed the two of them. Jeanne couldn't resist a sudden desire to leave her sleeping place and slip out into the hallway.

There stood a table with the thermos jugs with tea and *amasaka* gruel as well as jugs filled with water, ready for the hungry and thirsty. Really the children weren't supposed to drink any more water later in the evening, because it was almost impossible to look for a toilet. Today thirst served as an excuse for Jeanne.

She poured a glass of water, began to drink slowly, and carefully squinted down the hall. Along the walls, between open doors that led to other offices, sat men and women on chairs or on the floor. They had fled into the building when it started raining. Jeanne knew that outside there were just as many crowded onto the veranda, which offered them only meager protection from the heavy rain showers.

She discovered Suzanne and her fiancé at the end of the corridor. Gaspard was holding Suzanne's arm and speaking to her. She listened to him in silence, her head raised. Her posture looked curiously stiff. Now and again she shook her head, which each time seemed to make Gaspard still more excited, until he finally became angry and tried to pull her out with him.

She freed herself with a shake. Turned and left him. Hurried down the hall without once turning around to look at him. Gaspard stood there staring after her, his arms at his sides.

When Suzanne came level with Jeanne at the table with the drinks, she threw her hands over her face and began to cry.

A crying bride, Jeanne thought. But she couldn't believe that it meant happiness.

She felt it clearly: In this place, at this moment, happiness was as far away as Heaven is from the earth.

"You fight with Mama!" says Massamba.

Our drum teacher from Senegal. He comes to us twice a month, and we make our house shake. The neighbors obligingly close their windows.

I'm the white spot in our circle. But I'm carried away by the sound of the drums to a part of you, of Africa. In the beginning it was hard for me to get into the strange rhythm. But since then it has reached my vitals and my beats make their point.

When I can differentiate the interplay of sounds, when I begin to understand the language of the drums, I plunge into an existence outside of established boundaries. I realize that each voice is an important element of a whole. That it is incorporated in the whole, yet remains audible individually. And that it fulfills its purpose by speaking with the others. Outside of time and space. In the circular movements of life.

We attend a wedding. We are fishing, we throw our nets out. We greet an important guest.

The voice of Africa.

Massamba brings it to us without many words.

*Through his hands. Through his laugh. Through his spirit,
which fills the room.*

He says that you're supposed to fight with me now.

*We exchange a look and laugh. Will we be able to do it
this time? Give up our unison? Set our beats against one
another, hesitate for a fraction of a second so that we fight
with one another?*

*As usual, we don't last long. Our beats grow closer
until they cover each other again. Unison means security.*

Massamba grins. "Yee-e-es . . . , it's hard," he says.

*Nevertheless, we've already fought each other. You
and I.*

Without drumming.

*Sometimes you can be really beastly. You snarl at me.
You storm. Tears of rage in your eyes. I can be hard at such
moments. Hold out against them. Let you feel my strength.
So that you have to fight with me.*

You do it unhesitatingly.

*I'm so glad that we can dare the closeness that a fight
requires. Without seriously injuring us.*

*Since you fight with me so often, I'm certain that you've
regained your strength and are entirely at home.*

When she awoke, Jeanne found the place on the mattress
beside her empty.

She dressed hurriedly and left the building. The rain
had stopped, but the sky was still overhung with clouds and
the water had collected in numerous puddles on the plaza.

She saw Aunt Pascasia and Claire at one of the fireplaces. She wandered over to them.

Claire was stirring something in a big tin pot.

"Good morning, Aunt!" said Jeanne.

"Good morning, Dédé! Would you like some *igikoma*?"

"Just a little. I'm not very hungry."

Aunt Pascasia took the pot from the fire, handed Jeanne a mug, and poured the *amasaka* gruel into it. Some ran over the edge.

Jeanne sat down on a stone and began to lick at it. "Can I have some more sugar?" she asked.

Her aunt shook her head.

Jeanne set the mug aside.

She looked over to the eucalyptus wood, where several men with spades and axes were digging two huge pits. Some men were standing in them and shoveling out the dirt from there. Only their heads were visible. Thick clumps flew threw the air and plopped between the bushes. The men had begun their work yesterday afternoon. Jeanne, Claudine, and Saphina had approached curiously, but they were sent away.

"What are they digging there, anyhow?" Jeanne asked.

Aunt Pascasia and Claire exchanged a look. Her aunt seemed annoyed, and Jeanne was afraid that now she'd raise her hand and give her a slap.

"Those are supposed to become our toilets," she answered finally. It was easy to see how very repellent this thought was to her. "A few people have gotten sick, so we're not allowed to use the outhouses anymore. For our own protection, they say." These last words sounded bitter.

Jeanne was horrified. No one could ask that of her! That she'd have to crouch over that gigantic hole. There where everyone could see her. No! She wouldn't go to the bathroom at all anymore either, then. Just as if there were a bad spell put on her, she immediately felt a powerful pressure on her bladder. Thank goodness the holes weren't ready yet. Leaving the half-full mug behind, she ran to join one of the lines that soon would no longer exist.

When she came back, Saphina and Claudine had settled down in the plaza. Claudine drew boxes for hopscotch on the muddy ground with a stick. A cross made of eight rectangles, into which you threw a stone according to a certain order, after which you had to hop through the boxes without touching any of the lines.

"I'll play too!" Jeanne cried, and the toilets were forgotten.

Now her entire attention was taken up with the game, where she was having a hard time outdoing her two opponents. She fought to keep her balance, and she never could if she jumped and landed on her left foot, which offered her uncertain support. But she absolutely did not want to slip and fall in the mud. She had hardly any clean things left. So she preferred to put up with losing by stepping on a line.

The girls broke off their game a little later when a transport column noisily approached.

Four open trucks rolled up.

They drove back and forth a few times, engines roaring, leaving deep tire ruts in the wet ground. Young men were standing or sitting in their open cargo areas. A rowdy bunch, armed with rifles, grenades, machetes, and axes. Their heads and faces under heavy helmets camouflaged with grass and leaves. They bawled a song and drummed on the sides of the trucks in time to it. Let out a piercing war whoop, striking their palms against their lips. At the same time they were passing banana beer around, as if there were something to celebrate. There was a megaphone on the back of each truck. They sang at the top of their lungs:

Muze tubatsemba tsembe
muze tubamene ibitwe
muze twishyirehamwe
Interahamwe turaganje
Interahamwe twaratsinze

Come, we will wipe them all out,
come, we will cut off their heads,
come, we will do it together.
We Interahamwe are everywhere.
We Interahamwe have won!

Jeanne had already seen motor convoys like these several times. More frequently in recent months. But she'd never really taken in the exact words of the rallying cries that were called out through the megaphones—often accompanied by snappy radio music—and could be heard over a wide area. Sometimes the children had been sent home from school early on such occasions.

Almost in unison, the trucks now turned, rolled directly up to the eucalyptus wood, and stopped right in front of the pits, where the men had stopped digging. Puddle water splashed to all sides.

"Don't let us disturb you!" boomed out of one of the megaphones.

"You know what you're doing there? I'll bet you don't know!" Laughter. Yelling.

"We'll tell you. Those holes there, those are for you! Dig good and deep, so you'll all fit in!"

Again laughter. A chorus of honking. Shrill whistling in between. And as they slowly retreated, they started their song all over again.

"We'll be back! Tomorrow this'll be your graveyard!"

With this cry, which resounded over the plaza, they departed.

Their brief appearance brought everything to a standstill. The people were left standing there lifelessly. And this condition lasted for a long time after the Interahamwe had gone.

But Jeanne, Claudine, and Saphina took up their hopping game again as if nothing had happened. They played until noontime and even forgot to eat.

When a light rain began, Jeanne went inside. She had lain awake for a long time after last night's incident with Suzanne, and now suddenly she was unusually tired. Despite the unease that existed around her, she fell asleep quickly.

*

Until shouts from outside wakened her. Astonished, she realized that there was hardly anyone else left in the room with her. And the few besides her seemed to be leaving. She sprang up and ran across the hall to the exit, where she ran into Florence.

"There you are, Dédé! We've been looking for you. The mayor's called a meeting. All families are supposed to come. Even the children." She examined Jeanne. "Why haven't you showered yet?"

Jeanne stuck out her lower lip. She had no desire at all to go to a meeting. What were children supposed to do there?

"I have no more clean underwear!" she declared.

Florence moaned indignantly. "Then take the cleanest you have!" she advised. "I can't change that. Now go and wash! And hurry! You can get some warm water from me at the fireplace."

Jeanne turned around, ran back into the sleeping room, took a dress to change into, soap, and a towel. She skipped the underpants.

Florence was waiting to press a bucket into her hand. Filled to the top with warm water.

"Hurry now, you hear!" she warned her once more.

Jeanne disappeared into the washhouse, undressed, and began to soap herself from head to toe. She took her time. Perhaps that way she'd even miss the dumb meeting.

The noise outside increased. Jeanne heard the sound of a car driving by and right after that voices got loud.

"It's starting!"

"Hurry!"

"Everyone come here! The children too!" she heard in a tone of command.

The door to the washhouse was pushed open and Saphine stormed in.

"What are you still doing here, Dédé? Get dressed quickly and come on."

Jeanne stared at her soapy belly.

With a growl, Saphina snatched up the bucket and let a torrent of water slosh over Jeanne's shoulders. "Now, you get that soap off! I'll help you."

Together they struggled to rinse the light, smeary layer off her skin. They weren't especially thorough, for in the meantime Jeanne had been infected by Saphina's agitation. She slipped into her clothes without drying off. There was no time left for applying lotion.

Shortly after the girls left the washhouse, they were swallowed in an excited crowd. People streamed past from all directions.

The mayor's car was parked in front of the building holding the community center. A brand-new pickup truck. Its dark blue and chrome gleamed spotless under the band of bright sunbeams that angled down through a gap in the gray cloud cover.

Innocent was sitting in the passenger seat beside his chauffeur. He was looking through the closed car window. Jeanne caught sight of her mother, who was blazing a path straight up to the car. Jeanne wanted to go to her. She squeezed through the crowd but she didn't get very far because the press was much too thick. And she had already lost sight of Florence.

The mayor raised his arms. The noise ebbed away.

At that very moment, however, a woman near the car screamed out: "The Interahamwe! They're here! Behind the houses! They're going to kill us!"

The scream was multiplied. The people next to the car began moving.

Innocent rolled the window down and stuck his head out. Using a police whistle, he called for order.

"No need to get excited!" he shouted through a loudspeaker. "They've come to protect you!"

With these words he pulled his head in, quickly rolled up the window, and let himself fall back onto the seat. A nod of the head. The engine starting. Steady honking. The people fell back as well as they could, and the truck rushed away.

Some people had fallen on the ground where he parted the crowd, and the space suddenly gave a view of a troop of soldiers who'd appeared out of nowhere.

With rifles pointed, they moved in and began encircling the crowd and driving it in the direction of the community center. When some people ducked to try to break out of the encirclement, shots came from all sides. Those struck fell to the ground, and hardly anyone else dared to try to escape. Only a few people at the edge managed to get away. The circle closed ever tighter, crowding the people together, shoving them step by step up to the open door and stuffing them into the building.

"In there! Get along in there!"

Jeanne was caught in the stream as it swept along. She struggled against it, stayed behind a little, and got to the edge of the crowd. But then she had the soldiers close behind her and there remained no choice but to follow the others. She was also pushed into the building, one of the last ones.

She could only hold onto one thought: She had to get out of here! Right away! The building swallowed people. A man-eating building.

The door opened. A soldier shoved a woman in front of him, the barrel of his gun pointed at her neck. She stumbled over the doorsill and stopped a moment, standing there panting and swaying. The soldier yelled something and poked his knee into her back. Beside him appeared other soldiers, holding out hand grenades. Ready to throw. The woman took a step forward.

In a flash, Jeanne dropped to her stomach. Slithered past the soldiers' boots to the outside, sprang up, and raced away. Along the low hedge that separated the paved path from the houses around the plaza. The way was open.

Right afterwards a deep, powerful explosion shook the air. It struck her between the shoulders and terrified her. Further explosions followed at short intervals. In between, shots. Shattering wood. Breaking glass. Screams.

Jeanne reached the end of the hedge and now looked back at the plaza, where innumerable people lay bleeding on the ground. Others fled in zigzags toward a house. Or tried to escape into the bordering shrubbery. Until shots struck them down. Until someone caught them and simply clubbed them down.

And then she saw her mother.

Florence was lying only a few yards away, at the feet of some soldiers and Interahamwe, who were striking at her. Clubs and machetes rained down on her body. Feet were kicking at her. Over and over again. Obeying an impulse, Jeanne was about to bend over the hedge and run to her mother, but a soldier was coming toward her and blocked her way.

Jeanne spurted away.

Looking back for a last, breathless moment, she saw Florence raise her head as though she wanted to stand up. The club blows followed the movement, and they did not miss their target.

Jeanne ran on. Ran for her life.

They were her legs that were running. A race without mind and heart. Every thought, every feeling was extinguished. The little plaza with its houses was like a trap. She saw others also running haphazardly. Here and there. Suddenly her father, who dashed out from behind one house and disappeared behind another. Her legs turned in his direction. Carried her toward him without her knowing what she was doing.

"Teya! Teya!" The tearful cry of a little voice. A little hand that grasped at her. Jeanne stopped and sank to her knees.

"Teya, hold me! Where is my mama?" A sob. Arms that wrapped around her and clasped her tightly. It was hard for her to breathe.

I'm not Teya, she thought desperately without saying it.

"My mama . . . ! Where is my mama? Teya, take me with you!"

The loud weeping drilled itself into her consciousness. She stood up.

It was Alain who thought she was Teya. A little boy, three at the most. His grandmother was a colleague of Florence's.

Alain's hands clutched at Jeanne's dress.

"Come with me! We've got to get away from here, fast!" she said.

He stopped crying. She loosened his hands, pulled him along with her, and headed for the wall of the house behind which she'd seen her father disappear.

Ananie came into view again. She called to him before he could get too far ahead of her. He stopped running. Turned around and ran up to her.

"Dédé!" He was breathing hard. "Come, we have to go on!"

Holding Alain between them, they hurried toward the little eucalyptus wood, using the houses as protection. Pursued by the sounds and the voices of the dying. Others in front of them and behind them were fleeing in the same direction.

They fought their way into the bushes. Dove into the eucalyptus wood. Between running figures. And suddenly, miraculously, Jando was also beside them. His face was contorted. Sweat streamed down his forehead. He gasped, said nothing.

He'd also escaped the trap!

"Up we go!" Ananie cried, swooping Alain up so they could cover the ground faster.

They reached the end of the wood. Stormed across a road, to dive into a banana grove on the other side.

The greenness enclosed them. Them and the others who were wandering about among the tall palms. But there were too many people. The vigorous movements with which they parted the plants betrayed them.

And soon they were already hearing the voices of the pursuers. Shouts were coming from all directions in the hills around them. The voices gave each other directions and were accompanied by shots, leaving no doubt that the hunters intended to carry their extermination plan to the end.

"There's some running! They're coming down the mountain to the road!"

"Yes! We see them!"

"Run up to them! Catch them!"

"Come from the other side, quick! We have to surround them!"

Voices compelling them to turn back.

The fugitives pushed ever deeper into the plantation, where the thicket of plants now became so impenetrable that progress was almost impossible. Yet they fought their way through, distancing themselves yard by yard from the invisible callers, whose voices became increasingly faint, and finally even the shots were almost inaudible. Blocked by the green wall.

Here the fugitives finally halted.

Jeanne was holding her side. A knife-sharp stitch robbed her of breath, leaving no room for other feelings. Ananie gasped for breath as he set Alain on the ground. Jando, his face ashy, leaned against the trunk of a palm.

Some twenty other people had collected there. They acted dazed. Unable to do more than catch their breath. For a long time they all just stood there. Each contained within himself. A sudden silence enveloped them, only interrupted now and then by sounds of exhaustion.

A woman spoke first. "What can we do? They're on our trail and will be here soon. There's no chance of escaping them anymore. We're surrounded."

"I can't take any more. I'm going back to the community center and giving up. We haven't a chance," said another.

"Are you crazy? To volunteer to go be killed! No, I'm not giving up so fast."

"Where are we supposed to go, then? What do you think they'll do when they find us? And they certainly will find us. They saw from the hills where we ran. They're already behind us and in front of us. I don't want to be just slaughtered. I'd rather go back and let myself be shot. It'll be fast that way."

"Do you think they'd do you the favor? For shooting you have to pay."

"Yes, that's right. I saw it myself before. Someone gave them money and was shot for it," someone said.

There was silence for a long moment after this

exchange.

"I'm not giving up! I'll wait until it's dark. Then I'll try to make it through to Joseph. He's my friend. He'll hide me," cried a young man.

"We have no more friends," murmured the woman who had spoken first.

"And I have no more money," said one of the group.

"The best thing would be for us to pool our money, go to the community center together, and give up."

"Yes, you're right. What else can we do?"

Some of them actually emptied their pockets and put their money together.

"No, I'm not going to let myself be killed," the young man insisted. "Joseph will help me."

Jeanne was observing her father, who had followed the exchange of words in silence. What would he do?

When he didn't move, she hoped that he had his own plan. The stitch in her side didn't hurt so much anymore. But her feet were burning terribly. And she was thirsty. There was an emptiness in her head.

"Then what are we waiting for? They'll be here pretty soon!"

The group started moving. Others followed. Then Ananie gave the children a wave. The breathing spell was over.

When they again came to the spot where they'd forced their way into the banana plantation, the group that had decided for their own death went in the direction of the community center.

The others scattered.

Jeanne held Alain firmly by the hand and followed her father, who together with Jando, was fleeing parallel to the main road. Through a little wood, across small fields, and along side roads hidden from view. Thus they circled the commune and came out near houses situated on a hill far away from the main road. Ananie obviously had a goal.

Over a hill they came to a small house, surrounded by fields, the last one behind a development.

A man was standing outside, at the door. Children were playing in the yard. When the man saw Ananie, Jeanne, Jando, and Alain approaching, he quickly sent the children into the house.

Ananie raised his hand in greeting. Jeanne wondered if she had ever seen the man before. But she didn't remember him. He was smaller and less robust than her father. He came toward them, his thin, wiry arms crossed on his chest. His graying hair thinned back from his forehead to a partially bald head. No. Jeanne was sure now. She didn't know him.

"*Bonjour*, Bernard!" said Ananie when they stood opposite each other.

"Ananie!" replied the other. "How did you make it here? There are gangs and militia all over the place!"

"I know. Perhaps you can advise me what to do. Where we should go."

"Not back to the center, under any circumstances. There's no protection there anymore."

"I know," Ananie repeated and waited.

"Unfortunately, I can't hide you with me, Ananie. I would gladly do it, but it would be too dangerous. We're being checked constantly."

Ananie looked him in the eye. "Have you any other suggestion?" he asked.

"Maybe the reed area up there!" Bernard gestured up this hill with his outstretched arm. "It's very thick and set back quite far. Probably no one will find you there. Not tonight, at least. Otherwise, I don't know. I'm sorry."

Ananie nodded.

"*Merci*," he said tersely. "Let's go!"

"I'll look after you later, when it's dark," Bernard promised.

Again a nod of the head. Ananie turned to go.

The thin reed grasses grew nearly nine feet tall, with almost no space between them. In order to enter the field, you had to bend their thick, hard stems apart and so, unavoidably, you created a broad trail that anyone could follow.

A few times, Alain fell over the stalks lying every which way. His short legs had trouble getting through. But he bravely kept on. Jeanne fought her way past the grasses and tried to keep the sharp edges from scratching the bare skin of her arms.

Somewhere in the middle of the field they stumbled on a figure curled up on the ground. They stopped. On a closer look, Jeanne recognized the young man who'd intended to hide with his friend Joseph. He didn't move, but panting showed that he was alive. He'd probably run in from the other side of the field. His trail would also betray to searchers that this was a hiding place.

It made no sense to go any further.

Ananie pressed a few reeds flat and sat down. The children copied him. Alain stretched out and put his head on Jeanne's lap. His little hands balled into fists, he closed his eyes. Jeanne looked over at her brother. He seemed to be far away.

"Has any of you seen Florence?" asked Ananie, after they'd all caught their breath again.

Jeanne winced. The picture of whirling clubs and machetes blazed up garishly before her.

After a brief hesitation, she reported what she had seen.

Ananie took off his glasses, stared at the lenses, and rubbed his eyes with the back of his hand.

"Was Teya with her?" he asked.

Jeanne shook her head. Only at that moment did she become conscious that Teya was missing. That she had entirely forgotten Teya. And at once she began to feel guilty.

"And you?" her father directed his words to Jando. "Have you seen Teya?"

The lips moved in her brother's sunken, stony face and formed a voiceless no. Jeanne shuddered. Whatever was wrong with Jando? He looked like a ghost. Had he lost the power of speech? Or his mind? She would have liked to crawl over to him and shake him. But she was held back by the crackling sound of tramping steps suddenly approaching.

Seconds later a gang of teenagers broke through the bamboo stalks. There were six or seven young men, among them also two boys hardly older than Jando.

"We got 'em!" cried one.

Jeanne automatically thought of the street boys who had often washed her father's motorcycle. But they'd been armed with polishing cloths, not with axes and machetes. Jeanne put her arms around Alain.

As she did so, her eyes fell on Zingiro, her family's former houseboy, who, though he held himself a little away from the others, looked just as grim and determined as his half-grown buddies. Jeanne had never seen him again since Florence had let him go about a year ago. He'd grown quite fat.

His unexpected reappearance in this place loosed a rage in her that was even stronger than her fear. She could have flown at him. What did he think he was doing, threatening them! Certainly he wanted to get revenge.

Now one of the boys walked up to Ananie and spat in front of him. He was obviously the oldest and the leader of the gang.

"Well, how do you feel now, Professor?" he sneered.

Jeanne's indignation grew. How dared this fellow speak to her father so disrespectfully!

"Without your beautiful house and your motorcycle!" he continued spitefully. "Now you don't have anything anymore! Who do you think's riding your motorcycle now!"

Jeanne threw an angry look at Zingiro. "But you know us! You worked for us. So what do you want from us?" she burst out at him.

The leader answered in Zingiro's place. "Well, what else

191

would we want! The money you have on you! So hand it over!"

"I have nothing," Ananie declared.

"Then your shoes, for all I care. Or your shirt, Professor!" He waved his machete unmistakably. "If you have nothing to offer, we'll kill you!"

Ananie pulled a bundle of money out of his pocket and handed it to them.

"Well, now! There, you were lucky again." The leader waved the notes triumphantly and then pointed to the young man on the ground. "Is that one there one of you?"

Immediately Ananie answered the question in the affirmative.

But then Zingiro chimed in. "I know the family very well!" he growled. "That one has nothing to do with them at all."

He barely had the words out when they all stepped forward, as if on command, and hacked at the man on the ground.

Jeanne buried her head in her arms. She only lifted it again when she heard, "We're finished here."

The young murderers grabbed their victim by the feet and dragged his body away behind them. They retreated, bawling out the glory of their exploit.

Jeanne tried not to look at the place where the body of the murdered man had crushed down the reeds. She wondered if he'd made it to his friend Joseph and been turned away there. Or if he'd just stopped to hide here temporarily on the way to him.

Slowly the dusk crept through the grasses in the field. It brought cool night air with it and a little later, voices again, which approached from far off. Then the crackling of the grasses under firm steps provided Jeanne with the certainty that the next troop was unerringly on its way toward them, led by the tracks of the others.

A group of teenagers pushed the reeds aside and stood in a semicircle. Civilians this time, too, but fitted out with everything they needed to kill. One just like the other. Interchangeable. Drunk with power. Driven by greed.

Because Ananie had no more money left, they took his shoes, his wristwatch, also his plastic ballpoint pen, and his glasses case. They also wanted his glasses.

That was too much!

Jeanne couldn't contain herself anymore. She protested, "My father can't see anything without glasses! What do you want with his glasses anyway? Please don't take his glasses!"

This time she pleaded. It had its effect. They withdrew and left Ananie his glasses.

After they were gone, Jeanne listened tensely and waited. She realized that her hands were clenched into fists so hard that her fingers hurt. Slowly she stretched them out, one after the other.

When the tension had ebbed somewhat, she began to tremble. She was miserably cold, for she was only wearing a sleeveless summer dress. Her pullover was back in the washhouse. Desperately she rubbed her arms.

"I'm so terribly cold," she wailed.

Jando turned his head in her direction and looked at

her. A fog cleared from his eyes, as if he had just woke up. He pulled off his sweatshirt and handed it over to her. He was wearing a second one under it.

She took the sweatshirt gratefully and slipped it right on. The inside gave off her brother's warmth. Gradually the shivering stopped.

They waited. No one said anything. In the silence Jeanne prayed that the gangs of thieves had gone to bed. If another of them were to turn up now, there was nothing left they could give them. Then they were lost.

Shouts awakened them.

"C'mere! Over here! Some of them went in here! They can't have gotten very far!"

"Search the field!"

This was the end.

"Stop! You can spare yourselves the trouble. We've looked all through it. There's no one left in there anymore!"

Jeanne was puzzled. She knew that voice. It was Bernard's voice.

"You sure?"

"Very sure. Others have already done your work."

"If you say so . . ."

The voices moved away. It grew quiet.

Very much later, after it was completely dark, Bernard found them as promised. He brought blankets, a flashlight, and cookies with him but he stayed only a few minutes.

"It will be better if tomorrow you're not here anymore," he warned. "I advise you to leave the field before daybreak. They'll come back. And then I can do nothing more for you."

"*Merci beaucoup,* you've already done very much for us," Ananie answered. "If we survive the night here . . . *on verra.*"

When Bernard had gone, quiet finally returned. Alain was already asleep. Jeanne wrapped a blanket around him and put one around her shoulders.

She remained sitting upright. Keeping her eyes open and staring into the night. The hard grasses and stalks cut her flesh. Her skin, dry and still full of the remains of the soap, began to itch. She became painfully aware of each part of her body. And inside her, a big, black hole.

Suddenly she was sure that her mother was dead. That she could not be alive anymore.

"Let's go back and lie beside Mama," she said. "Then they'll think we're dead too and won't do anything to us."

Now she'd said it out loud. Her words hung there in the darkness.

"The soldiers will come to bury the dead," Ananie finally answered tonelessly. "We can't go back, Dédé. Don't rack your brain. It makes no sense to think back over it."

But her thoughts wouldn't let her go.

She remembered the death of her grandmother. When Nyogokuru died, the family had mourned her for a week long. The children didn't have to go to school. All the relatives and the other mourners—friends and neighbors—had come together at Grandmother's house, where the old woman was laid out after her death, dressed in her most beautiful festival dress. Everyone could go up to her, see her once more, and take leave of her.

Outside in the yard they had lit a great bonfire for her. Until Nyogokuru's burial on the third day, it was watched over day and night to make sure that it did not go out. Now and then the children had joined the watchers and helped them lay wood on it.

As long as the dead were not buried, you had to keep watch at the fire for them.

There was no fire for Florence. No mourners either.

But Jeanne watched the whole night.

While the murderers slept.

You run away from me.

As you do every morning when we run our lap before breakfast.

For the first part we're still close together. But then, when the street begins to go uphill, you run away from me. I lose sight of you in the narrow streets of Biniaraix.

You're waiting for me at a corner at the end of the village. Then it's time for a little rest, because we're both out of breath.

Usually we go a few yards farther and stop at the highway above the valley. There, where there's a view over the orange groves, over the city of Sóller and its old towers, to the bay.

We always greet the morning at this spot, before the others are up. Inspecting Mallorca's vacation sky to speculate how the weather is going to be. Inhaling the stillness and the fragrance of the groves. It's rare for anyone else to be out yet. Here in the south the day doesn't begin until later. At this moment, everything we see or smell belongs to us.

Then we go down into the valley together: the incline,

down from now on, helps me keep up with you. Your lead only a few yards now. Then we go back into the house. And make breakfast for the others. Thus begins our day.

Today I'm even slower at the beginning than usual.

You've run way ahead of me.

Although it's still very early, the sun is giving off a warmth that pools in my legs. And as the streets become steeper, I fall into a tired trot. Biniaraix is such a picturesque village! Today the warm yellow of the rubblework walls under the brilliant blue sky seduces me into stopping here. I look around me. The morning shadows make the colors seem darker than they are. They are very high, up to the roofs, and block out the dazzling light of the sun. The colors gentle, softened, as if they were sleeping.

I find a little store. A bar. Let my eyes sweep over a small church square. It's beautiful here. Terrifically peaceful.

When I approach our corner, I can't see you anywhere. You haven't waited for me. And you aren't at our viewing spot, either. Well, wait, I'll still catch up with you somewhere! I run off.

I hope to catch sight of you around the bend, on the long, straight part of the street that leads to our house. But there's nothing to be seen of you here, either. You want to show me something today? Have you possibly put the coffee on already?

I arrive at the house out of breath. Open the big door. Walk into the entrada.

You aren't there. Not a sound to be heard.

I leave the house quickly. Run back to the street. Keeping my eyes peeled. No sign of you. I go back to the starting place. Look high up toward Biniaraix. Decide to climb up there once again to look for you.

The store has opened in the meantime, the door stands open. But far and wide there is not a human being to be seen. And not you either!

Not at our corner either.

I'm gradually growing concerned.

The shadows are so dark in front of the big gates that the inner courtyards of the houses are hidden behind them. I see a strong arm suddenly reaching out to draw you inside. You're a pretty girl!

And my imagination is boundless when it's fed by anxiety.

Perhaps you sprained an ankle along the way? But then I would have found you at the edge of the road.

My watch says that you've been missing for almost an hour. And that's not your way at all! My heart begins to pound. I have to do something—first, back to the house!

There you are, standing at the door, waiting. Safe and sound.

Anger and joy war within me.

"Where have you been?" I snap at you.

You explain to me.

Because I kept you waiting so long for me, you ran a little extra way for a change. And from then on we missed each other everywhere. You were also looking for me. And waiting for me.

Breakfast tastes especially good to us today. Good that

you're there!

Yes, I was afraid for you.

None of them had slept, except for little Alain. They had held out in the bamboo field, not looking toward the morning, for morning offered no promise.

They had no more money or anything else with which they might buy their lives, and there was no possibility of hiding from the killers. They were at the end.

And they knew it.

At some time, the lights in the sky were extinguished. A layer of cloud moved in front of them, announcing the rain that Jeanne had been expecting all night, because it was unavoidable, like everything else. Daybreak rose from the reeds before their eyes. Creeping closer was a day that promised only hopelessness.

Then the rain came and pelted down on them with hard drops. No longer a rain you could play tag with. It fell into their hiding place, slammed with cold wetness, dragged Alain from his slumber, and forced them all to stand up. An accomplice to the killers.

They huddled close together, pulled the blanket over their heads, and endured until the shower vanished as quickly as it had come. The sun came out in all its strength, fraying the cloud cover around it, and with fierce brightness announced that it was irrevocably day.

"*Venez, enfants! On y va,*" said Ananie.

They left the blankets behind. Jeanne had trouble getting her legs to move. She walked as if she were on stilts, her stiff limbs hurting and resisting every movement.

But Ananie, shoeless, swung along ahead of the children as if they were on their Sunday walk. On a direct road going toward the main road, which they reached after very few minutes. The way he was moving, erect and looking purposefully ahead as he walked, as if there were nothing more to fear, had something challenging about it.

Normal daily life had already started around the houses that lay on their way. Women were hanging out washing. Grain was being taken from the storage sheds and spread out to dry on large raffia mats. Children were playing in the yards. Their voices were as lively and lighthearted as usual. A boy and an old man were kneeling in front of a gigantic wooden trough, along with two women, arms and hands sunk deep inside the container, kneading tirelessly. Jeanne knew what they were doing. They were trying to press the juice out of the bananas into a mash mixture with grass, under steady pressure. If the juice was going to be processed into beer, they had to start early, for it was a very time-consuming, difficult production process that needed a whole day of preparation. The kneading demanded all the strength of their fingers, and the effort of it could be seen on their faces.

If some of the other houses hadn't been destroyed and abandoned, if besides Ananie and the children there hadn't also been Interahamwe, armed farmers, gangs of youths, and a few members of the militia on the main road, there would have been no perceptible sign of menace or the recent atrocities at all.

What kind of a war is it, Jeanne wondered, when they hang out their wash while the others next to them are killed for no reason? What had she and her family done, what had their friends done to deserve death?

They were Tutsis. Jeanne knew now that all Tutsis were supposed to die. Without exception. But why?

As she dragged herself along behind Ananie, battling the pain in her legs and holding little Alain tightly by the hand, she lost the connection to what was going on around her. She was trapped in a bad, confusing dream, snared among its images.

Therefore it did not surprise her that her father was walking with her, Jando, and Alain in the middle of the main road among the murderers, who were even marching along in the same direction as they were. Nor that they remained unmolested as they did so, no one doing anything to them. It was as if they were wrapped in an envelope that protected them from the outside. As if they were really not there at all.

Now they were overtaken. Hostile looks and spiteful words were hurled at them.

"What d'you want here? Are you lost, maybe?"

"What are you looking at, then? You still think you're someone better? That's over for you now!"

"Well, Professor, on the way to class? You're a little late today! But we'll wait for you, you can count on that."

Ananie remained unmoved, not allowing himself to be flustered by anything. Jeanne hadn't the least idea what he had in mind, but she trusted him. Shortly before they reached the center, Ananie placed his hand on Jando's shoulder. "We're going to the mayor," he said.

This time they approached the small dwelling from behind, and again they met the mayor at his door, just about to go into the house. He was not dressed. He only had a large towel wrapped around his mighty belly, as if he'd just come out of the shower.

He turned toward them, clearly displeased, as Ananie walked up to him with the children.

"*Bonjour*, Innocent," said Ananie. "Excuse the interruption, but you must help us! Tell us of a place we can stay!"

"Ananie, you know perfectly well I can do nothing for you! I'm not allowed to take in anyone else here. I have no right to!"

"Innocent, *pour l'amour de Dieu*! Help us! Can you not at least protect the children?"

"Impossible!"

The door slammed behind the mayor, and its dull thud spoke the last word.

They stood there in front of it, numb. Now there was no one left to whom they could turn. Jeanne looked at her father. He stood there with sagging shoulders, his face gray and tired like that of an old man. Staring hard at the door.

"Come over here! Quick!"

A voice from the gate to the yard. Too soft for a shout, yet clearly a summons directed at them. The mayor's houseboy, half hidden behind the large pillar at the entrance to the yard, was beckoning them. They followed his signal imme-

203

diately and ran through the gate. The yard was empty.

"I'll hide you here with me, but only for a short time," the houseboy said. He hurried forward, opened the door to his bedroom next to the kitchen, let them enter, and quickly closed the door again.

"Probably no one will think of looking for you here for now," he said. "You can stay until I've found something else for you."

"*Merci*!" Ananie said.

The room was very small and too full with them in it. Two tiny, high windows allowed very little light inside. There was a bed, which took up a large portion of the room, a set of shelves filled with boxes and food, and a large, open suitcase with pieces of clothing spilling out of it.

"Bosco! Where are you?"

Innocent. Very irritated.

"All right then, I'll see if I can find something for you!" Bosco whispered, before he opened the door a mere crack and slipped through it.

Ananie watched him go. And then he said, "*Bon, mes enfants*, now I'm going to leave you for a short time. I want to see if I can get something for us to eat and drink."

Jeanne, her eyes on the filled shelves, wanted to contradict him.

But all at once Ananie appeared to be in a great hurry and to want to use the instant in which he could probably get out unobserved.

"No matter what happens, wait here! *Compris*?" And he was gone.

After he left them, she listened intently without being entirely sure what for. Shots? It remained quiet. For quite some time. Long enough so that she could assume that her father had left the yard without being seen.

But then shortly after that the noise started again. Heavy steps, a racket from outside. People came running into the yard.

"Hey! Where are those people who came in here?" someone shouted.

Jando ducked and disappeared under the bed. Jeanne looked for another hiding place, but there wasn't any.

"Quick!" Jeanne whispered and pulled Alain up next to her on the bed under which her brother had hidden. She hoped that their dangling legs could serve as a screen.

At that moment the door was thrust open. Two men stood on the threshold, a tall youngish one with a shaved head and a smaller but very stocky older man. Both were armed with machetes. Jeanne peered past them into the yard, where three more men, also armed with axes and machetes, had taken up posts.

The older one now entered the room, followed by the younger one. Both looked around them. Then the older one leaned over close to Jeanne. An unpleasant smell was coming from his clothing. He wore a tattered, dirty suit, whose jacket didn't match the trousers, over a greenish-yellow patterned T-shirt. And his hair was stiff with dirt, bleached by the sun, and little knots of reddish colored dust covered his head.

His face looked coarse, the skin rough and scarred.

When he opened his mouth to speak, he revealed rotted stumps of teeth.

"Where are your father and your brother?" he barked at Jeanne.

Afraid the fear in her eyes could betray her, Jeanne bent her head, and her eyes fell on the elegant, shining leather shoes into which the man's dirty bare feet were crammed.

With the sudden awareness that another man must have lost his life for sake of those shoes, she was over- whelmed by uncontrollable fury.

She looked up. Naked rage in her eyes.

"I don't know," she answered in a trembling voice. "Maybe you just killed them!"

The man hauled back his arm. He struck her full force in the face so that she fell back. She rubbed her burning cheek. Her eyes were burning too. But she held back her tears. The rage was stronger than the pain.

Now the man grabbed her by the arm, pulled her vio- lently off the bed to take her outside into the yard. She resisted. Alain, whose hand was still firmly clasped in hers, was dragged along. The youth with the shaved head stepped in and tried to separate the two children. When she wasn't able to hold Alain's hand any longer, Jeanne threw herself onto the ground, trying to resist that way. As she was dragged across the yard, she saw one of the three men who had been posted at the door enter the houseboy's room. Alain ran after Jeanne. At the courtyard gate she grabbed one of the gateposts, clung to it, kicked her legs, and screamed with all her might.

"Let go of me! I won't! I won't!"

Alain was standing right beside her.

Still other armed farmers and young men had gathered in front of the gate. They appeared to be waiting for something. Slowly Jeanne stood up. One of them came up to her.

"Who are you? You're Tutsi, aren't you? Where are your parents?"

Jeanne didn't answer.

"My mama said my papa is coming from Zaire to get me," said Alain in a very small voice.

A slight man detached himself from the group and seized Alain's hand. "I know his father," he asserted. "I'll take him with me." No one seemed to have anything against it, and so the man went away with Alain.

As the little boy stumbled along after him, clearly against his will, he looked back at Jeanne. "Teya! Teya!" he cried pitifully. And for the first time since she'd found him and brought him along, he started crying again.

A club struck Jeanne on the shoulder. She screamed.

"Now, talk!"

A second blow followed.

"Stop it!" she screamed. "I'm a Hutu!"

Scarcely were these words out of her mouth when she saw that two men were dragging Jando across the yard, while others behind him were hitting him with clubs and kicking at him. He must already have been beaten inside and injured, for he could hardly stand on his legs. His eyes half closed, his head bent to one side, he hung between his tormentors. They beat him through the gate. He made not a sound, as if he were already unconscious. But Jeanne caught a look full of agony. She was beside herself.

"Let him go! Right now! He's my brother! He hasn't done anything to you!"

"You lied to us!" The cold voice of the man in the shoes that didn't belong to him grazed her ear.

She had to look on helplessly while Jando was driven with unceasing blows and kicks to the plaza in front of the community center, where still others intent on murder and a few soldiers and policemen had gathered.

She tore herself loose and ran after her brother. But before she could reach him, she saw a farmer walking across the plaza. Apparently without purpose.

As he was passing the group with Jando, however, he quickly lifted his long-handled field hoe and drove its point into the back of Jando's head. Jando collapsed. He lay there and moved no more. But still the blows rained down on him. The farmer disappeared.

At the moment the hoe struck its target, Jeanne began to scream. She screamed with every fiber of her body. She screamed in place of her brother as he died.

No one came to her.

Finally the murderers left their victim and moved on. Only the young, bald-headed man stayed behind. He tore Jando's clothes off his body and put them on over his own. Jando's short pants, his T-shirt, his sweatshirt.

When he was done, he grabbed the dead boy under the arms, picked him up, carried him to the pit, and threw him in.

Jeanne stopped screaming.

She didn't cry either. She couldn't cry. Her tears were locked in.

The jailers were patrolling.

We eat melon with ham.
Tears run down your face.

You have simply pursued me all day long. With your words.

We lay on the beach. We sat in the café. We took the little railroad through the wild gardens of the harbor inlet back to the city of Sóller.

It is our first vacation on Mallorca. We have come alone. We are planning to begin the work. On our book.

Even at breakfast you began to tell.

Like a button pushed. Like an automaton. Couldn't be turned off, not for a moment. You kept on talking to me while we walked through the narrow streets together.

Pressed against the wall of a house to let the traffic go by, I listened to you. Listened as the horror poured from your lips. I heard words that were seeking their way to the outside. Without any order. Fragments of memory. I listened to you the entire day. On the way to the supermarket. As we went through the shelves, as we put the items we needed for supper into the grocery cart. Only once did I interrupt you. When we were in the long line in front of the deli counter.

"One moment," I said. "I have to get some ham. Then I'll listen to you again."

Not until supper does calm gradually return. The explosion of words is over.

In the silence you now put the question that has haunted you for so long. Why weren't you killed too? You feel guilty. Just because you survived. Just because! That's how you see it. A little bitter, as it sounds to me. The others were worth more, you probably mean to say by that.

What can I answer? I grope my way toward something I've been feeling for a long time, and after today I almost know for sure.

"You wanted to live! Every minute, and you want it now. You fought for it then and you're still fighting. Your reason for living is you yourself." I say that to you as I cut the melon piece by piece into small slivers. I look up and continue, "There's still another reason why you survived. This moment, in which we're here together. There's you for me now. That makes me happy. Your life has a reason for me too. And for the others."

You look at me and say nothing.

I go around the table. To you. Hug your shoulders. Pull you very close to me. "You do feel that, how important you are for us!"

But still you say nothing.

"What did you actually feel that day you came to us?" I ask.

Your eyes fill with tears. "I trusted you," you say.

"Right away." And begin to cry. For the first time.

The tears run down your face. They also continue to run unstopping as you eat. A stream that does not dry up for a long time.

It is the rainy season. Life is returning.

Jeanne stood alone in the middle of the plaza in front of the community center and looked around her.

Where was her father? He'd promised to come back. But he would not come back. Not ever. He was dead. Certainly. All were dead. All except her. Why not her too? She wanted to be dead too. Where should she go now? She didn't stir from the spot.

Around her the groups broke up. Some of the soldiers and Interahamwe withdrew, and the civilians began to clean up. Carried some more bodies to the pits. There weren't many anymore. Obviously there'd been a thorough clearing up the day before.

But now individual people were brought out of those houses that had served the Tutsis as sleeping places during the recent days. Their grenade-shattered bodies.

Jeanne watched, no longer affected inside. Once, a considerable distance away, she fleetingly caught sight of a man standing between two policemen who raised his hand, as if he intended to greet Jeanne. A gesture from another world, which she didn't understand. She turned away from him.

Then the door to the community center, from which she'd fled just at the last moment yesterday, was opened and a woman brought out.

Her body lay on a large, colorful cotton cloth with a pattern of birds. Perhaps it was that pattern, perhaps something else familiar that made Jeanne unconsciously take a few steps in her direction.

It was Aunt Pascasia. She had no legs anymore.

Her eyes were turned toward Jeanne but without any sign of recognition.

"Please give me some water!" she moaned.

Jeanne ran. The word *water* streamed through her head like a spring, which kept her from going mad at that moment.

Water. Water . . . when someone asked for water, you weren't allowed to refuse it.

She ran to the water place. No container there. And it had to be fast. Jeanne formed her hands into a bowl, filled them with water, and ran back. The water dripped through her fingers, it ran out through the crack between her hands.

When she got back to the place where she'd last seen her aunt, there was no one there anymore.

She held her hands in front of her, still formed into a bowl. The inner surfaces gleamed in the sun. Damp. But her hands were empty.

She lifted her head to the sun. Against the light a swarm of birds, the flicker of wings in the air. She blinked. Her eyes returned to the plaza, scouring it. Stopped, fastened to the edge of the pit.

No, she could not look into the hole.

From behind heavy steps hurried up to her. Someone

took her by the arm. She turned slowly around. Certain that now she would meet her own death.

But it was the man who had waved to her.

"Come, Dédé," he said. "I'll try to take you with us."

He led her gently from the plaza. Completely without will, she let it happen. Thus they headed toward a group of women, young girls, and children who were sitting down on a small patch of grass at the edge of the road. Motionless figures, watched by the two policemen and a few farmers who were still there. Some of the women and girls were wounded on the arms and legs. Somewhat to one side squatted a girl about sixteen years old.

Chantal! A former pupil of Florence's, who had sometimes cared for Jeanne when she was a small child and had been taken to school by her mother. Beside Chantal sat her sister Carine, who wasn't much older than Jeanne.

Wordlessly Jeanne sat down beside the two of them. Chantal had changed. She had always been very tall and slender, but now she looked skinny. Her small face emaciated and its length increased by the broom hairdo that was very fashionable at the time: the hair cut very close on the sides, longer on top, standing in a low brush from front to back.

Her round eyes glittered feverishly, and in them lay the unspeakable, which Jeanne also carried inside her. The back of Chantal's right hand and her little finger, as well, were swollen, pierced by grenade shrapnel. She was bleeding. She kept trying to wipe off the blood on her long, colorful summer slacks.

"Hello, Dédé," she said softly.

Jeanne was not able to return the greeting.

"Dédé..." Chantal began after a pause, "...besides Jando have you seen anyone else from your family?"

Jeanne understood immediately what Chantal intended to say with these words. That she had also been a witness to Jando's murder. To speak about it that way made it easier.

"I saw my mother," she answered faintly. "Yesterday. On the plaza in front of the community center." She swallowed. "My father was still with us this morning. He went to get us something to eat. That's what he said anyway. I haven't seen him again since then."

Chantal nodded silently.

"I haven't seen Teya either."

"I saw Teya," Chantal replied. "She was with us in the community center when it blew up. Right near me." She regarded her injured hand. "We were standing very far back, so I didn't get very much. Teya wasn't hit, Dédé, I know that for sure. She only fell down. Just like that."

In Jeanne's thoughts flared the moment when she had crawled between the legs of the soldiers through the door to the outside.

Teya! she thought. Teya! She was inside there. And I didn't know it.

Now the man who'd waved at her and later led her from the plaza detached himself from the group of farmers.

"Dédé, if you want, I'll take you with us," he said, repeating his offer from before. And then she suddenly realized who he was.

Vincent. A friend of her Aunt Theresia, who owned several houses, a bank, and a restaurant in Kibungo. Vincent had worked for her as a property manager for a long time.

During the days when Jeanne and her family had been staying in Birenga, now and again a message from Aunt Theresia was brought to them. The last had been written news that her aunt had hidden herself somewhere in her restaurant. After that they had heard nothing more of her.

"Do you want to come, Dédé?" asked Vincent gently.

Two of the farmers standing there intervened.

"What's all this, Vincent! What do you have to do with this family! You'll leave the girl here!"

Their tone and the way they moved toward him was doubtless supposed to intimidate him, if not actually threaten him. "It's enough that you've taken Theresia's things with you!"

Vincent drew back. "I'm sorry, Dédé. Don't worry. I'll see what I can do for you," he said regretfully before he left.

When he was gone, Jeanne collapsed and sank into a condition of complete exhaustion.

Meanwhile the work of cleaning up in front of the commune's center went on. They began to fill in the pit with the soil piled up around the edges. Jeanne observed it like a distant happening that had nothing to do with her.

More women and girls joined the group of survivors on the grass strip. Before they were allowed to sit down they had to undergo a short interrogation.

Some of them were later taken away with someone. Especially younger girls, who would be offered a place as a housemaid or a marriage.

At the word *marriage*, Jeanne pricked up her ears.

When Tutsi women married Hutu men, the women became Hutus. And later their children were also Hutus.

Marry or kill, Jeanne thought. It all comes to the same thing!

Shortly thereafter a young woman with five children walked straight toward them. Her manner as she came seemed almost brazen. Jeanne looked at her. She knew her.

It was Maria, a neighbor, who had lived with her husband Gasana and their children not very far from Jeanne's family on the same hill. However, Jeanne knew the children only by sight because she had never played with them. And the older ones, three sons by Gasana's first marriage, had gone to a different school from her. Besides them, Maria had two smaller children with her, a small boy about four years old and a girl, scarcely a year old, whom she was carrying wrapped in a cloth on her back.

She was a corpulent woman with a chubby face and a double chin. She marched heavily up to the group. She rocked on her hips as she walked, as if she had to find the ground for each step. Head and body were wrapped in bright cloth.

After she reached the grass strip, she stopped, breathing hard, and turned to the police.

"Tell me where I have to report if I want a pass!" she demanded bluntly.

The policemen looked the woman over mistrustfully, obviously not prepared for her bold request.

"Where are you coming from and where do you want to go?" one of them asked sharply.

"I was just now with friends. They advised me that we should report here to the commune."

"Why didn't you stay in your house?"

"It's destroyed. Gasana, my husband, was killed. He was Tutsi." She stopped a moment before she continued. Now markedly louder and in an arrogant tone. "But I am a Hutu! I want to go back to Zaza, where my parents and relatives live. These are my children."

"They are all your children?" The question sounded scornful.

She confirmed her assertion with a vigorous nod.

"So young and already so many children and such big ones?"

With a tentative smile she nodded again.

"Sit down there with the others. We'll see!"

Maria and her children dropped onto the grass not far from Jeanne, Chantal, and Carine.

Meanwhile the clearing up seemed to have been completed, for at the pit and on the plaza there was hardly anyone else to be seen.

The few farmers who were still standing by the waiting people to watch them got ready to leave.

Some of them moved off in the direction of the church.

"Wherever there's something left for us to do," Jeanne heard one of them say as he left.

Others, who intended to go home, took a few of the girls from the group of refugees with them. Finally there were only Maria, her children, Jeanne, Chantal, and Carine left behind. And with them the two policeman, who appeared somewhat at a loss.

Maria leaned over to Jeanne and Chantal. "What's happening with you?" she asked. "Don't you know where you can go?"

Chantal explained that she wanted to go to the hospital to get her wound treated there. Jeanne was silent.

"You can forget the hospital!" Maria said to Chantal. "And without a pass you won't get anywhere!"

"If you have no idea where you can go," she finally went on after a pause, "then come with me to Zaza! Maybe I can do something for you." She looked sideways over at the police and lowered her voice. "I'll tell them that I know your parents and that you're Hutu," she added. "Come, we'll ask them if they'll give us a pass so that the soldiers will let us through the roadblocks." She got up. "Now come along!"

The children stood up and followed her.

"I want to get on the road to Zaza with the children," Maria informed the policemen. "Can you help me or should I rather turn to the mayor?"

"Those surely aren't all your children?!"

"No, only these five. But I know the other three and also their parents well. They're related to me."

The police acted uncertain. It was clear to see, however, that they wanted to bring the matter to a close quickly and wanted to leave themselves.

"All right! I'll make a list of those you are traveling with. The mayor has to sign it. Wait here until I come back!" commanded one of them harshly.

He asked Maria once again about her exact origin, her name, her destination, noted it all on a slip of paper, and added that she had eight children with her who belonged to her.

He then took it to the mayor's house.

While they waited for him to come back, they suddenly saw two boys running up a narrow path between the houses. They had their arms raised and were waving a white T-shirt as a banner between them. Jeanne knew who they were. Friends of her cousin Claire. Hot and panting they approached them.

"It's all over! It's all over!" they were crying in chorus.

With a brisk movement the policeman raised the barrel of his gun, aimed at the boys, and shot.

The two of them whirled around in a vain attempt to escape. The next shots hit them in the back. Jeanne saw them fall.

It's all over, she thought.

The policeman didn't move from the spot. He didn't even look over at the boys. He held the rifle carelessly in his hand, now pointed at the ground again as if nothing had happened.

The sun stood vertical in the cloudless sky and burned pitilessly down on the plaza in front of the community center, which was as empty as if it had been swept.

A little later the other policeman came back. Without taking any notice of the boys on the ground, he handed the pass over to Maria.

"You can go," he said.

A deathly stillness reigned everywhere as they left Birenga.

You explain to me what the names mean.

The African ones.

They are your first names, you say, although they come second. The name is chosen right after the birth of a child, when the parents see it for the first time. It means something that is given to the child as a direction or as a gift to take on its way.

You say that who the baby looks like, for example, could determine the name. Or some thing that happened while the baby was still on the way. Or the first impression the baby makes on the parents.

So the second name is not a family name. It has nothing to do with relationship.

That confused me a great deal in the beginning. But now I understand that your name does not have a bureaucratic use. That it is a legacy that accompanies you. Your whole life long.

The first names only come later. At baptism. And from them nicknames, usually.

Florence **Muteteli**—Parents' darling

Ananie Nzamurambaho—He for whom I would do all
Jean de Dieu Cyubahiro—The honored one
Catherine Icyigeni—What God has planned for you

These are the names of those who shared your life before death took them. They are now all as close to me as if I'd known them myself. Especially your mother. She is almost as close to me as you are.

In your diary, which I gave you once and you gave back to me a short time ago so that I could read it, you ask the question whether, if Florence could see you today and know how you've managed, she would be proud of you.

I see you with her eyes.

Yes, she would be proud of you. We are very proud of you.

Jeanne d'Arc Umubyeyi—She who gives life.

That is the name they gave you to take on your way.

They could have made no other choice that fits you as well as this one.

Nyogokuru's mother, your great-grandmother, gave you the nickname Dédé. Really Bébé. She no longer had teeth and couldn't speak properly anymore.

Everyone called you Dédé.

For us you are Jeanne now. For me Jeanne d'Arc, the fighter.

Florence Muteteli
Ananie Nzamurambaho

Jean de Dieu Cyubahiro, Jando
Catherine Icyigeni, Teya

We will remember them. And all the others who died at their sides.

I think of the story that Nyogokuru told. The story of the voice of Africa. Of Kalinga, the great royal drum, which can be heard everywhere. The story of the hill where Heaven and Earth touch. Where the great king of Heaven and the Earth king met and joined their families together, and afterwards a time of peace began. Nyogokuru knew that place.

Let us go there in our thoughts. Let us listen to the great voice and the voices of those who loved you. You are joined with them beyond place and time.

We will kindle a flame for them and watch over it, that it does not go out.

PART III

the long way home to us

MU BIHE BIBI
NIBWO UMUNTU AMENYA INSHUTI
N'UMWANZI!

*ONLY IN THE WORST MOMENT
WILL YOU KNOW:
FRIEND OR FOE!*

The route to Zaza was via the main road. You just had to keep following your nose. The road led over many hills, up and down, through the commune of Kigarama directly to Zaza. Jeanne knew the way. She'd driven to Zaza with her parents a few times to visit a friend of her father's there, Jando's godfather. By car it took barely an hour.

It was uncertain how long it would take them on foot. Every thousand yards they came to a roadblock, where they were stopped each time by heavily armed civilians and had to show their pass. There were frequently difficulties with that because Jeanne, Carine, Chantal, and also Gasana's sons from the first marriage were immediately recognized as Tutsis. They were still in a district where people knew them, so one of the posted guards always knew who they were.

There was an incident at the very first barrier, a tree laid across the road in a small wood. A young man walked up to Jeanne and blocked her way.

"What's this one doing in your group? I know this one. This is the daughter of the white professor! She looks just like him!" he said, pressing the handle of his axe into her stomach.

The white professor. Her father was called that by some of his students because he had very light skin.

"What are you doing here, you have no right to go with this woman!" the young man barked at Jeanne. "And you have no right to take the girl along with you!" he said, turning to Maria. Maria did not reply.

But Jeanne lifted her chin and looked him in the face. "I don't know where my parents are," she stated. "So I'm going with our neighbor."

"You're going with no one," he said firmly. "You're coming with me! My wife can use help. It's time your like finally learned to work. Your hands are too soft." He struck at her right hand with his axe handle.

Jeanne winced and hid her hands behind her back.

"I am not going with you. I won't be your slave!" she said firmly.

He hit at her once more and struck her on the chest, with full force, making her totter. "Lie down on the ground!" he screamed. "Get moving! Face up. And uncover your neck!"

She kept her gaze fixed on him. Filled with contempt.

"If you're going to kill me, then I can die standing up just as well," she answered, without knowing where she found the words.

He avoided her eyes. "I hate your royal arrogance! You're nothing anymore now! Just dirt! But still too proud!" He spat at her feet.

An older man, apparently his father, pulled him aside. "Let her go," he advised. "She's got the evil eye and can put a curse on us. And she won't get far anyhow. At the next block the others will take care of it for us!"

With a growl, the young man gave up. Maria and the children were allowed through.

Maria went on again as quickly as possible. But after about a hundred yards she stopped short, snorted angrily, and lit into Jeanne. "How dare you be so fresh! What were you thinking of! If you go on like that, you'll put us all in danger!"

Jeanne said nothing.

Chantal put her arm around her shoulder reassuringly. "What on earth should she have done?" she defended Jeanne. "Besides, what are you so upset about? After all, they let us go!"

Maria growled something angrily under her breath and started moving again.

They made hardly any progress at all for the first six miles, still in the vicinity of Birenga. Despite their pass, they were held at the barriers. A few times Maria complained and pointed out that she had the signature of the mayor. But the sentries, clearly determined not to let them pass so easily, would only give them permission to go on after long argument and with threats.

In addition, looters kept appearing, triumphant and burdened down with their booty. Jewelry, household items, clothing, and frequently big pieces of the meat of freshly slaughtered cattle, sheep, or goats. They made no secret of whom they'd murdered for it but boasted loudly of their deeds. "You really missed something there!"

Jeanne looked at the machetes, their bloody slaughtering tools, and thought, first the people, then the animals!

Hours later they came to a small rural settlement, which lay halfway up a hill surrounded by banana plantations and sweet potato fields. Here the inhabitants had erected a barrier of boxes, cans, and tree stumps. About fifteen men and boys were collected there. Some of them were standing in front of their houses, casually leaning on the fence or against their front doors, as if they had been waiting for Maria and the children and were hoping for a show of a very special sort.

Three armed men stood guard at the barricade.

"Halt!" bellowed one, even before Maria and the children had reached them. "You there, stand aside!" He pointed along the row to Jeanne, Chantal, Carine, and Maria's stepsons. They obeyed.

"Lie down on your backs, heads back! Necks uncovered!"

They hesitated.

"Make it snappy!" he screamed and strode toward them.

Chantal was the first to follow the order. The others copied her. They crowded close together.

"Close your eyes!"

Jeanne kept her eyes open. Staring at the man and staring at the machete over her head, raised to strike. She felt nothing inside.

Then, in a clear voice, Chantal demanded: "We want to

pray. Please! Let us pray!"

The machete sank slowly.

"All right," he said.

Chantal sat up and knelt. When none of the men stopped them, the others knelt beside her and began softly to murmur to themselves.

Jeanne found no words for a prayer. And what she understood from the others didn't sound like prayers either.

"We'll try to draw things out somehow," Chantal whispered to them.

When the sentries became restless, however, she raised her voice and said the Our Father loudly. The others immediately fell in with her. Then they said the Ave Maria in chorus. A few times, without a pause for breath. And again lowered their voices to an incomprehensible murmur.

"Make an end of it!" snapped one of the men. "How long is this supposed to go on?"

"Before we die, we have to confess all our sins," Chantal explained to him. "You know that! Or aren't you Christians?"

"I've had enough of this," interjected a younger man who'd been standing to one side. He acted uneasy. "As far as I'm concerned, they should go on. They won't get far anyway. Rukara is waiting at the next roadblock. He won't let them past in any case. He's really collecting heads!"

They actually let them go.

Shortly after that the girls broke into nervous giggling. As if they'd just succeeded in a daring trick, whose consequences they couldn't foresee.

But the echo of the threat haunted Jeanne for a long time during the next leg of the journey. There was nothing more she could trust in, and her thoughts detached themselves from everything that had been familiar to her. She felt that death was on the road with them. It was their constant companion. It had nothing to do with a war, just with naked hatred, which had suddenly burst out and shown itself to them undisguised. She knew now: however she might behave, she couldn't change the fact that they wanted to annihilate her.

Strangely, her fear had receded. Her instinctive resistance, formerly kept obediently concealed, won the upper hand and took up the fight. She had no respect for anyone or anything anymore. She intended to be the only one who would decide what she did.

In this she wasn't thinking of the future. Life could be over at any moment. And she didn't even know if she wanted to live. But fear she would not have! Fear made you weak and without will. When you were ruled by fear, you could no longer protect yourself. Were completely surrendered. Like Jando in his last moments.

Keep going. Hold out. Don't put up with anything. That's what it came to now.

They got through the next two roadblocks without any noteworthy incidents. Rukara, the collector of heads, appeared to be busy elsewhere. They did not meet him.

Thus, in late afternoon, they approached the top of a

hill in the commune of Kigarama, and even from far off they could see a large house, entirely enclosed by fencing, sitting beside the road up there. Recognizably the house of a rich person.

The road was blocked here, too. But only with two big tree stumps, between which there was a space for cars to go through.

A man was sitting on one of the trunks. Unarmed. Besides him, there was no one else to be seen far and wide. Only a white dog dozing peacefully beside him in the sunshine. So they could hope that it might not take long here.

But when they came nearer and Jeanne recognized the man, her breath caught. She fell into a panic.

For the ugly, fat man with the mirror-smooth bald head and broad, fleshy nose was no one else than Kanuma, "the dove," a man about whom Jeanne had heard the most grisly stories since her earliest childhood. People said he had an evil eye and would steal little children, whom no one ever saw again afterwards.

He was a merchant who owned several businesses in the town of Kibungo. One for clothing. One for children's things. And one for agricultural tools. Because he was a good friend of Aunt Theresia, Jeanne had met him several times at her grandmother's house when he was visiting Theresia. He had no sooner appeared than the children would scatter and hide. For the older cousins had often threatened the smaller children with him if they wouldn't be good: "Watch out, we're going to Kanuma. He'll come and get you!"

Kanuma or the devil, one was like the other.

When Jeanne, in the company of her mother, encountered him on the street in Kibungo now and then, and Florence had stopped for a moment to greet him, Jeanne would quickly sink her head as deeply as possible and not raise her eyes from the ground, to keep him from looking at her. But one time he'd smiled at her from far off. Then a chill went down her back, and she'd been frightened to death for days.

When she met him again here so suddenly, her heart began to beat wildly, just as it used to, and she hid herself behind Chantal.

Kanuma asked Maria for her pass. And where she was going with the children. His voice boomed in Jeanne's ears.

"I'm on my way to Zaza," Maria reported. "My family lives there. When we get there, we'll see what's next."

Kanuma shook his head. "Who'll take on so many children in these times? And especially such as these!" he remarked dubiously, and as he spoke, he looked directly at Jeanne, who shrank under his penetrating eyes and quickly looked aside.

He's going to take me away right now, she thought despairingly.

"You're Dédé, Theresia's niece, am I right? I've seen you a few times at her place," she heard him say.

Jeanne bit her tongue but dared a quick look in his direction. He was still looking at her, and now his face split into a wide grin, which made his eyes disappear into rolls of fat. She was sick with fear.

"Wait here a moment," Kanuma commanded Maria and the children. "I'll be right back." He slipped from the tree trunk and disappeared through the gate into the yard.

Now he's gone to get his weapon, Jeanne thought.

She would have liked to run away. But she stayed, as if she were spellbound. They had to wait a while before he returned.

When he finally came, he was carrying a fat bunch of ripe bananas with him. A little ceremoniously he began to divide them among the children, one by one, and with a wink he even handed Jeanne two.

"You're sure to be hungry for bananas," he rumbled heartily. He gave Maria what was left over. "You can go now," he said. "What terrible times! Take good care of the children! And just get them all home safe!"

"I'm sorry for you, my child!" he added seriously, again addressing Jeanne.

As they walked on, she stared at the bananas in her hand. She was completely confused. Kanuma, the bogeyman, had shown himself to be a friendly man who wouldn't hurt a hair of anyone's head. Her picture of him had been utterly and completely false. And neighbors whom she had once thought were friends had turned into murderers. From now on, she would never know who she was talking to.

Only at the very worst moment can you tell friend from foe.

Who is the person facing us?

We never know exactly.

Do we even know about our own selves? More and more, I understand that our life is a tightrope walk. Along the edge of its own abyss, as well.

And yet, there are encounters that last only a moment and create a closeness between people that ordinarily takes an entire lifetime. It occurs in a gesture, a smile that says to you: I have recognized you.

Something like that has happened to me so often. I've never forgotten any of those moments.

Do you remember the day on which we three, Papa, you, and I, were invited to the Family Court to once again, in person, declare our wishes to the judge who was going to decide about your adoption? Yet it had all been presented in writing already! Your papers, the death certificates of your parents, a notarized declaration of intention from all of us, the report of the youth welfare office after someone visited us, checked us out, spoke with us, and found us "mature." And Papa had already been your legal guardian for years.

A lot of time had passed before it got that far. Month upon month, long after the three of us had decided. The bureaucrats give themselves plenty of time.

Therefore, I asked the judge on the telephone whether it would really be necessary for us to come before her personally. Yes, she would very much like to meet us. Tuesday morning. Nine o'clock sharp.

Well, good. Then so it must be.

The day arrives. For you, two hours out of school. For me, a trip to the city, during which I can also get some other things done. For Papa, an interruption during office hours, a little inconvenient because the waiting room is full.

We meet at the entrance to our District Court. You and I are all dressed up. Papa in his everyday suit and just on the run.

A brilliant blue day.

Elevator to the third floor. Room 308. We are punctual. Knock on the door. Weary "Come in" from inside.

Expectantly we enter the small room. A file room, or something like that, without anything that catches the eye. Behind a desk piled high, a thickset woman of middle age, who acts almost startled when she sees us. As if she doesn't quite know why we're there.

That's how she begins, too. Hesitant. Stiff. She addresses you formally, treats you as if you were your own mother. As she talks, she leafs through the file as if she were informing herself for the first time right now. Hardly lifts her eyes once to look at one of us. We feel out of place, as if we'd intruded uninvited.

I've forgotten what she said. It was nothing important. Only once she asked you casually what would now change for you. Because of the adoption.

"Nothing," you said with a small, amused smile. "They're already my parents."

Was it more than ten minutes we spent there? I don't know. Probably even fewer. We met a judge who decided something vital for us. But she didn't meet us. She hid herself behind her desk.

Outside again, we laugh. Teetering between annoyance and amusement. A quick farewell, our paths separate. You go to school, Papa runs back to the office, and I stroll over to the bank, which is opposite the courthouse.

The man at the teller's window knows me. And I him. A man with full, bushy white hair, a small mustache, rosy skin, and glasses behind which gleam very bright eyes. He's sitting in a high booth behind bulletproof glass.

When I approach the window, the sound of classical music flows toward me. Something wild, melancholy, which suddenly captures me and also stirs me. For a moment I forget why I've come here. I listen. On a small table in the booth sits the tape player that is producing the sounds. Dark, demanding they reach for me. The teller sees me and smiles, sunk in music.

"What is that?" I ask after a while.

"Isn't it marvelous?" he asks back. "It's Franz Schubert's String Quartet in D Minor. 'Death and the Maiden.' I have to listen to it over and over."

"Yes, really!"

I feel like celebrating. We both smile.

"And you find time for that with your work?"

"Yes. And if I'm interrupted, that isn't so bad. I know it very well already."

—Death and the maiden.—

This particular theme on this day in a place where I never expected it! In my bank. I think with regret of the judge in the district court, who missed a celebratory moment.

When I leave the bank, still filled with the music and also with the smile of the teller, the day is still bright blue. A postcard day.

Filled with tenderness, I think about you. And cordially toward the man who does his work in this way. Attending to people and accompanied by music that means much to him.

Suddenly I feel very cheerful.

You know? This is a moment in which I unexpectedly discover the whole breadth of a life.

They passed the night in a small village. They'd arrived there about six and made a stop because it was slowly growing dark and the first raindrops were falling. It was high time to rest, for Sophia and Olivier, the two youngest ones, had been crying without interruption for the last hour. Sophia, although she'd been asleep on Maria's back for most of the journey. She needed her mother's milk.

The village lay at a fork in the road where the highway divided for Saka or for Zaza. From here on it was the commune of Mugesera, to which Zaza also belonged.

They found shelter on a narrow stone terrace under the veranda roof of a small abandoned store. After they'd been checked, they were allowed to go on in peace. No one refused them the sleeping place. Only a few people made disparaging remarks about Maria. That she couldn't be quite right in the head if she was on the way to her parents with eight children.

"They'll be overjoyed to have so many mouths to feed soon!" they sneered.

Little by little the villagers retreated into their houses, all except for a few sentries, and stillness returned.

Maria and her children stretched out full length and soon fell asleep. But Jeanne, Carine, and Chantal remained sitting up. They moved into a corner of the terrace close together, so that their bodies were touching and mutually warming. Chantal moaned softly to herself and sucked on her wounded finger.

Sometime during the course of the night, Jeanne tipped over onto one side in complete exhaustion. But she didn't want to go to sleep. Tensely she kept her eyes open, directed into the darkness, so that no one could descend on her unseen. And now and again she heard a whisper beside her, "Are you still awake?"

Making sure that they were watching out for each other. Chantal and Carine didn't close an eye either.

They next morning they set off about eight o'clock.

The road that lay before them now wasn't as wide as the part they'd already traveled. And that made them hope that they'd get past the roadblocks faster, for no one here knew them anymore.

Maria, who seemed to be somewhat rested, drove the children on. "We have to reach Zaza before evening!" she insisted.

In fact, they made good progress in the first two hours.

At the roadblocks, they let them go on unhindered after a cursory look at the pass and a few scornful remarks about Maria's large group of children.

Although Jeanne had scarcely eaten anything for two days, for some strange reason she felt no hunger. There was never anything edible in sight, so that eating didn't even enter her mind. But once the sun was high in the sky, she was tormented by thirst. Her tongue was sticking to her gums. She tried to collect some saliva and to swallow, but that made it even worse. Her lips grew chapped and split.

To distract herself, she counted her steps, the way she'd done long ago during the summer holidays on the way to the water place.

The road was in bad condition. Everywhere were deep potholes, with muddy rainwater standing in them. Stones large and small littered the ground.

Suddenly Jeanne stumbled. She almost fell, but she just caught herself. Yet when she tried to walk on, she noticed that the sole of her right sandal had come loose and was now rolling under her foot at every step.

She stopped to see if she could repair her shoe. But the

straps were torn and couldn't be fastened anymore. The shoe was finished! Nonetheless, it was impossible for her to separate from it. She tried to go on, pulling the right leg behind her. But it was very difficult to make any headway, and the distance between her and the others was getting larger and larger.

When Chantal and Carine saw it, they ran back to help her.

Now Maria also became aware of it. She stopped and waited until the three came up to her.

"What's this all about?" she scolded Jeanne. "Why don't you take your shoes off?! We'll never get to Zaza this way."

With heavy heart, Jeanne obeyed. When she had to leave her shoes lying by the roadside, the loss hit her so hard that she could only keep the tears back with difficulty.

Although she had often joyfully removed her shoes and stockings in the summertime while playing, she wasn't used to walking barefoot for a long time. The small stones dug into her naked feet, it felt as if she had warts, and she had to be fiendishly careful not to stub her toes on something. She walked as if she were on broken glass. Even without the hindering sandals, she found it difficult to keep up with the others.

Chantal and Carine remained at her side. Carine was silent, the way she had been most of the time.

But with her voice lowered so that Maria couldn't hear, Chantal began to express some misgivings. "Do you really suppose that Maria's family will take us in with them? Even though we aren't related to them at all! I don't think they'll want to have us. Why should they?"

"Maria promised us," Jeanne said. "She was our neighbor. Her husband was Tutsi. Her children are Tutsi too."

"I don't know . . . ," Chantal said doubtfully. "We should consider what we'll do if they won't take us."

"I know a few people in Zaza . . . ," Jeanne answered and stopped herself right there because she remembered what Gatori had reported about Uncle Alphonse and the Tutsis in Zaza. She hadn't thought of that anymore during the experiences of the last few days, but now suddenly she was afraid to be on the way to that place. ". . . but I don't think they're still there," she finished somberly.

"We'll see," said Chantal. "If we can't stay, we'll just have to go back."

Maria turned around to the girls with impatience. "Now don't talk so much! When do you think we'll finally get there if you go poking along like that!"

Toward noon it got very hot, and Jeanne didn't know which burned more: her throat or her feet, which had meanwhile become sore from the hot ground. She was sweating. In spite of the heat, she was still wearing Jando's sweatshirt. She'd been unable to bring herself to take it off, for fear one of the barrier sentries could have taken it away from her.

Olivier was whining and whimpering because he couldn't walk anymore, and Maria, who was obviously exhausted and becoming very irritated, pulled him impatiently by the hand. He burst into tears.

"Wait, I'll take him!" Chantal offered.

She lifted the little boy up high. She carried him piggy-back until they reached a settlement half an hour later.

"We'll take a rest here and ask somewhere about water," Maria gasped. "They have to give us that." Fat beads of sweat stood on her forehead. Her lips were cracked.

At the very first courtyard she trudged purposefully through the wide, open gate. The children followed her. She found a young woman standing at a fireplace. A few children were squatting around a large mortar and crushing something. They looked over at the intruders curiously.

Maria headed straight toward the young woman, who turned around and put down her stirring spoon.

"Could we please have some water?" Maria asked.

The woman nodded. Not unfriendly.

"Louis, go and get water for the people!" she ordered one of her boys.

He picked up a plastic glass next to him and ran with it to the rain barrel, returned with a filled glass, and handed it to Maria, who let Olivier drink first, then Gasana's sons. The boy ran back to the rain barrel a second time. After Chantal and Carine had drunk a few swallows, they handed the glass on to Jeanne.

Although her thirst had meanwhile become almost unbearable, she hesitated. She didn't like to drink out of the same glass with others. Besides, the water could be poisoned. She squinted into the glass mistrustfully, and when she discovered something black in there that stood out against the bottom, she was so disgusted that she just poured the water on the grass without thinking.

Maria exploded. "What do you think you're doing! You should be grateful that the people here are giving us something to drink!"

"I don't want to drink anything that's so dirty!" replied Jeanne stubbornly. "A person can get sick from that!"

"All the others drank it. Don't act like that!" Maria barked. Then she asked embarassedly once more for water for herself.

A little later, as they went on their way between banana plantations, manioc and sweet potato fields under the stabbing sun, and there was nowhere another house in sight, Jeanne's thirst became so agonizing that she almost regretted having given in to her disgust. But the resistance against everything that wasn't clean and that came from strangers was so deeply ingrained in her that she couldn't overcome it.

So she was very glad when they were surprised by a mighty cloudburst at the next barricade. They waited under the protection of the corrugated iron porch roof of an unoccupied house until it was over.

Maria used the time to put Sophia to her breast, and Chantal held her injured and now infected hand out in the rain. As the storm was raging, Jeanne looked longingly at the gigantic quantities of water the heavens were pouring onto the earth. The puddles were filled to the edges in an instant.

And even before it stopped raining, the sun broke forth again. Its beams shone through the drops, now glittering and glistening as they fell from the sky. Jeanne took one step forward, stretched out her hands, and tried to catch a few of them. Suddenly she remembered something Nyogokuru had said once when it was raining and the sun was shining at the same time. "Now a white man has died, and God is weeping."

When the rain stopped, she rushed over to a puddle, scooped up the water, and slurped it in greedily. That it was mixed with earth did not hold her back. This dirt was familiar to her. Maria observed her with a frown, but she let her alone.

Later the children plucked large leaves from the plants at the side of the road as they passed and licked off the water that had collected there.

Zaza finally came into sight in the late afternoon. However, it was a different Zaza from the one in Jeanne's memory.

Entire sections of the town were destroyed. Faced with the missing roofs and the house walls blackened by the fires, Jeanne thought of her parents' house, of its peaceful look when she had seen it for the last time, and the idea that it must now look just as desolate made her throat close. Again Gatori's report went through her head, and she wondered what she might expect in Zaza.

The main road led straight through the business district. Jeanne had never noticed before that the Tutsis and Hutus had lived in close proximity, it is true, but in separate neighborhoods where they were always among themselves.

Here, anyway, it showed very clearly: On one side of the street, the houses and stores deserted and looted! And on the opposite side houses and stores to which nothing similar had happened.

Jeanne wondered whether Tutsis had shopped in Tutsi stores and Hutus in Hutu stores. Nonsense, she thought. It had never been like that. At least she couldn't remember it.

There were a lot of people around, and when Maria came through the town with the children, she was stared at from all sides.

Gradually they left the center behind them. The closer they came to the end of town, the more perceptible it was that Maria was nervous. Here they occasionally met people whom Maria obviously knew. But no one greeted her. Instead, waves of hostility came surging at them.

For instance, someone said, "Where are you going with those children? Surely you don't believe that Habimana will let them live?"

Maria kept her eyes straight ahead and did not respond.

"Maria, why are people saying things like that?" Chantal asked her uneasily.

"Because they just like to talk," replied Maria curtly. "Don't worry about it!" But it was clear that she was not certain and that her tension was growing from minute to minute.

When they had the town behind them, she stopped suddenly and pointed to a farm that lay up a hill away from the road. It was surrounded by fields.

"That's my parents' farm," she said. "When we get there, try to behave yourselves, all right? My grandmother still lives with us. She's almost blind and very frail and she

247

scolds quite a lot. Don't make anything more out of it but just leave her alone!" She looked grimly at Jeanne. "And you, don't always give so much fresh backtalk, you hear? Just answer yes if you're asked, and do what you're told! You'll have to get along without your sensitive stuff here. Don't make such a fuss but take what people give you!"

Jeanne bit her tongue to keep from contradicting.

The houses and stables of the property enclosed a large inner yard. When Maria and the children entered it, Jeanne's eyes first fell on a round, straw-roofed mud hut, in front of which squatted an old woman on a raffia mat. She was holding her face up to the mild evening sun. Her eyes were closed and her fallen-in mouth was moving up and down, chewing. That must be Maria's grandmother. A few chickens pecked around her.

Besides the old one, there were a young woman and a girl about seventeen in the yard. They were busy at the fireplace. The woman was cleaning sweet potatoes and the girl was picking over spinach. When they noticed the new arrivals, they both raised their heads at the same time, but they showed no surprise at all.

"Those are my sister-in-law Béata and my sister Agnès," Maria murmured.

"Béata, who did Maria bring here with her?" the grandmother called.

Either she could still see or she had also already heard of Maria's arrival in Zaza.

At once the woman hurried over to the grandmother, without greeting Maria and the children, who had stopped in the middle of the yard.

"Maria has brought her children and then three other children with her," she explained. "They're sure to be relatives of her husband."

The young girl ran joyfully over to Maria, embraced her, and whispered something in her ear.

"Hello, Agnès," said Maria. "Where's Mama? Is she in the house?"

Now Béata came over too. She greeted Maria with an embrace, pinched Olivier tenderly on the cheek, and lifted him up. She only gave the other children a quick nod.

"Yes, she's in the house," she murmured. "Come on, you'll have to explain this to her."

Maria and Béata disappeared into the main house.

"Oli!" called the grandmother. "Are you there? Come here and get a hug!"

Olivier ran to the grandmother, who embraced him, and began to feel over him with her crooked fingers from top to bottom.

"Agnès," she commanded her granddaughter, "get the little one something to eat! He's completely wasted away!"

Agnès, who until then had been standing indecisively next to the group of children, waiting, obeyed at once, ran to the fire, and scooped something out of the great kettle into a dish, which she then took over to Olivier.

The little boy sat down beside the grandmother and fell hungrily on the food. With his fingertips, he first picked a large piece of meat out the dish and bit into it.

At the sight of the meat Jeanne suddenly felt so sick

that she began to retch. Her stomach wanted to turn out everything and vomit it all up. But it was empty. However, the horrible retching didn't stop. Her body convulsed. She thought she was going to choke. Something biting came up inside and burned her throat. She closed her eyes in anguish. It calmed her a little when she felt Chantal's hand on her back. But before she dared open her eyes, she turned away from the grandmother's hut.

Just then Maria, Béata, and a farmwoman came out of the house and hurried over to the group of children. The farmwoman, who might be about fifty, was the spitting image of Maria. She regarded Jeanne disapprovingly while she still gasped for breath. Then she greeted the children with a brief hello, but she did not offer them her hand. Not Gasana's sons either. Her hands and bare feet, cracked and covered with calluses, betrayed the daily fieldwork.

"Sit down somewhere. And if you want, take something to drink," she commanded gruffly. Her teeth were colored brown from chewing tobacco.

The children squatted on the broad mud step that encircled the main house, and Jeanne looked around. Where should they get something to drink? They didn't know their way around.

Maria walked slowly over to her grandmother. When she bent over her to greet her, the old woman clutched at her wraparound dress and thundered:

"What are you thinking of, Maria! How could you let the poor boy walk so far! You ought to have carried Oli. And he hadn't eaten for two days! A fine mother you are!"

"What else should I have done? After all, I had nothing to eat myself either. And I had to carry Sophia. And she needed my milk," Maria defended herself.

"Then why have you saddled yourself with even more children? You really must be out of your mind!" the old woman snarled.

Maria sighed in resignation. With few words she described what had happened in Birenga. That she'd lost husband and house and was left with nothing. And she tried to explain why she'd brought the children with her.

"The three girls there are also relatives of Gasana," she asserted, pointing to Jeanne, Carine, and Chantal. "I couldn't just leave them to their fate."

"I don't know if that was very smart of you," her mother remarked pointedly. "Your brothers Habimana and Maboko are still out with the other men. They'll be anything but enthusiastic!"

Her words awakened an unpleasant presentiment in Jeanne. What are we doing here, where we're clearly not welcome, she thought.

We quarrel.

A lively discussion starts after a reading with all of you. The others want to know how it's possible for a mass murder by hand to happen. How many murderers did there have to be to carry it out? Whether that might mean that there were almost as many perpetrators as there were victims. And whether all who let the murder happen, even if they weren't actual perpetrators, made themselves jointly guilty. And why then did no one offer resistance.

Weighty questions are being asked there in that room.

"Yes! There was resistance too," I assert.

And I tell about a book that I've just been reading. Written by a journalist from the United States. In recent years he's had conversations with victims and killers from all groups in the Rwandan population. Also with politicians and church people, with members of the militia. He spoke with survivors in Rwanda. And outside the country with those who had fled.

I tell you about a Hutu, a hotel manager in Kigali, who's mentioned in the book. He saved a great many people. He took them in and bargained for their lives. And he was openly in resistance.

"I did not agree with it. And I said so." His exact words were something like that.

You interrupt me. With unusual violence.

"I don't believe that!" you shout.

"Oh yes, I think one can believe it," I reply. And substantiate my opinion by giving details. But you don't want to hear it at all.

"If so, then he did it because there was some sort of advantage for him in it!" you pronounce in a hard voice.

I would so like to convince you.

"You really ought to read this book yourself," I suggest. "I'm quite certain that the author is unbiased and that you can rely on his portrayal."

"Oh, yes? It doesn't interest me!" You're getting more and more upset. Your stubborn opposition intensifies.

That provokes me.

"But it's important!" I insist. "Important for you too, above all. That in your country there were people who risked their necks to save others. Who didn't take part in the madness. I'm even convinced that there were others besides him who also acted that way. And it's really important to know that!" I repeat.

Now you are absolutely infuriated. Furious with me, which I can feel. Your voice breaks.

"I've had enough of this, you hear? I don't want to listen to any more of the story! I can't anymore! I feel nothing but hatred!"

You clench your fists. Weep with rage. Jump up and run

upstairs to your room. Leave me and the others behind. Shocked. At a loss.

It's already late. It makes no sense to follow you now. Besides, you have a right to your anger. I don't want to deprive you of it.

I wait until the next day.

We talk about it once more. Just you and me.

I say that I understand you. Also your hatred. And that I want under no circumstances to hurt you. Or to call up something that is much too painful for you.

And that perhaps one can never really be certain oneself. But that sometimes one simply must believe something.

We are dependent on that which we believe.

"If it's getting to be too much for you, we'll stop now. You're more important to me than this book. The book is important, but you're more important! We'll only keep on going if it's good for you," I say.

And I tell you about me.

When I was your age, it meant a great deal to me that at the time of the genocide in Germany there were people who offered resistance. Who protected others from death at the risk of their own lives. Although I was only born the year afterwards and wasn't involved personally, the mountain of dead that was piled up because of the Germans also weighed on me. So it has remained up to this day.

Everything always comes to the point in the question: "What is humanly possible? Or: What is possible for *humans?"*

Humans between God and Devil.

I believe that everywhere—even in Rwanda—there are some who stand either on one side or the other. The majority, and perhaps we are a part of it, range somewhere in between. The majority can never be sure of itself.

"Yes," you say. And that you would like to keep on going.

Habimana and Maboko didn't make them wait long for them. They returned shortly after six.

A few minutes before they walked in, dark clouds had rolled up in the sky, heralding the next rainfall. The yard, still illuminated by the evening sun a moment before, suddenly lay in gloom, as if someone had turned out the light.

Jeanne was frightened when Habimana, accompanied by two large sheep-dog mongrels and his younger brother Maboko, came through the open gate. The two brothers seemed to her as ominous as the sky.

Habimana, of small, compact build, might be about thirty years old. He had an angular face with a hard expression around the mouth. His black suit trousers were baggy at the knees and frayed at the bottoms. His checked, short-sleeved shirt revealed muscular arms. Maboko, perhaps half his age, was a younger edition of his brother.

It was obvious that the men had been on a looting expedition. Both were heavily laden. Habimana with an armchair and an overstuffed shopping bag, Maboko carrying several plastic bags, filled to the tops with pieces of meat, which shimmered reddish through the plastic of the bags and gave off the smell of blood. Once again Jeanne had to struggle against a gagging feeling.

Habimana's eyes swept expressionlessly over Jeanne and the other children. Then, followed by Maboko, he headed quickly to the fireplace where his mother and Béata were tending the boiling pots. Maboko handed his mother the meat. Habimana set down the chair and the bag.

"We have more yet! We'll be right back," he said.

His voice, surprisingly light, confused Jeanne. She watched Maria, who was squatting beside the grandmother with Sophia at her breast and looking over at her brother uncertainly.

However, Habimana took no notice of Maria at all but left the yard with Maboko. The dogs stayed behind. They lay down beside the fireplace, ears cocked as though they were waiting for a few treats to be dropped for them.

Béata left her place at the fire and slowly began to unpack the bag. Taking the things out one by one to appraise them. First, pieces of clothing of various sizes, then cups, plates, and finally a silver knife, fork, and spoon, which she handed over to her mother-in-law with a satisfied smile.

A few minutes later the men were back, and this time they brought two wooden chairs, stools, and several slashed mattresses, with shreds of the foam rubber hanging out of the cuts.

Chantal poked Jeanne in the side. "What are they going to do with those? You can't sleep on something like that!"

she murmured.

After Habimana and Maboko had piled up their plunder in the yard, Habimana summoned Maria to him in a brusque voice.

At once, Maria took Sophia from her breast, laid her on the mat, and hurried over to her brother. Sophia began to scream.

"What's the meaning of all this, Maria?!" Habimana interrogated his sister loudly, so that everyone could understand his every word. "What do you want with so many children here? With these"— he snorted scornfully—"Tutsi brats? How did you think to feed them all? With your mother's milk maybe?"

Maria let his attack pass over her with lowered head. She replied nothing.

"You really should have thought it out better!" he said angrily and left her standing in order to go over to the children. Maria slowly followed him.

Jeanne immediately took a deep dislike to the furious man as she watched him coming toward them. For his pitiless expression left no doubt that she and the others were not welcome to him.

He stopped directly in front of them and examined the row from head to foot. Under his sharp, disparaging look Jeanne suddenly felt dirty.

She hadn't washed for days. Her summer dress was full of spots, the dark line of dirt stopping at the edges of Jando's sweatshirt, her naked feet were encrusted with mud, her hair stuck in matted little knots on her head. All too clearly she was aware of the smell of her own sweat. She knew that she looked like a street child but that the aversion in the man's look did not apply to her undignified condition but to her, and on that account alone she was that much more ashamed of herself.

"The girls we can probably use . . . ," Habimana growled, " . . . but the boys . . . " He stared at Eric, Gasana's oldest. "A wonder you made it this far at all . . . the way you look . . . " He let his eyes slide disdainfully over Eric's small figure and the small face with the long, straight nose.

"Maria, have you lost your mind, to saddle us with Gasana's litter?!"

Maria seemed to have lost all her courage in her brother's presence. She acted completely changed. Silent and embarrassed, she plucked at her dress.

"I'll talk with our village headman and the other men tomorrow!" he decided in a tone that promised nothing good. "Then we'll decide what we're going to do with the boys."

Maria's hands clenched. It was obvious that she wanted to say something, but she didn't dare.

Abruptly Habimana turned away and followed Maboko, who was just carrying the chairs into the house.

Maria ran to Sophia, who was crawling across the yard, screaming.

After she was far enough away from them, Eric whispered to his brothers, "I knew from the beginning that Maria couldn't help us! It was crazy of us to come here. We'd better disappear right now."

It was the first time since they'd left Birenga together that Jeanne heard one of the boys express himself about their situation. She could understand Eric's fear. Also his wish to run away.

"Where do you intend to go now?" she joined in softly. "Nothing more will happen today, for sure. Early tomorrow morning we can go to the cloister. I know a few monks and priests there. Maybe they'll help us."

On the way through the village she'd noticed a sign pointing to the cloister. Since then, the idea of fleeing there would not let go of her. For the cloister and some of its inhabitants were familiar from the years when her father had taught at the priests' seminary there. And Jando's godfather lived in the neighborhood. Now she clung to the vague hope of finding people in the cloister she knew and who were perhaps still alive.

At the crack of dawn the children got up, sat down again on the step in front of the main house, and silently waited for Habimana's appearance. Only when he'd left the farm did they intend to risk an attempt at flight.

Jeanne felt numb and miserable. Her feet burned worse than the day before; the stresses of the long march to Zaza made themselves felt in her whole body; her limbs were heavy and they hurt; and since Chantal had awakened her, another, still much bigger pain threatened to burst her chest.

A restless night on the thin raffia mats that Maria's mother had spread for the children in the living room of the house lay behind her. They had taken turns keeping watch while the others slept, but Jeanne had hardly rested during the times when the others had watch. The smells and sounds of the strange, unfriendly house had gotten her down, and in the middle of the night, the howling cry of an owl, the harbinger of death, had plunged her into terror.

Only two hours before daybreak, relieved by Chantal, who'd taken the last watch, Jeanne had finally fallen asleep briefly and very deeply. She even dreamed, and now this dream still filled her mind.

Hiding from Jando, his right shoe pressed to her, she was crouching under Florence's writing desk.

"Have you seen Dédé at all?" she heard her brother ask, and through Florence's legs she saw his feet with one shoe missing.

"I?" asked the astonished voice of her mother. "No, why?"

"I'm looking for her. She took my shoe again."

"Oh, well, go look and see if you can find her in the garden . . . in any case, she hasn't shown up here."

Jando's feet left. Giggling, Jeanne crept out from under the desk onto Florence's lap, and her mother caught her, laughing, and pressed her close. . . .

Even now, the images of the dream were still so much with her that she felt her mother's arms, and the reality seemed to her like a bad nightmare from which she needed only to awaken again at last.

Despairing, she looked across the gray yard, sodden

with the nightly rainfall. Not a sign of life anywhere, not a sound to be heard.

Half an hour later, something moved by the stalls. One of the herdboys shoved the wooden door of the biggest of the mud huts to one side and five goats and three sheep trotted outside, one after the other. Their bells jingled at every step, as they greeted the day with bleating and baaing, running obediently ahead of the herdboy. Right after that, the door of the next house opened and out walked Habimana and Maboko, armed with axes and machetes.

When Habimana noticed the children, he strode across the yard to them.

"Don't think that we have servants, the way you're used to!" he snarled at them. "At least make yourselves useful, and don't just sit around here!"

Then he took a police whistle from his pants pocket to call the dogs to him with an ear-piercing blast, and they obediently crept around the corner of the house to him at the first sound and trotted sleepily across the yard.

"Come! There's work waiting for us!" He beckoned his brother to him impatiently. And shortly thereafter the two vanished through the gate with the two dogs.

Frowning, Chantal watched them leave, then suddenly stuck out her tongue and made a couple of sharp bleating sounds. The effect was a release. They all laughed, made faces, and joined in bleating.

Eric jumped up. "Come, the time is right and there's work waiting for us!" he mocked Habimana with his voice screwed up to a falsetto. "Don't think that the servants will take care of it for us! So, what are we waiting for?!"

Crouching, they slipped along the hedge and out the gate.

When they had left the farm behind them without being seen and were running along the first stretch of road, the knot in Jeanne's chest gradually began to dissolve.

"The best thing would be to go back exactly the way we came here yesterday!" she proposed. "I saw a sign. And I'm sure I'll find the cloister from there."

The night quiet still lay over the town. But on the way into the center they would occasionally encounter groups of armed men. Each time they were afraid of meeting Habimana and being sent back. Or worse. They tried to act as casual as possible, going along markedly slowly. But the men took hardly any notice of them. They seemed to be in a great hurry.

From the direction sign, the road led on through a residential area to the edge of the town on the other side.

Beyond a long curve, which wound around the summit of the Zaza hill, they finally came to the cloister. They saw its extensive estate before them: the church with the great cross on the top of the roof, the church plaza, the other buildings of the cloister, the dormitory, the elementary school, and the kindergarten.

When Jeanne glimpsed the monks' luxuriant orchards and flower gardens between the buildings, her memory traveled back. It was of course long ago, at the time when her father was still working at the seminary. She and her family had often visited Jando's godfather and she had played hide-and-seek with Jando and Teya in the cloister garden.

Now there was not a soul to be seen. The school buildings were deserted. No wonder. It was the last week of the Easter vacation. However, it seemed unusual that there were neither monks nor nuns in the gardens or in front of the buildings. If Jeanne remembered correctly, they usually began their work in the early morning hours.

The residences of the monks and priests lay to the left of the church. Jeanne led the others there. They stopped in front of the door of the first and largest of the houses, still uncertain of what they should do. The voices of many people came to them through the walls, and Jeanne guessed that other fugitives had already found refuge here. Her hope grew. Feverishly she tried to remember the names of priests she had known personally in those old days. But she couldn't think of any.

"Who should we say we want to see?" asked Chantal quietly, as if she could read her thoughts.

Jeanne shrugged her shoulders. "Right now, I can't remember any names," she said regretfully. "Never mind! Here they have to help us anyway."

Eric gave a couple of strong knocks on the door, which opened to them almost immediately. A stout priest in a white robe, spanned by a broad purple sash, stepped onto the threshold and stuck out his head. A rosary hung around his neck, he held a second in his hand, and on his rotund chest, fastened to a leather cord, a large wooden cross with a crucified Jesus made a magnificent show.

When the priest saw the children, a sound of indignation escaped him, and before they even had a chance to frame their request, he took a step toward them and shooed at them, hands fluttering. The beads of the rosary clicked hard against each other.

"Be off with you!" he cried. "Quick, before anybody sees you. It's full here already. We can't take anyone more. And tomorrow it'll be a cemetery here anyhow!"

Without giving them a chance to answer, he withdrew into the house and let the door slam behind him.

They looked at each other in disbelief.

Now God has abandoned us too, Jeanne thought.

Chantal drew in her breath audibly. "What's the big idea!" she burst out angrily. "Why all of a sudden do they all act as if they never had children!? I just don't understand it!"

"Oh, that's quite clear," Eric said bitingly. "After all, priests aren't allowed to have any children!"

In spite of their hopeless situation, they had to laugh at his words.

"That was supposed to be a priest? Not on your life!" Chantal blasphemed. "He was just dressed up as one!"

But the priest's warning had aroused their fear and they left quickly so as not to be caught.

Jeanne's thoughts were racing. She did not intend to give up.

"There is one other possibility," she said, thinking aloud. "My brother's godfather is a professor at the priests' school. He lives here in the neighborhood. Perhaps he's still there."

She didn't let on to the others that she didn't know exactly where the house was anymore. She was convinced that she'd find it, if she followed her earlier play places. They had to walk past the garden, of that she was sure. Then they would come to a small development of houses. And one of the first houses there belonged to her father's friend. She'd certainly recognize it when they came to it.

Once again she took the lead. Trained her eyes carefully forward, searching for a tree on which she had sat, a hedge behind which she had hidden, the guideposts of childhood. But it was still hard for her to find the right way. Everything had grown, and one orchard looked like another. As did the flower gardens, multicolored seas of flowers, in which the rains had hammered and torn some of the flower heads from their stems. Now they covered the soil, drowned in muddy water.

Finally Jeanne's eyes were caught by something she remembered exactly: a very tall papaya tree. Its branches were full of the fat, pear-shaped fruits, whose sweet flesh under the yellow peel was soft and delicious. The memory of the taste made her mouth water, but she had something more important to think of right now.

"I know where I am now. It isn't much farther," she said with relief, convinced that behind the garden the first houses would soon appear, and one of them would be the one she was looking for.

In fact, she found it just little later. She recognized it right away, but it was in a condition that demolished all her hopes at one blow.

The entire development was in ruins.

The big house was, like that of her parents, surrounded by a high cypress hedge. But part of the hedge had been cut down, someone had removed the wrought-iron gate, the roof of the house was missing, windows and doors were broken out of the exterior walls, parts of the walls were pulled down. Through the great holes you could look into the former salon, into its dreadful emptiness.

Jeanne looked at the bare back wall of the room. She and her family had often been guests here. In recollection she saw the huge cupboard on which stood the white raffia baskets with the artistic black decorative borders she had so admired. Beside them the *icyansi*, an exquisitely carved, gleaming wooden pitcher, in which milk was kept. Her parents had also had such a pitcher. It was a traditional wedding present that was given to the bridegroom, together with a cow. At the ceremonial presentation, the newly married couple must drink milk out of it together.

"That was it," said Jeanne softly. She couldn't bring herself to look at the others.

"Oh, no!" moaned Eric. "What are we going to do now?"

Simon, the youngest of the brothers, dug his fists into his eyes.

"We have to go back," Chantal decided. "There's nothing else for us to do." Her voice sounded hoarse. With a jerk, she turned around and led hastily away. "Come on, let's go!" she cried irritably.

The others hurried after her. Fear was written on the

boys' faces.

"I don't want to," Simon whimpered.

"We have no other choice. So the best thing would be for us to get back to Maria's family's house as quickly as possible," Chantal said as she marched determinedly on.

"How are we going to explain where we were?" Eric objected. "When Habimana notices it, he's not going to be very nice to us."

"We won't say anything at all! Just act as if nothing happened," Chantal advised.

Eric shook his head. "Didn't you hear how he threatened us? We're burdensome to them. It's very clear that we're not welcome there. The way they treated us! We had to sleep on the floor! Wait, Chantal! I don't want to go back there again."

But she wouldn't be stopped. "Do you have a better idea?" she asked challengingly.

"Yes, I'm just going to stop here right now!" He grabbed her arm.

From the hill you could look out over the valley. With outstretched arm Eric pointed to a swampy area that lay between banana and coffee fields.

"You see that swamp there? Right in the area behind the banana fields there's a lake, you can't see from here. They grow rice and vegetables in the swamps. I know my way around there quite well. We can hide in the reeds. Between the plants and in the water, no one will look for us."

"And how long do you intend to stay in the water up to

your neck?" asked Chantal snippily.

"Until the Rebels get here," he returned promptly.

Chantal could not be convinced. "We don't know if they're coming at all. And when! We can't stay in the cold and wet all day long without anything to eat or drink. And without sleep!"

Jeanne, who until now had heard only the worst rumors about the Rebels, also had objections to Eric's proposal. "How do you know that the Rebels won't want to kill us too?" she asked.

Eric finally gave up. "All right," he conceded. "Then we'll go back."

The decision was not easy for any of them. Silent and downcast, they made their way back. They hurried, so as to be at the house before Habimana. Sometimes they were stopped and asked where they were going. Then they boldly claimed to be out on an errand for Maria.

Shortly before noon they finally reached the farm unmolested, and when they found only Maria with Sophia and Olivier and the blind grandmother outside, they breathed a sigh of relief. Maria was sitting on a mat and feeding Sophia. Like the evening before, the grandmother sat in the sun and smoked her pipe. In a shadowy corner of the yard, Olivier knelt on the ground, absorbed in playing with stones.

Guiltily they approached Maria, who awaited them resentfully.

"Where have you been? Why did you leave without saying anything to me?" she upbraided them. "Isn't my family good enough for you?"

"We didn't want to be a burden to you," Chantal explained.

But Maria would not let herself be appeased. She was insulted.

"Hmph. If you don't want to be a burden to us, make yourselves useful, will you!" she said in a cutting tone. "You girls can go clean vegetables right now. And afterwards get some water. Agnès will show you where the spring is. The boys should stay here."

Jeanne gulped. She didn't see why the boys didn't have to do anything. They had more strength for getting water, too! She thought that was unfair. Besides, she didn't like being given orders like a serving maid. But she didn't want to anger Maria any more. So she held back and followed Chantal and Carine to the fireplace.

The boys, with nothing to do, again took their places on the low sitting wall in front of the main house.

But they had scarcely sat down when Habimana and Maboko marched in with a troop of armed farmers.

In recent days Jeanne had so often seen gangs of men carrying clubs, axes, and machetes that at first she thought nothing of it. It seemed almost normal to her. But when the farmers, with Habimana in the lead, made straight for the boys, the knowledge went through her like a shock: They had come to kill them.

"You're going with us!" commanded an old farmer bluntly.

The boys stood up.

Habimana detached himself from the group and walked determinedly over to Olivier. "And you're also coming with us!" he said.

When he lifted the little boy up, Olivier began to kick and scream. Habimana held his mouth shut and grasped him firmly.

Jeanne couldn't believe her eyes. Olivier was Maria's son!

Only now did Maria seem to realize what was happening. She sprang up and rushed to her brother.

"No!" she cried in horror. "What do you want with Oli!?"

Habimana looked stonily at her and said nothing.

"But you can't do that!" Maria implored. "He's just weaned from my breast!" She began to weep.

"He's a boy," replied Habimana, unmoved. "And Gasana's son."

With these words he left her, carrying the kicking Olivier under his arm, and rejoined the men, who were leading Eric and his brothers from the yard. The three boys did not attempt to defend themselves. They didn't look back at all. Jeanne watched them go away forever, with lowered eyes and immobile faces, surrendered helpless to the violence, as it had also been with Jando.

Only Olivier screamed unceasingly. He kicked his feet against Habimana and hit around him. "Mama! Mama! I don't want to! I don't want to! Let me go!"

After the men had left the yard, his cries died as if cut off.

Maria stood there, where her little boy had just been

playing with stones, and wept silently to herself.

The stillness that followed made Olivier's screams echo in Jeanne's ears a thousandfold. She saw Maria dissolved in tears, saw the grandmother sitting there in silence, smoking her pipe, the wrinkled face turned to the sun.

And she believed she would never in her life be happy again.

You wept when you told me about it.

I wonder what Habimana is doing today. Whether he was brought to justice for the murder of Maria's and Gasana's sons. And whether Maria condemned him for it. Whether he considered himself guilty.

How many murderers are running around free? Perhaps the nameless murderers of your parents and siblings?

I can hardly bear these thoughts.

Your friend Mireille, who, like you, lost her parents and siblings during the genocide, told us once of her young neighbor, just twenty, a friend of the family, who killed her little sister.

"He came to us so often," she said. "He loved my little sister especially. I still see him before me as he threw her into the air, laughing, and caught her again. Yes, he loved her! I simply can't understand it! One day I would like to ask him why he did that."

I doubt that he would have an answer for it. Probably it's beyond what a person could explain. And perhaps, like many others, he's not conscious of any guilt.

"The really guilty," you say, "they planned this murder a long time before. They stirred up all the others, paid them, and exerted pressure on them. They haven't gone to prison. They're abroad somewhere. Probably they're doing well. The other perpetrators were their victims."

"I don't know," I say. "But I understand what you mean. The ones who ordered the murder and prepared the way for it, they're guilty in a special way. But the others are too. Even if someone else brought them to the point where they functioned like a tool. The step you take to doing wrong is your own step. When you lift your hand to destroy another human being, you do it yourself. And you alone bear the responsibility for it."

"What would it be like if I were to go to Rwanda today?" you wonder. "I'd certainly meet people who helped me but who've killed others. How do you prove all the wrongdoers guilty? There were way too many."

You are certainly right.

But the thought that the murder of your parents and siblings, of your aunts and cousins, might perhaps remain unpunished makes me angry. Emotionally, I want retribution.

At least those who walk over corpses without a scruple should feel the dead clutching their heels and drawing them down to them. They should never walk free and upright again!

The following days dragged on and vanished in an uncertain, oppressive existence. Everything in Jeanne resisted staying at the farm.

The three girls drew closer and closer together. They hardly spoke with each other, not even when they were by themselves, for fear of being overheard. Also, it wasn't necessary for them to speak, they understood each other without words. They hardly ever came face to face with Maria, who had completely withdrawn into herself. Béata now called the shots in her place.

Jeanne resigned herself to having to earn her keep. Besides, the work helped her to keep the worst thoughts at a distance. She had to help with the cooking and washing and fetching water. Sometimes with harvesting sweet potatoes or manioc in the fields. When she lay down on her mat at night, Jeanne was tired and drained enough to scarcely feel the hard floor anymore and eventually fall asleep. Without prayers. She had stopped praying.

As well as they could, the girls tried to avoid an encounter with Habimana. Since he was out every day with the other looters, they were usually able to keep out of his way.

Once they heard Béata discussing with Maria's mother whether they should perhaps be separated and dispersed to relatives. Lest it actually come to the point that they tried to run away.

Mornings and afternoons they went with Agnès down into the valley to the water place, a natural well hole between stones, which was fed by a spring. As long as the water cans were empty and the path went downhill, this trip was no trouble for them; on the contrary, if nothing unexpected happened to them, they enjoyed it as a little bit of freedom.

But coming back was a torment. It demanded all their strength to manage the steep climb with the big water cans, filled to the top, on their heads. Jeanne, who ate little and had lost a lot of weight, sometimes thought she was going to sink to her knees under the burden.

After the word got around that the girls came to the water place daily, a few young people from the village turned up to wait for them there and play a cruel game with them.

They blocked their way, grabbed them, held them fast, and bent their fingers so far back that they almost broke.

"Let's see if you're really Tutsis!"

"Just look! How soft their hands are!"

The light skin on the palms of their hands stretched under the hard pressure until it was white. Dark red spots formed where the blood was stopped.

"And that there is definitely Tutsi blood, or isn't it?!"

Jeanne's limbs were very flexible. But she too sometimes reached the point at which the hyperextension caused unbearable pain. She screamed and resisted. Once she sank her teeth into the arm of her torturer, who now also bellowed with pain, flung her from him, and kicked at her.

While this was going on, Agnès chatted with a few women who were standing by and watching the girls being tortured, calmly got her water, and when it was all over, called them to leave as if nothing had happened.

When the rains became heavier and lasted for many hours, enough water collected in the barrels for washing and cooking. From then on they only had to get drinking water now and then, and there was no longer a daily walk to the spring.

All at once, toward the end of April, remarkable changes occurred.

Streams of refugees, fleeing as the Rebel troops moved closer, poured through Zaza. But now it was Hutus, who had left their houses out of fear of reprisals and were trying to escape over the border. Some of them were temporarily housed at the farm, and the girls had to share their quarters with them.

A nervous disquiet spread through Maria's family. Habimana and Maboko stopped their looting tours and remained at home.

One day a motor convoy of soldiers and police drove through the village. They were also in flight and warned the villagers about the Rebel army, which was already very close and could no longer be halted.

That same afternoon Habimana gave the order to leave. Everything that anyone could carry or load onto wagons was hastily packed.

In an unobserved moment, Jeanne, Chantal, and Carine slipped behind the goat shed to discuss what they could do. They considered whether they should oppose Habimana and simply stay there. But fearing the consequences of his anger, they discarded the thought.

They left the farm with about fifty people, to join the long procession of fleeing villagers. Only the grandmother stayed behind with a few animals after she'd obstinately refused to leave her hut.

At the beginning, they moved forward very slowly. As long as the road was through Zaza, more people kept joining them, crowding into the thick stream of fugitives and holding it up.

The walk was arduous. Jeanne was balancing a large basket of dishes and cutlery on her head, Chantal carried shopping bags with clothing, bananas, and avocados, and Carine bore several rolled-up sleeping mats. It was raining buckets and after a short distance they were already soaked to the skin. Jeanne wondered how her clothes would ever get dry again if the rain held till evening. She had carefully stuck Jando's sweatshirt in the basket and covered it with a plastic cloth so that at least that would remain dry.

We ought to have stayed back there, she thought.

She felt weak, close to collapse. The mud under her feet swelled up between her naked toes at each step. And on top of that, itching was causing her discomfort that was hardly endurable.

Several days before, she'd discovered that her things were infested with lice. When one of the little gray bugs had crawled out of the sleeve of the sweatshirt, she screamed in horror. It was the first time she'd ever seen such vermin. Together, the girls had searched the seams of their clothing and found little white eggs. Chantal and Carine had them too. There was nothing they could do about it! Since they had no clothes to change into and didn't want to run around naked, they couldn't undress to wash their clothes and get rid of the vermin.

Jeanne wondered if she would ever be clean again. With bad conscience she thought of her mother, who never tolerated these conditions.

Now the wetness on her skin seemed to have aroused an entire army of lice and goaded them into action. It tickled everywhere, and the thought that the bugs were running over her body in throngs made the itching worse. The desire to scratch was overpowering. But her hands were not free. They held the basket.

When the stream of people reached the edge of the village, it partially dissolved, for from that point they went on in different directions.

Habimana obviously had a specific destination in mind. He turned off into a narrow track that ran around the large lake that Eric had spoken of that day on the cloister hill. When they reached the shore, Jeanne thought of Eric's proposal to hide there, and she kept furtively looking for heads that might appear somewhere among the water plants or in the reeds. But there was nothing other than the dark gray surface of the water, stirred up by the rain. If people really were concealed under it, they must be dead.

It was a lonely area. A lightless place, in which any voices were missing, even those of the animals. As if all life had left it. Isolated abandoned houses lined the track.

At regular intervals, however, protractedly long exchanges of gunshots shattered the stillness, a sign that there was fighting somewhere, not very far away at all. Jeanne noticed that Habimana strode on somewhat faster every time.

Now the war is here, she thought.

It was late evening and had finally stopped raining when they halted in front of a farm similar to Habimana's in a small, remote settlement. Here too the houses seemed to be deserted, but when they entered the large interior courtyard they found a number of fugitives there already, sitting on the ground near the fireplace.

A young woman came across the yard. Her great resemblance to Maria and Agnès struck Jeanne immediately, despite the darkness. Her belly curved out like a gigantic ball under a long cloth dress. It was obvious that she was expecting a baby very soon.

"*Wiriwe*, Felicitée!" Maria's mother embraced her daughter.

"Where is Maurice?" Habimana asked.

"He's leading our soldiers against the Rebels," the young woman answered softly, not without pride. "Come, you must be hungry."

The women followed her to the fireplace and the men joined a group of refugees, who were leaning on the fence and debating about something. Jeanne, Chantal, and Carine stayed behind, without anyone's paying any attention to them.

Near the fire, Carine unrolled one of the mats she'd been carrying, and the three girls sat down on it. Jeanne had cold shivers running down her back, and they wouldn't stop. Her wet things stuck to her body, her skin was sodden and completely chilled. Chantal undid the cloth she'd temporarily wrapped around her wounded hand and held it in the air to dry.

"I can't move my fingers anymore," she moaned.

Shivering, Jeanne jumped up, picked Jando's sweatshirt out of the basket, and disappeared behind a tree with it. Quickly she stripped off the wet dress, also her underwear, and pulled on the sweatshirt. It reached down to her knees. Then she came back, spread the wet things out on the mat, and moved near the fire to let herself be warmed by the flames.

She stared absently into the glow. Her eyes were burning with weariness and with the tears she couldn't shed. She didn't want to think about the coming day, she wanted only to sleep and forget.

You are indignant.

"The kids in my class are mean!" you say when you come home.

For just under two years you've been going to a private school. You're very popular and are invited to one party after another. This time by a girl named Svenja, who is the outsider in your class.

You've already told me about her. That she was new in your class this year because she had to repeat the grade. That she is big and fat and unattractive. Slovenly and unkempt. And awkward. Smart, but lazy. She's absent all the time. Often without a reason. She always keeps to herself. No one can stand her.

Now she's asked you and your crowd of girls to a birthday party. She wants you to go to a swimming pool with her.

"The others are planning to just stay away. Without declining! And they don't want me to go either. I think that's mean!"

"Well?" I ask. "What are you going to do?"

"I'm going, of course," you say decidedly.

When you come home, you report that the afternoon was a real disaster. The others actually did not come. And the swimming pool was closed. Svenja had to take you home with her. No one was there. The little apartment was dirty and messy. And Svenja was in a bad mood. When her mother came home from work, you had a piece of cake.

"Good thing the others didn't come," you say. "Then they would have talked about her even more."

"And what about you? Are you sorry you went?" I ask.

You shake your head vigorously. "I never used to be able to stand children who were poor and dirty," you say. "I looked down on them. And then I was poor and dirty myself. I stank. And I had nothing, not even a home! Never again. . . , " you say, and now your voice gets loud, "never again will I look down on someone just because he's poor or dirty!"

I don't yet know very much of your story. But the anger in your voice lets me guess what you went through and that for you this is a matter of dead seriousness.

The next morning the sun was shining.

After breakfast the girls were sent with Agnès and a couple of boys to get water. When they got the canisters from the cookhouse, Jeanne noticed that there was still enough of a supply there. She suspected that they were just being kept busy.

Before they started out, they were warned not to dawdle. If the Rebels came closer, they would have to leave immediately.

Agnès knew the way.

They had to go back to the lake. It was more than a half hour's walk to get there. As they went, Jeanne kept looking mistrustfully over at the boys, but they seemed to have no interest in them, and about halfway along, the boys ran ahead and were already starting out on the return journey by the time the girls got to the water place.

It lay in a swampy area beside the lake. Crystal clear spring water burbled between stones into a little pond.

Chantal set down the canisters. She unwrapped her hand, let a calabash fill with water, and poured it over the wound. Finally she rinsed out the bandage, sat down, and stretched out her legs. Carine drank some of the spring water and sat down beside her sister.

Jeanne realized that the girls wanted to delay the return to the farm, and it was also all right with her to stay longer. After a restless night in which she'd had to endure the smell of sweat and the noisy breathing of strangers beside her, she felt exhausted, and her head was throbbing. She filled her scooping dish with water and began to wash. First her face, then her itching arms, and finally her dusty feet. The ice-cold water refreshed her, her skin began to tingle. Once more she filled the dish and poured the water over her head. It ran down her face, cooling and invigorating, her vision became clearer, and the dull pain behind her forehead subsided. She approached the bank of the lake slowly.

It was transformed.

Under the clear morning light its smooth surface shone a brilliant blue, the slightly curling blades of grasses were reflected in it, dragonflies hovered shimmering over the shallow spots near the edge. Now and then a frog leaped out of his hiding place in the reeds to dive headfirst into the water again. At the spot where he'd disappeared, tiny waves made their circles, spreading wider and wider, until they were no longer visible.

Sweet potato fields bordered the bank and the air was drowning in the scent given off by the countless lilac-colored flowers of the potato plants. Mixed in was the smell of mud and goat dung. Jeanne inhaled deeply. She followed the flight of a dragonfly and lost sight of it behind the reeds. She thought sadly of Eric and his brothers.

Meanwhile Agnès had filled her canisters and was hopping impatiently from one foot to the other.

"Now hurry up and finish! We have to go back," she urged. But she obviously didn't dare use her usual commanding tone.

"Ohhh, reeeaally?" Chantal asked, drawing out her words. "But it's so beautiful here."

"The Rebels might come!"

"So?" Chantal put her head on one side, looked at Agnès out of the corners of her eyes, and leered at her. "So what?"

"They'll force you to join the army or kill you! Anyone knows that!"

Chantal stopped smiling. "I've seen many dead in recent days, but not one single Rebel!" she said coldly. Her eyes flashed.

"Habimana is sure to be furious if we stay away so long!"

Chantal shrugged her shoulders. She seemed to be intent on irritating Agnès. "You could always go on ahead," she suggested.

Jeanne knew that Agnès wasn't allowed to leave their sides. And of course Chantal knew it too. Jeanne followed the dialogue intently, wondering how far Chantal would push it.

"I'll tell my brother it's your fault we're late! You'll see what that gets you!" Agnès threatened.

Jeanne didn't doubt that Agnès would carry out her threat as soon as they got back to the farm. Although she would love to have stayed, she grew uneasy. Besides, the thought that they might in fact meet Rebels was not comfortable.

"Oh, we might as well go," she said and began scooping up water.

With a sigh, Chantal stood up. "All right," she conceded, but still she calmly drank her scoop empty before she filled her canisters.

Finally they started on the path back.

Agnès stared grimly ahead as they went along. Chantal, on the other hand, acted unconcerned, even humming softly to herself, and Jeanne was convinced that she was just doing it to upset Agnès even more.

They had just gone a few hundred yards from the edge of the lake when suddenly two young men in uniform walked out of a side path and came directly toward them.

Agnès flung her hand to her mouth and choked back a scream, and Jeanne also shrank in fright.

The two men appeared to be unarmed, and they were not wearing camouflage as Jeanne knew it but olive-green suits with thin black horizontal stripes. They must be foreign soldiers. One of them walked up to Chantal, smiling.

"Could you perhaps tell us the fastest way back to Zaza?" he asked. "We've gotten ourselves lost."

It sounded very polite. Jeanne noticed that he spoke unusually slowly and also clearly, without the northern accent. Pure Kinyarwanda, which she had sometimes heard in school.

Chantal returned his smile, sent a triumphant look toward Agnès, who'd retreated a few steps, and answered energetically, "I'm sorry! We don't know the way around here very well ourselves. We fled . . . from Kibungo!" she stressed. "Agnès, perhaps you can tell them the way? After all, you're from Zaza!" she added sweetly.

Agnès flinched, shook her head, and looked to one side.

The second soldier now approached Jeanne. "Can you please give me some of your water?" he asked pleasantly.

She hesitated. Probably the men had nothing bad in mind. All the same. You could never know. They were soldiers, after all. But you were not allowed to refuse anyone water, not even an enemy. So she took the canister from her head and held it out to the soldier.

The young man drank in great gulps. Some of the water ran down his chin onto his shirt collar. "Ahh!" he groaned. "Your water tastes better than milk! I thank you, Gacyecu!"

Smiling he gave the canister back to Jeanne.

His jokingly calling her "little grandma" awakened something familiar in her, and she relaxed. Jando's godfather had sometimes called her that too. Now she was almost certain that the men meant them no harm. She pointed in the direction of the watering place.

"If you keep on along the shore, you'll come to the main road," she explained. "Then you can ask there."

"I thank you, Gacyecu," said the soldier, smiling. "And also thank you for the water!"

When Jeanne turned around as they walked away, she saw that the men were standing and looking after them.

"Those were Rebels," Chantal whispered excitedly. "They've come to Zaza!"

Agnès was out of hearing distance. She was rushing on as fast as she could with the full canisters on her head.

"We ought to have told them about us. Maybe they would have taken us with them!"

Yes, Jeanne thought. Better than going back to Habimana! She turned around once more, but the soldiers were no longer there.

The farm had barely come into sight when Agnès began to walk even faster.

"Now she's definitely going to tattle on us!" Chantal prophesied acidly.

And she proved right.

When they arrived, Habimana, with Agnès at his side, was standing in the middle of the yard waiting for them,

287

snorting with rage, ready to light into them.

"What do you have to do with the Cockroaches?" he began. "It was certainly no accident that you met them! Agnès says you dawdled on purpose until they came. Did you know the men?"

They shook their heads.

"How should we know them? They were foreigners. We've never seen them before. Otherwise we'd certainly have stayed there!" Chantal declared in a challenging tone.

Habimana raised his hand as if he intended to strike her. "Shut your mouth! I don't believe a word you say. I'll soon find out what this is all about!"

Then he began to interrogate each of them individually: Why they hadn't gotten the water and then come right back, as ordered. Why Chantal hadn't listened to Agnès when she told them to leave. Why they hadn't run away from the Rebels. What they had spoken with them about.

They told how it had been. And assured him over and over that they did not know the men.

Finally Agnès jumped in. "Jeanne even gave one of them water. He drank out of her canister!"

"So you do know them! Or how did you think to give water to our enemies? You planned to meet them there, now admit it finally."

Jeanne did not answer. There was no point in answering. Chantal and Carine were also silent while he went on and on, talking and raging at them. Chantal turned away and rolled her eyes. Finally he gave up.

"I forbid you to leave the farm from now on! Understand?" he said viciously before he left them.

After lunch, quiet descended.

Some of the refugees stretched out on their mats to sleep. Béata and Agnès withdrew into the house with the other women. Habimana sat with some men under a tree. Several large pitchers of banana beer were handed around.

The three girls were lying down to one side in a shady corner and acting as if they intended to sleep too. In reality they were observing the yard closely. Since the quarrel with Habimana, they were afraid. He was unpredictable. If he thought they were traitors, they were in danger.

"Look there," Chantal whispered suddenly.

Habimana got up and went up to the main house. Three of the men followed at his heels.

"Wait here!" said Chantal, after they had all disappeared into the house. "I'm going to find out what they have in mind."

Looking around to all sides, she followed the men and whisked up to the door. Jeanne, her heart pounding, watched her disappear into the front room. Was she out of her mind? What if Habimana discovered her? Carine grabbed Jeanne's arm and clutched it hard. Her hands were damp.

The minutes dragged on, and Jeanne could have screamed with relief when Chantal finally reappeared, waved briefly to them, and looked around her once more before she came back as slowly and casually as possible. She dropped onto the mat.

"I knew it! We have to get away from here fast!"

"What's the matter?" Carine asked.

"They were talking about us in the living room. The door was closed, but all the same I could hear every word. They think we're spying for the Rebels."

"What are they going to do?" Jeanne asked.

"They're going to leave this evening and head in the direction of the border. They aren't agreed yet what they should do with us. One of them suggested killing us beforehand because we could betray them. But Habimana said we could maybe still be useful to him. If the Rebels catch him, he means to say that he saved us. We're his security. Especially you, Dédé!"

"Why me?" Jeanne inquired.

"Because your father was a professor. He thinks they know him."

"Well . . . what should we do now?"

"I don't intend to wait until they decide. Besides, I don't want to go any farther with them!"

"If you go, then I'm coming with you!"

"But how are we supposed to get away from here without anybody noticing?" Carine asked anxiously.

"It's siesta now. Most people are sleeping. Habimana is in the house. The best thing would be for us to try it now. Each of us goes in a different direction. I'll wait just a little so that it isn't so noticeable. You two go on ahead! Get going! We mustn't lose any time!"

Jeanne stood up.

"I'm off," she said. "See you later!"

They believed they'd made it when, half an hour later, they saw the lake not far ahead of them. No one had followed them and they had met no one along the way. Obviously, their escape had remained unnoticed so far. Only once in passing did they see a couple of unknown refugees, who were having a midday rest under the wide fan of shade of an ancient foliage tree.

They halted at the bank of the lake for a short time.

Rain clouds were collecting from all directions of the sky, as if this spot were a gathering place. They made the calm reflection on the water appear spotty and gloomy here and there. In the reflection, the clouds and the reeds changed their colors among green and gray and brown. The lake in camouflage. The cloud cover had still not closed over. But there was concentrated moisture in the air, and whenever a cloud moved in front of the sun, it became noticeably colder and the smell of the mud grew stronger.

"It's going to rain," said Chantal. "The best thing would be for us to take side paths the rest of the way, in case Habimana follows us. . . ."

They wanted to go to Zaza. In the hope that they would run into the Rebels there, who might help them further. So they turned off sideways into the fields. Walked on narrow tracks, which you could scarcely have called roads. In a green labyrinth of fields, small woods, and plantations they soon lost their bearings. Occasionally they passed lonely farms, abandoned by their owners. They were in no-man's-land. When it began to rain, they plucked large banana leaves and held them over their heads as umbrellas.

The drops drummed on the leaves. They filled Jeanne with their monotonous rhythm. A whisper that resounded from a thousand hills and grew to a thundering. From which one word detached itself. Always only that one word. Death, death, death, death, death, death, death, death, death, death, death, death, death . . .

Once they stopped to rest for a moment. They leaned on the trunk of a banana palm and sought protection under its crown. But the leaves were no longer able to hold back the quantities of water.

"Do you think the Rebels are still in Zaza?" Jeanne asked Chantal. She had a feeling that the entire country was deserted.

"Certainly," Chantal said. "They were still there this morning. . . ."

"And what if they don't recognize who we are . . . if they take us for enemies . . ."

"It doesn't matter, I'm not going back for anything!"

Once again Jeanne's memory traveled back to her grandmother's farm. One place to which she could return in her thoughts any time without hurting too much.

If Sakabaka, the advice-giving bird, were there now, she would ask him, she thought.

But there weren't any birds there at all anymore. They had vanished like the people.

Nyogokuru had told them of Sakabaka, the wondrous big black bird with the white collar, who predicted the future. You could ask him everything: where the king's cows were grazing, whether you would ever become rich, whether you would go to heaven when you died. . . .

The bird didn't show himself often. If you were lucky enough to see him somewhere, you had to seize the opportunity and quickly put to him the questions you had on your mind.

Once she and Teya had discovered him on a lower branch, close enough to be able to speak with him. They had been terribly excited and had squabbled, as usual. Each wanted to be the first to ask him something. Finally their excited quarrel had scared the bird away. "It's your fault," Teya had screamed.

Teya, Teya, where are you? I want to squabble with you.

"Come on," said Chantal, with a worried look at the sky, "we have to find the main road. I think we're lost. We've been going for much too long."

Jeanne threw away her umbrella. It was no good anymore, for the water was streaming out of her clothes and the rain was slacking off.

When they finally reached the main road, they could already see the first houses of Zaza from a distance. But the clouds had not dispersed. The solid, dirty gray layer swallowed the light. Although their legs would hardly cooperate, the girls began to run.

Jeanne had no idea how late it was. The first of the houses at the beginning of the village was a little white house with a green corrugated iron roof. To their amazement, they saw a woman in a narrow front yard without a fence. She had her back to them as she bent over a flower garden.

At that moment the woman turned around.

She was very old. Her back was quite crooked so that she could no longer stand upright. Her eyes widened in surprise as she saw the girls running toward her.

"*Muraho*!" Chantal greeted her, but without stopping.

Now the old lady came alive. Supporting herself on a stick, she walked out of the yard, more quickly than they could imagine, and blocked their way.

"Stop!" she cried and raised her stick. "Where are you going? You must turn around!"

Chantal stopped unwillingly. "We're going into the town!" she declared.

"You mustn't do that!" shrieked the old lady. "The Cockroaches are there! They'll kill you! They killed my children."

"I don't believe that." Chantal made an effort to remain polite. "We want to ask them for help."

"Oh, no, don't do that, my dears!" begged the old woman. "The Cockroaches are dangerous. They are wicked, wicked! They come to me every day. Ask if I have enough to eat. I don't want that! They're checking up on me. They want to drive me out of my house. But I won't go away from here! I was born here."

She's confused and doesn't know what she's saying, Jeanne thought.

"We have to go on now!" said Chantal firmly and made an attempt to start moving again.

The old woman brandished her stick. "Please, please, children, listen to me!" she cried, fell on her knees, and lay across the road. Her body a barricade. "God will help you, but don't go there where death lives!"

"We have no other choice, we'll see what happens to us."

With these words Chantal tried to get past her. When the old woman stretched out her arms to hold her, she slipped to the side and ran on. Jeanne and Carine followed her.

"Stay here, children! Come back! Come back!" pierced the air behind them.

They didn't look back. After a few hundred yards they stopped and burst out laughing.

"She's crazy!" gasped Chantal. "If she knew where we've come from and why we don't want to go back, she wouldn't be making such a scene!"

When you say lice *instead of* rice,
free market *instead of* flea market,
I could kiss you . . .

But I just pinch you in the ribs. Or on the behind. You sound-shifter! You syllable-chopper! What, I ask you, are you doing to our words? When you talk fast or are excited, you chop the ending off a word and put it on another one instead. And you're simply at war with the vowels. Especially with the short ones. You squeeze those out to long ones.

You learned our language very quickly. You can now say everything you want to, but there's a little monster lurking in your speech center and thwarting your plans, cavorting on your tongue, so that sometimes it doesn't obey you.

I suspect that this monster is a relic of your early childhood, when you had polio.

A few weeks ago you started going to a speech therapist. She's prescribed exercises for you: Every day you're supposed to talk or read with a cork between your lips for ten minutes. Out loud, of course. You're finding it hilarious. So are the rest of us. Suddenly the corks are always disappearing from the empty bottles. The corks have become the family thing. I can't drink my wine that fast!

How does one sharpen sounds?

With corks clenched between the teeth. Lips and tongue must do terrific gymnastics to maneuver the sounds past the obstruction to produce words that people can understand.

If people were to come by and glance through our kitchen window, they'd see us conversing with cork mustaches while chopping vegetables. And they might have the impression, perhaps not entirely wrongly, that the Jansens were crazy.

It's great fun! As is the breakfast ritual on Sunday mornings.

Niklas, our oldest, who's giving you lessons in German, has assigned you a sentence for homework. You're supposed to be practicing the short u/oo sound.

"The awful butcher put a bullet in the cushion—bad neighborhood. The cook took out the sooty footprints. The book now looks beautiful."

Sundays we take our time over breakfast. Often the entire morning. There's also much more on the table than other days. When everyone has slept as long as they want to, they arrive one after the other. Then we eat and chat. And you appear too at some point.

"All right, Jeanne, let's go! How's it going with the awful butcher?"

You pout. Grin and groan. Reluctantly you begin: "The awfool bootcher poot a boolet—"

At this point, at the latest, the chorus interrupts: "The

awful b<u>u</u>tcher p<u>u</u>t—"

"*Yes, yes!*" *you shout, waving until we are quiet.* "*The awful . . . ?*"

"*Super!*"

"*b<u>u</u>tcher . . .* "?

Thumbs up!

"*p<u>u</u>t . . .* "

"*Yes!*"

"*a boolet . . .* "

"*b<u>u</u>llet!*" *sings the chorus.*

Laughter! Again! Over and over: minutes long, until you've muddled your way through the sentences.

Finally, though, you get it. At least for this time!

They approached Zaza's business district. Jeanne thought back to the moment when they'd arrived here with Maria. Now all the houses and stores were abandoned, those of the Hutus as well. Nothing was moving anywhere. It was growing darker, and a cool wind had come up. It penetrated her damp clothes, crawling over her skin. She felt as if they were going through a ghost town.

Suddenly figures detached themselves from a dark corner. Carine screamed.

Three soldiers in Rebel uniforms, rifles on their shoulders, came toward them.

"Hello! Where are you going?" called one of them.

Carine clung to Chantal.

Another said something in Swahili, grinning broadly as he spoke. It looked as though he was baring his teeth.

Jeanne thought she understood a few bits. What he said sounded like, "Look out, we're going to eat you right up!"

"Well, where are you going?" the first one asked again.

"We don't know," replied Chantal evasively. She seemed uncertain.

"And where are you coming from?"

"We don't know that either."

"Well, well. You don't know much at all. Then you certainly don't know who we are!"

"Yes, you are Rebels."

Now all three of them laughed.

"We're the Cockroaches," said the soldier who had spoken Swahili before, now in their own language, but with a foreign accent. "Haven't you heard what the Cockroaches do with unaccompanied children? Aren't you afraid of us?"

Chantal raised her head abruptly. "It doesn't matter! We were going to be killed where we just came from, too!" she retorted belligerently.

The third soldier, who'd been silent until then, approached her and gently took her arm. "You don't have to be afraid. We won't do anything to you. You can come with us and stay with us for the time being."

Jeanne was surprised. Judging from the voice, this soldier was a woman. You couldn't have told at first sight. The full shirt of the uniform concealed her figure. Her hair was close cut, and besides, she was no smaller than the two men.

"My name is Consolée," she went on in a friendly voice. "You're sure to be tired and certainly hungry, too. You really don't need to be afraid. No one here is going to kill you. Sometimes Jimmy talks a lot of hogwash."

In corroboration, Jimmy opened his mouth wide and gave out a few exaggerated grunts.

"So, how about coming with us?" asked Consolée.

It was reassuring that there was a woman among the soldiers. The children hesitated no longer and followed her and Jimmy down the street.

As they went along, Consolée asked them about their parents.

"They're dead," Chantal answered shortly. She left it at that, and Consolée didn't pry any further.

They didn't have to walk far. The soldiers led them to a big house in the center of town, whose lighted windows revealed life inside. Yet another house just opposite appeared to be occupied. All the other houses nearby were without light.

Consolée took the girls along a big corridor to a wide-open double door, which led into an inner courtyard. A group of soldiers, in the company of two young girls not much older than Chantal, were sitting on stools, under which empty beer and lemonade bottles had collected. Laughter and cheerful voices filled the courtyard, which was lighted by an outside light. From one of the small out-buildings Jeanne heard a familiar sound. The regular hum of a motor. The generator.

There was also light on in the cookhouse on the opposite side. A man's voice sounded through the open window. It called something in a foreign language. Jeanne thought she recognized it as English.

As they entered the inner courtyard, the talk died for a moment and those present turned their attention to the newcomers. Two soldiers stood up and fetched stools.

"I'll get you something to eat and drink first." Consolée disappeared into the cookhouse. Jimmy followed her.

One of the girls bent curiously toward Chantal and greeted her with a hello.

"Are you survivors too?" she asked softly.

Chantal nodded quickly and turned away.

Consolée came back with a tray on which were three mugs and a plate of cookies.

"This is for a start. There'll be more later," she said. "They were just baked."

Jeanne squinted at the mugs. She smelled buttermilk! She could not drink buttermilk, try as she might. She considered what she should do. She didn't want to be impolite.

"I can't tolerate any milk," she said.

"No problem, I'll get you something else then," said Consolée, who went back to the cookhouse and shortly afterwards brought Jeanne a mug of *amasaka* gruel.

A tall, thin man, clearly older than the other soldiers, came out of the main house. Gold-rimmed glasses were clipped to the end of his nose. He wore a jacket whose shoulders were decorated with epaulettes. The soldiers stood at attention.

The man ordered something in a foreign language.

Immediately the soldiers stood up, took leave of their visitors, and left the courtyard. The young girls also left soon afterward.

The man pulled up a stool and sat down next to Jeanne, Chantal, and Carine.

"Hello, whom do we have here now? Who are you three pretty girls?" His careful pronunciation betrayed that he came from a foreign country.

They didn't answer right away. In his presence, Jeanne felt a shyness similar to that she'd felt with her father.

"Won't you tell me your names? I'm Afande John," he introduced himself.

They said their names.

He carefully studied their faces. "I'm wondering how you managed to come through the war . . . ," he said thoughtfully, "looking the way you do . . . ," his serious expression changed to a small smile, "I mean, as pretty as you are. . . ."

Jeanne understood very well that he meant something much different.

"Now, you certainly have something better to do than to chat with an old man . . . ," he went on when they didn't answer him. "We can talk together some more tomorrow. Consolée will take care of everything. Just tell her what you need."

With another cheering smile he got up, wished them a good night, and went back into the house.

"Before you shower, we should first find a few clothes for you," Consolée suggested. "There's a store right across the way. The best thing would be for you to look for something for yourselves there."

"We have lice," Chantal informed her.

"Yes, I was afraid of that. So you'll have to shower thoroughly and change your clothes. And tomorrow we'll cut your hair. It's too late to do it now."

Chantal made a face. She obviously didn't like the idea of sacrificing her broom mane.

Consolée and Jimmy accompanied the girls across the road to a small house that lay in complete darkness. Jeanne hung back. It didn't seem right to her to go into a strange store at this hour and simply serve herself there.

The door wasn't locked.

"We'll wait outside," said Consolée, taking up a post with Jimmy on the threshold. The two directed the beams of their flashlights into the small, dim room.

"Now go on," Consolée urged the girls. "There's sure to be something in there that will fit you!"

There's everything here, Jeanne thought when she looked around. And nothing destroyed!

The store must have belonged to a Hutu family who had only fled a short time before.

On the walls were several shelves filled with colored cloths, bolts of fabric, and reels of yarn. Ready-made clothes were hanging on racks, and in a corner Jeanne discovered a mechanical sewing machine that was similar to the one her mother had had.

Chantal and Carine began to burrow among the clothes on one of the racks. Jeanne, however, turned to a door in the back part of the room, which was standing half open. Apprehensive, she hesitated in front of it and listened.

Nothing! Without knowing why, she pressed against the door and stumbled into a small room, a sort of storeroom. It held only shelves, no furniture. As she took a careful step forward, her foot struck against something that lay in the way, and at the same moment the penetrating smell of something decaying rose to her nose. A wave of nausea rose in her, she bent over to see what was there, and in spite of the darkness she recognized the outline of a crumpled figure.

She dashed out and slammed the door behind her, screaming, "There's a dead person in there!"

Chantal and Carine were no longer at the racks but holding on to one of the shelves.

"I saw two also. Two women," Chantal croaked. Carine was crying.

"Let's get out of here!" Chantal grabbed Jeanne and Carine by the arms and pushed them ahead of her to the doorway, where they encountered the beams of the flashlights.

"Why haven't you brought any things with you?" asked Consolée.

"We don't want any clothes from dead people! That's disgusting!" Jeanne cried.

Consolée and Jimmy exchanged a look.

"That's all right," Consolée tried to calm them. "Then we'll go somewhere else."

But Jeanne didn't want to go anywhere. She didn't even want to take her things off anymore. She stood there stock still and shook her head.

"There's another store a little way on up," said Consolée. "You've got to put on clean things after you shower! Think about the lice!"

Jeanne clenched her hands into fists and shook her head again. Carine kept on crying, her shoulders shaking.

"We don't want to anymore!" Chantal now decided too.

Consolée raised her eyebrows and looked from one to the other. "Very well," she finally conceded. "Then we'll have to find another solution for today."

When the girls, after long, thorough showers, appeared for supper in much-too-large, colorful soldier's track suits, their entrance caused general merriment. The soldiers were unsparing with clever observations about the "new recruits," and during the entire meal their future assignments were discussed amid loud laughter. Jeanne suffered through it, feeling embarrassed.

Only unwillingly had she been separated from her own clothes. She'd especially not wanted to surrender Jando's sweatshirt, but this time Consolée firmly insisted that it had to be everything so they could be washed.

Now Jeanne was lying in bed, tired and full, and enjoying the cool, fresh sheets and the soft mattress under her maltreated body.

She finally felt clean again! Her skin glowed. She had worked over every inch with soap and rinsed many times. At the end she had rubbed lotion on thickly from top to bottom.

Chantal and Carine lay beside her. They had all three

crawled into a wide double bed, although there were enough other beds in the room. Protecting each other in sleep and being close had become habit for them.

Their bodies smelled of lotion and soap, a narrow fluorescent tube glowed on the ceiling above them, and voices could still be heard from the inner courtyard.

"We're safe," murmured Chantal as she rolled onto her side.

A little later she was breathing deeply and evenly, and Jeanne also sank into a dreamless sleep.

An excited voice ripped her from her slumber. Someone was calling over and over for her and for Chantal.

Jeanne groaned. She didn't want to wake up. But the voice took on an anxious, shrill tone. Jeanne started up. She didn't know where she was. It was pitch dark.

"Carine, what's the matter, where are you?" asked Chantal sleepily beside her.

Jeanne stretched out a hand to feel and touched Chantal, who was sitting up in bed. But Carine's side was empty.

"Chantal, I have to go, I can't get the door open!" came desperately from the other end of the room.

"Wait, I'll turn on the light!"

Jeanne heard Chantal feeling her way through the room. She was now wide awake, for all at once she also felt the need to go to the bathroom. Too much lemonade!

"Darn, where is that light switch, it was here ... wait ... yes ... I found it!"

The fluorescent light flickered on. Chantal stood there,

tousled and blinking. At the door, Carine, very agitated.

"Just a minute, I have to go too, I'll come with you!" said Jeanne, and she climbed out of bed.

"But the door won't open, it's locked," Carine wailed. As proof, she rattled the handle.

"Nonsense, it's probably just stuck. Let me try it!"

Chantal pressed down the handle and put her shoulder to the door, but it didn't open.

When Jeanne came over, they tried it together. In vain.

"They locked us in," Chantal stated in surprise.

Carine was crying. "I have to go so badly. I can't wait any longer!"

Jeanne felt panic rising in her. She began to beat wildly on the door with both hands.

"Open up!" she shrieked. "Open up right now! We want to get out of here!"

Outside there was nothing. Except for them, there seemed to be nobody there.

Infected by Jeanne, Carine and Chantal began to pound on the door. They screamed and hammered on the door for minutes at a time. Without success.

When they finally gave up, the silence everywhere was sinister.

"What are we going to do?" Jeanne asked with a glance at the window, which was covered with a grill of iron bars. "We'll never get out of here again."

Carine was whimpering to herself.

"I don't understand it. There must be an explanation," Chantal said thoughtfully. "Maybe they're out and locked us in for safety. Come on, we'll go back to bed."

But Jeanne would not be reassured. The wonderful feeling of security that had cradled her before she went to sleep was swept away. They were trapped! And the worst thing was that she had to go to the bathroom very badly and couldn't. It hurt! She definitely would not be able to hold out all night.

"And what if the Rebels are attacked and killed?"

"The fighting is over here," Chantal said. "Believe me, tomorrow morning they'll open up and we'll be free. We can't change anything now. So come back to bed."

Jeanne remained where she was. She wondered bitterly where Chantal got her trust in the Rebels. Besides: She wanted out of here right now, not early in the morning!

Carine did not respond to Chantal's urging either. She seemed not to have heard her sister at all. Her nose was running. She was staring tearfully into the distance. Jeanne reached reassuringly for her hand. And at that moment she saw a pool spreading between Carine's feet.

Oh, no, she thought, horrified and filled with sympathy. That mustn't happen to her for anything! And if it did, she would never forgive the Rebels for it!

Barely a week later, the girls were sitting beside each other on the backseat of a pickup, which was to take them to Kibungo. Three shorn, deloused, and extremely clean girls.

Consolée and Jimmy were going with them. Jimmy was driving. Consolée sat beside him.

Jeanne held a large travel bag on her lap. Filled with

trousers, dresses, T-shirts, and sweaters. There were even a nightgown, slippers, and sneakers in it.

The morning after their arrival at the Rebels' each of them was supplied abundantly with clothing. Consolée had brought it to them. Jeanne had chosen not to ask where the things came from. In spite of the promises, she hadn't gotten her own clothes back.

"They were really impossible to get clean again," Consolée explained regretfully.

Jeanne swallowed it without protest, just as she had the dreadful night in which they'd been locked in. As it turned out, the Rebels had in fact been out very late and had locked the door of the girls' bedroom so that they couldn't run away.

"Only out of concern for you! We didn't want anything to happen to you," Consolée asserted. And even Afande John had apologized.

All the same. Jeanne would never forgive the Rebels for that!

She missed her clothes, especially Jando's sweatshirt, badly. They had been the last things that connected her with her earlier life. Now she was nobody's child. Herself a stranger, for she possessed nothing more that belonged to her. And she felt more alone than she ever had been in her life.

For since they'd been living with the Rebels, something had come between her and Chantal that disturbed their former unquestioning concord. Chantal's uncritical enthusiasm for the Rebels provoked Jeanne's annoyance. And also a gnawing jealousy. When Chantal discussed things or joked with the soldiers, which happened often, she felt shut out. It seemed almost like a betrayal to her.

She cast a glance at Chantal's distinct profile as she faced front. Without her broom on her head, her friend looked very different. Younger. And not so dashing as before.

Jeanne clutched the handles of her bag. Being on the road to Kibungo filled her with fear and resistance. She didn't want to go back to that town!

It was Afande John's idea to go there, to look for relatives.

"If there's someone still alive, relatives or friends of your parents, perhaps you could live with them. Then you'd have a home again."

What nonsense!

There was no home anymore. Not anywhere. And everyone was dead!

She looked past Chantal out the window. The truck kept jolting through potholes. Trees and fields bounced before her eyes, and once the vehicle went into a skid so that the girls almost slid off their seats. Jimmy swore. Consolée turned around and smiled at them, as if trying to assure them that everything would turn out all right. Jeanne looked through her.

Her insides clenched when they reached Kibungo and drove slowly into the town. She knew every corner again. But nothing was the way it had been anymore. The images were only a colorless streak that went past her without touching her. Eternities separated them from what had been familiar to her.

They were approaching the hospital area, driving past the hospital, and shortly afterwards, they pulled up in front of the Chinese House, a large residential complex consisting of four row houses built on the diagonal.

"We're there!" said Consolée. She was the first to leave the truck and held the door open for the girls. "I'll take you to Annonciata. You're sure to get along well with her."

Unconsciously Jeanne expected to meet one of the Chinese faces as she got out. But she saw only a few soldiers standing guard at the entrance. No doubt about it, the Chinese House was in Rebel hands.

Annonciata turned out to be a motherly person in her early thirties with a soft, warm voice and a bosom that no man's shirt would conceal. Her broad hips fitting tightly into her uniform trousers and her Afro hairdo, a full cloud billowing around her head, made her look like a woman who was just borrowing the uniform. She took over the care of the girls with enthusiasm, doing things for them and constantly asking in those first few days whether they needed anything or how they were doing.

On the whole, life in the Chinese House was more bearable than Jeanne had expected. She was left alone. The leader of the group, Afande Brian, was still young. He took care of Chantal's wound, kept it open, and kept removing little grenade fragments. He told her that he had broken off his medical studies to join the Rebels.

The month of May came to an end. All around there was an explosion of green. The plants grew as fast as they could, covering over the traces of the genocide. Rain fell only rarely. Life took place outside. Eating, playing, wasting time. No more work. And so passed one day after the other.

However, a legacy from the Chinese provided diversion of a special sort: They had left behind a Ping-Pong table and equipment. It was an attraction for the girls as well as for the soldiers.

Chantal and Carine often left the house and went looking for relatives or acquaintances who might still be alive. Each time they asked Jeanne to go with them, but she refused, and so she was frequently left alone. Often she just sat there quietly and observed the doings of the others, like a spectator who has gotten into the wrong performance. The strength with which she had fought for her life and that had kept her going until then was now flagging.

She had been sleeping alone again for some time, each of the girls having been given her own room. Now she battled through restless nights and tormenting dreams. When sleep deserted her, she lay awake for a long time, sometimes until morning, and tried to remember something. But the pictures slipped away from her. All that was left was a pain so overwhelming that it displaced all else.

One morning, lured outside at the crack of dawn by the sunshine, she was walking aimlessly around the building. She'd often felt cold recently, and then she usually went outside to warm up.

When she came around a corner, she encountered

James. He was one of the youngest among the soldiers who were stationed in Chinese House. Fifteen at the most. His face, emaciated and marked by privation, still had the soft features of a boy. He was a *kadogo*, a child soldier, and served the *afande* as bodyguard. He didn't seem military at all, more like a student.

Although Jeanne had hardly exchanged a word with him, she liked him. He was always playing tricks, and whenever he saw her he winked at her.

Now he was sitting on the wall that separated the grounds from the valley, and cleaning his machine gun. Jeanne had often watched while the soldiers cleaned their weapons. With sober interest she had followed how they took the guns apart and would wait to see whether they succeeded in putting them back together correctly again.

James had removed the cartridge belt and snapped open the breech mechanism. When Jeanne approached behind him, he turned around and grinned at her over his shoulder. He looked as if he'd been awake all night, his eyes deep in their sockets and bloodshot.

"Well, Little Sister, are you bored? Come over here! It's safe for you to talk with me. I don't bite."

She had stopped. Undecided whether to stay or run away.

"You look like Gasasira," he said. "Are you related to him?"

"Who is Gasasira?"

Really she hadn't intended to say anything, but the question slipped out of her.

"He was a businessman in Kibungo. You really look a lot like him. You could be his daughter."

"You're just saying that! You can't even know him yourself. You aren't even from here!"

He laughed. "Oh, yes! I know him. Relatives of my father lived in Kibungo. I visited them very often. But that was a long time ago. Gasasira was a friend of ours. Well, are you related to him?"

"No, I don't even know who that is."

"Too bad . . . ," he said, and he turned to his work again.

Suddenly she badly wanted him to keep talking with her.

"What do you have to learn to become a Rebel?" she asked, approaching him with small steps.

"Not much. The main thing is that you can shoot."

"Is shooting hard?"

He grinned. "No, not especially. You naturally have to be able to aim. And just pull on the lever here. Then the shot goes off. It's no harder than with a slingshot. Shall I show you?"

She nodded eagerly. She had often shot with a slingshot. Before, together with Jando. They targeted a tree and counted who had the most hits. Jando always beat her.

"Well, then, come here, Little Sister. I'll hold the gun for you. You can do everything else by yourself!"

James placed himself sideways behind her and directed her hand to the trigger lever. "You have to look straight ahead through the little notch there, then you have your eye on the bead. That little black thing on the end of the barrel . . . see it? Right behind that is your target."

She laid her cheek on the stock the way she'd seen the soldiers do it, closed her left eye, and concentrated with the other on the small, triangular notch, in whose center a black thorn at the end of the barrel came into her field of vision.

Before them lay the wide-open valley. When Jeanne fixed her gaze on a particular point above the thorn, the chain of hills swam away. She tried to direct the barrel so that it was targeted at an old tree trunk nearby. Obediently James followed the pressure of her hands and steered the gun in the right direction. She felt his body behind her back. His nearness gave off warmth. Comfortable and also disturbing. Suddenly she took a step to the side and pulled on the trigger lever.

A short, dull crack shattered the air, and James was immediately thrown back against the wall with a powerful jolt.

"Damn!" escaped him. He stared dumbfoundedly at the gun and uttered a torrent of curses.

Jeanne looked at him in dismay. What was wrong? After all, he'd said that she should shoot.

The unexpected shot had also caused alarm in the house. Windows were thrown open and Afande Brian ran up with a couple of soldiers. The *afande* was visibly upset.

"What's going on here? Are you mad? Why did you shoot?" he bellowed, after he'd made sure that nothing had happened and also that there was no enemy in sight.

In utmost embarrassment James scratched his neck. "I'm . . . sorry, Afande!" he stammered. "It went off while I was cleaning it. I had no idea that it was loaded . . . the bullet was still stuck in the chamber. . . ."

"You idiot! How could you overlook that! What if you had hit the child!"

James sent Jeanne a warning look, which gave her to understand she'd better keep quiet. But she couldn't have said anything anyway.

"I know . . . ," he admitted apologetically. "I'm really sorry and it won't happen again, Afande! Word of honor."

"I hope not!" growled the afande and turned to go. "But with the likes of you, one never knows. . . ."

When they were alone again, James slapped himself on the side of the head several times. "Damn it, that shouldn't have happened!" he said crossly.

"It was my fault," Jeanne said sheepishly.

"Mhm," he growled and frowned, as if he had to consider her confession.

"That's exactly right!" he announced finally. He squinted at her. But then the corners of his mouth twitched and he was grinning again. "Well, I'll tell you one thing! If they'd thrown cold water on me . . . or even locked me up, then I'd have taken you with me, Little Sister!"

You dance around our kitchen.

The adoption decree is here. It came by mail this morning.
Three letters with the same contents. Addressed to you, to
me, to Papa.

You're skipping around the kitchen with yours. You're
bursting with joy and telling everyone who comes to the
house.

It's good to see you this way.

Infected by your exuberance, I grab you, whirl you
around, and we both dance around the kitchen.

"We'll celebrate this! Congratulations!"

"Yes!" you say, laughing. "To you too."

On a Sunday morning in June, at Annonciata's side, Jeanne
went to town again for the first time. They were on the road
to the hospital, where one of Kibungo's two refugee camps
was set up. Annonciata had talked Jeanne into accompany-
ing her.

"I need to go see some people in the camp. And you can
help me collect the mail," she said.

All public institutions were still closed. When there was

mail to be delivered, it had to be transported from camp to camp by soldiers.

The post office was on the way. As was the jail. Empty buildings that served no purpose at the moment. Jeanne wondered where the prisoners were. Had the war freed them?

It was an unusually hot day. Annonciata pulled her uniform shirt out of the trousers and opened some buttons. She fanned herself with the folders she was carrying.

"You'll see, Dédé, there are many new people coming again. Every day there are more. There's hardly any place to house them," she said chattily. And she began asking Jeanne a few questions. How she had done in school. If she liked living with the Rebels.

But Jeanne only answered monosyllabically. She wasn't comfortable to be nearing the hospital. She knew, of course, that there were no shots awaiting her, but she feared the memories.

A few yards before the large, open gate of the hospital there was a water place. Once there had been a kiosk there, where Florence had always bought the consolation candy at the end of the hated hospital visit. The kiosk was abandoned. But at the water place, several women and also a few children were splashing about.

"Teya! Teya!"

A joyful scream from their midst. Jeanne stopped short.

And then he shot toward her. Both arms outstretched. It was Alain!

Shortly before he reached her, he stopped and stared at

her, his eyes large with wonder. "But Teya, you're dead! Who killed you? I'll kill him too! When I'm big, I'm going to be a soldier!" he announced with a serious expression.

She smiled, but it hurt. "I'm not dead, Alain!"

A young woman left the water place and walked onto the road. As she came closer, Jeanne's heart rose into her throat. The woman was Esther, Alain's mother. He'd found her again!

"Dédé! *Uraho*! *Mon Dieu*, how are you?" Esther cried joyfully. She grasped Jeanne's arm with both hands and pressed it. "Dédé, that you survived . . . where are you living now and with whom?"

"With the Rebels in the Chinese House."

"We just got to this camp yesterday. Come by sometime and we can talk . . . Dédé, I am so grateful to you. . . ."

Jeanne nodded dumbly. She could say nothing. She was happy for Alain and yet . . . it was hard to bear.

Annonciata noticed that something wasn't right with Jeanne.

"Come, Dédé, we have to go on," she said gently and pulled her away.

"Teya?" Alain asked in confusion.

"Don't forget to come by, whatever you do!" Esther called after Jeanne, who was already through the gate with Annonciata.

Jeanne moved as though she were in a dream. Something inside her hurt terribly, as if a gigantic wound had opened.

After a few steps she stopped.

People were camped all over the lawn, between the buildings and in the shade of the trees, some with all their bags and belongings, some with nothing but their skins. The refugees, the survivors in one town. Among them, stretched from tree to tree, lines on which their washing hung. In peaceful harmony. Smoke rose from countless fireplaces.

"Look around to see if there's anyone you know," said Annonciata, laying a hand on Jeanne's shoulder.

Jeanne wrenched herself away. She didn't want to! She left Annonciata standing and ran a few steps into the park. Against her will she now allowed her eyes to travel over the encamped people. Perhaps, she thought, her heart fearful, Jando's murderers were here too. She didn't know their names, but she would certainly recognize them. The thought was choking her.

In the shade of a tree, right near her, a few children were playing marbles. Suddenly Jeanne's eyes were drawn to something that set off an alarm inside her.

A girl, about her age, was sitting off to one side. And was wearing her poncho! Jeanne rushed at the girl and grabbed onto the poncho, digging in her nails.

"Where did you get this cape?"

"Oww! What's the matter?" The girl was frightened.

"The cape! Where did you get it?"

"My mother crocheted it for me!"

"That can't be so! That's my cape! I got it from my aunt in Europe! You can't get anything like that here. It's mine! Take it off! Right now!"

"Are you crazy? I certainly will not! Leave me alone, I'm

sick. My mother crocheted it for me. I'll call her if you don't leave me alone!"

Jeanne was utterly beside herself. She pulled on the poncho with all her might, trying to pull it over the girl's shoulders and over her head. The girl resisted, scratching, kicking, and hitting at her. Jeanne hit back, weeping, her hands striking everywhere, in a blind rage that could no longer be checked.

Then she was grabbed from behind and held fast.

"What are you doing to my sister!? Stop it! Have you gone crazy?"

Jeanne tried to get free, but the girl holding her was bigger and stronger than she was.

"That's my cape! You're thieves. You looted our house!"

"We didn't steal anything! We served ourselves like everyone else. There was no one there it belonged to."

"You're thieves, thieves, thieves . . . !" Jeanne howled. Again she tried to get free to go at the girl again.

When Annonciata noticed what was happening, she hurried over and freed Jeanne from the hold. "Calm yourself, Dédé. What's the matter? What's got into you?"

"They . . . looted . . . our . . . house," Jeanne gasped out between sobs. "That's . . . my cape!" She tried to run back.

But Annonciata took her in her arms and pressed her to her breast. "Don't get so excited, Dédé. You've already seen worse things. Who knows where those people got that cape! They probably weren't in your house but in the one belonging to the people who looted it. . . ."

And while she slowly pulled the balking Jeanne toward

the entrance, she tried to explain to her how very much the times had changed. Because many people were no longer there. That each one took what he needed. And that people who took something from thieves were not themselves thieves.

Her words swept over Jeanne. They had no meaning.

Thieves! Thieves! All thieves, she thought, undeterred. The entire country is full of thieves!

Gradually her weeping slackened, leaving behind an indifferent emptiness. A head that could comprehend nothing more. A heart scorched to its deepest corner. She stumbled along beside Annonciata, who continued to talk to her comfortingly without a single one of her words reaching Jeanne.

That evening a fierce attack of fever plunged her into tangled dreams. She screamed in her sleep. And heard her screams resounding through the room as if they came from someone else. Icy chills gripped her. A cold that shook her body, tossing it back and forth. Every fiber of her skin hurt, as if she were being stabbed. She could not open her eyes. She no longer knew where she was.

Strange voices over her. Or maybe not? Suddenly everything was much brighter. Blurry faces beside her bed. Mama? Is that you?

"She's burning up! And she's wet through with sweat. We have to get her things off. She has a very high fever." A man's voice. A man's hand.

"No!" She clutched at her covers. Curled up in self-defense. But not undress! She was so terribly cold.

"Let her be. She's completely disoriented. We can't force her." Far away, a woman's voice.

Words whirling in confusion. Individual ones blazed a path to her ear: "exhausted . . . must do something . . . need an antipyretic . . . stay with her . . . must drink . . . serious. . . ."

The faces swayed, forward and back. They lost their contours and Jeanne sank into darkness.

In the following week she slept through the days and nights without transition. Sometimes her sleep was like a faint. Then she perceived nothing more. When she surfaced, the fever held her captive, she suffered agonies, could not defend herself. A lump sat in her throat, taking her voice and her breath, and she coughed until she brought up blood. And she was always cold. When she was able to be aware of herself, she wept.

In her dreams she was in flight. They left their house. Were on the road. Without end, without destination. And once she dreamed she was floating in the sky. She could see the town of Kibungo below her. The way it used to be. Before. The streets full of life. People in the bustle of shopping. And suddenly she saw her mother. At her side Teya and herself. Could understand exactly what they were saying. She called to her mother. But her call was unheard.

Annonciata watched at her bedside. Sometimes Chantal, too. And others. She saw them far away from her. A wall between her and them. She was at their mercy. Someone forced her to drink milk, which she immediately threw up again; she had to eat something, although she was not hungry at all; against her will, she was washed and dressed in clean things; someone carried her to the bathroom and stayed with her until she was done. It was painful for her. Still, resistance stirred in her: She hated to be helpless.

One morning when she woke up, for the first time since she'd been sick, her eyes took in the objects in the room with clear outlines. She was alone. And she was cold. There was no sound to announce that someone was on the way to her. Through the closed window she could see the sun. A blazing ball that promised warmth and was casting its incredible light through the windowpane. On the floor in front of the window, an illuminated rectangle. It must be warm there!

Jeanne tried to sit up. She sank back onto the sheets a few times. But she finally managed to sit up and push her legs over the edge of the bed. When she placed her feet on the floor, the room began to revolve. She swayed. Her legs had no feeling. But she was bound and determined to hold out. She intended to get into the square of sun. Absolutely.

With two wobbly steps she reached the wall. Tried for a hold there with both hands. The cool, hard surface made her shudder. With difficulty she groped her way forward. Only an inch at a time. Filled with the desire to reach the spot of light. Too weak to let go of the cold, repelling wall. Suddenly her legs buckled, and she fell. When she crashed on the floor, her body, merely skin and bones now, felt as if it shattered. She screamed. Then the room dissolved in a garish shimmer and a red wave carried her away with it.

When she came to, she was lying in bed again and was no longer alone in the room. Beside her bed there was a second one and she discerned a small, motionless figure under the sheet. She tried to lift her head.

"That's Uwera, Dédé. She's very sick. We brought her to you because we think she has the same thing you do." Annonciata was standing at the foot of Jeanne's bed with a steaming bowl. "You gave us quite a scare. Don't do that again! You're still much too weak to stand up. Now you have to eat something."

She sat down on the chair next to Jeanne's bed and began to feed her hot *amasaka* gruel with a spoon. Jeanne swallowed reluctantly. After a few spoonfuls she pushed Annonciata's hand away. She'd had enough. Her bones ached. And she wanted to be left in peace.

After Annonciata left, Jeanne stared over at the other bed. The back of her neighbor's head was all that was visible. She hadn't moved at all. The sounds of her rattling breathing crept out of her sheets like small, invisible animals. Then a shudder went through Uwera's body. She began rolling from one side to the other, began to talk loudly. Meaningless words. In between she whimpered and moaned.

Suddenly her head flopped around toward Jeanne and remained facing her. She opened her eyes. Large, round eyes, which shone with fever. Her gaze fastened on Jeanne.

"I can't feel my legs anymore," she now said clearly. "They're already dead." After that she was quiet. And she didn't move anymore.

Jeanne called for help. Immediately Annonciata and Afande Brian came running into the room.

"The girl . . . ," Jeanne whispered.

The afande bent over Uwera, laid his ear on her chest, and stood up again. He looked at Annonciata and nodded.

Annonciata stroked Jeanne's cheek. "Uwera is dead," she said. "We must take her away."

That night, in spite of the fever, Jeanne did not close an eye. She was afraid, terribly afraid. She resisted falling asleep because she was afraid she might not wake up again. And her legs, too, seemed to be already dead. And Annonciata had said that she and Uwera had the same illness.

The empty bed stood there next to her. Jeanne could barely see it in the dark, but she felt its presence and the threat exuded by its emptiness. Death was nesting in the bedclothes. It was lying in wait.

Jeanne fought desperately against her weakness. And a loud voice grew inside her, and other voices mixed in. That of Teya, that of Olivier.

"I don't want to! I don't want to!"

I tell you of my dream.

For a week it was the terror of my nights. I was still a child, five at the most, but I still see all the images of that dream clearly before me. They have never let go of me.

You must know that I grew up after the war in a street where there were only destroyed houses. Except for the one where we lived.

The ruins were my world. I would play there with the neighbor children, sometimes alone as well, until someone came looking for me. There were places where you could forget yourself. I balanced on iron girders projecting from the broken walls. A great hole beneath me. I dug objects out of the rubble: a teapot without a handle, a vase that had survived the bombing attacks without damage, pieces of cutlery, once even a bunch of keys. I didn't think about the owners. Everything I found belonged to me. I set up a house between stones, sat there for hours at a time, and dreamed.

But over all lay the echo of a great war whose horrors I could only guess at. I felt it at the back of my neck, I could still smell it, and fear was mixed in with my desire to capture its legacies.

It was an easy matter to get into the destroyed houses. Of course you usually had to climb, because the entrances were blocked, but otherwise nothing was secured.

Except for one of the ruins. It lay at the end of our block on the left side. The last house before you turned the corner. Its large, gray front towered against the sky. No roof. The windows were bricked up for several stories. Only the cellar windows, twenty inches above the ground, were open. Rectangular, blacker than night, so small that only a child could fit through the opening.

One time I squatted down in front of one to look inside. A cold breath of air hit me and a smell that I couldn't interpret. The darkness like a wall before my eyes, impenetrable, but I knew that it had depth. The depth of a nothingness.

Something strange reached for me, something that filled me with fear. From then on I avoided passing that house, crossing to the other side of the street before I got to it.

And a few days later I had the dream for the first time.

I dreamed that I was playing outside on the street with the other neighborhood children. Near the bricked-up ruin. We sat on the curbstone, exchanging pictures we had gotten from our fathers' cigarette packages or from an oatmeal package. A few of the bigger children were playing ball.

At first the ball disappeared. After that, a child. No one seemed to notice it. Except me. I saw a shadow rise from *the cellar window, a dark whirlpool that swallowed every-thing. At this point I would wake up bathed in sweat.*

The same dream, night after night. Except that each time another child became the victim of the ruin. Of the shadow monster that lived there.

I woke up. I cried. Called for my mother. But when she came, I was speechless. I was afraid to talk about it, as if the words would just make it real.

Every night a child was snatched from our midst. We were becoming ever fewer. Finally I was the only one left.

That night I lay awake for a long time. I fought against sleep. But when sleep did overwhelm me, I considered desperately in my dream how I could outrun certain death. And I found the solution for myself! I came to the decision to make friends with the monster. For if we were friends, it could do nothing more to me. Suddenly I felt strong. Yes, I was stronger! This thought was the last thing I dreamed. After that it was all past, like a bad nightmare.

Maybe it sounds a little crazy, but I believe that at that time I discovered in myself a strength that carries me today and that sometimes keeps me from sinking into the bottomless pit.

And I sense this strength in you.

After the fever was vanquished, Jeanne remained too weak for a long time to be able to stay on her feet for more than a few minutes. Her recuperation proceeded very slowly. Annonciata tried to build her up with quantities of fruit and vegetables. In the meantime, she'd given up trying to get Jeanne to drink milk at any price.

As often as possible, Jeanne allowed herself to be brought into the yard. There she sat on a chair or lay on a mat and turned toward the sun. Relieved that it was bright and warm around her. And that she could be aware of her body again without pain.

Chantal and James, too, came often to ask if she wanted anything. James brought her fruit: papayas, *maracujas*, fresh pineapple, and *amaperas*. And he always tried to wrest a smile from her with one of his jokes. But she remained quiet and turned inward. The illness had left her even lonelier than she'd been before.

Carine was no longer there. She and Chantal had found an aunt on one of their information-seeking expeditions and Carine had decided to stay with her. Jeanne only learned of it when she was able to think somewhat more clearly again. She accepted it with equanimity. Carine was just lucky. The time when they'd been there for each other like sisters already lay far in the past.

One afternoon at the end of June, Chantal came into the yard to see Jeanne. She walked gaily out the door, in shorts and uniform shirt, her broom already growing in a little, and at that moment she seemed to Jeanne almost the way she had earlier. Self-confident and bursting with energy. It was obvious that she had something to communicate.

As she sat down next to Jeanne, she burst right out with her news. "I'm going to be a *kadogo*, Dédé!"

Jeanne was not surprised. She'd been expecting something like that for a long time. Chantal's enthusiasm for the military was well known, and besides, she'd already said a few times that she might become a soldier. Nevertheless, it gave Jeanne a little stab. Certainly Chantal would also be going away now.

"I spoke with Afande Brian today. He's sending me to Afande Grace at Kayonza. I'm going to be her bodyguard."

So, she would become a bodyguard for a woman.

Occasionally Jeanne had also considered whether she should join the armed forces. Living with an *afande* had advantages. You lived well and were respected. But you had to follow strict rules and obey unconditionally. That was not possible for her any longer. Besides, she could never imagine taking a gun in her hand to kill someone with it. And she'd had enough of living outdoors.

"Why are you doing that?" she asked. "Why don't you go to your aunt, like Carine?"

Chantal looked at her. Her mouth hardened as she answered, "For Carine, it's good if she has a home again. She needs help, someone to look after her. But for me, there's no normal life anymore. I only want one thing: to fight against my parents' murderers; otherwise my life has no meaning."

Jeanne knew that she wanted revenge for herself, even if she didn't realize it.

"When are you going away?" she asked.

"There's a truck going to Kayonza tomorrow. I'm going with it."

As soon as tomorrow! All right, then that was just the way it was. It was fate.

"I wish you luck," said Jeanne. "Maybe we'll see each other again sometime."

"I'll write to you if I have time," Chantal promised.

Silent, the girls looked at each other. There was nothing more to say. Only *maybe* and *if*. The future lay in uncertainty.

"Good-bye, good luck, Dédé!" said Chantal seriously. *"Ngaho Urabeho."*

She stood up, hugged Jeanne, kissed her quickly on both cheeks, and left the courtyard.

Gradually Jeanne's strength returned. Day by day she felt able to do a little more. Including small walks around the nearby environs. She used every opportunity to be outside. She moved in this direction or that one, without a goal. Driven by an inner unrest.

About a week after Chantal had left for Kayonza, Jeanne encountered James and Dusabe in front of the building.

Dusabe was Afande Brian's second *kadogo*, though he hadn't been there very long. He was just twelve, and James had good-naturedly taken him under his wing. When they both had time off, they often roamed around the town. Now, too, they seemed to be just about to go somewhere.

They were a strange pair. Tall, thin James, black as night, and the delicate, light-skinned Dusabe, who barely came up to James's shoulder. They were both wearing their uniforms. Dusabe, however, only wore the trousers and visored cap; instead of the uniform shirt he had on a lemon-yellow T-shirt. The trousers were much too big for him, and the cuffs were rolled up to his knees so they wouldn't drag on the floor. James had his carbine. It hung loosely over his shoulder. When he caught sight of Jeanne, he waved at her with the gun barrel.

"Hello, Little Sister! Do you have a taste for *marie-angélas*? They're ripe now. Really good and red. I know a place where there a lot growing. Want to come along?"

Marie-angélas! A marble-sized stone fruit with sweet, crunchy flesh. They used to have two huge bushes in their yard. Yes, she had a taste for *marie-angélas*. And she was bored. A ramble with the boys offered a change. She agreed.

First James led them into town for a little way.

There hadn't been any clouds in the sky for days. Nevertheless it wasn't too hot. A soft, cooling breeze caressed her skin.

Jeanne walked silently beside the boys while Dusabe chattered uninterruptedly to James. She had trouble keeping up, needing two steps to their one. Dusabe was grumbling loudly about the *afande*, for whom he couldn't do anything right at all and who had recently sentenced him to one day's house arrest.

"Imagine! A whole day! Just because I overslept a few minutes," he complained.

"Don't get excited about it!" James advised. "He's always especially strict at the beginning. Later that settles down. He's okay."

"How did you get to the Rebels, anyway? Were you abroad?" Dusabe asked.

"Yes, my parents emigrated to Tanzania, because they

couldn't study in Rwanda. But they came from Kibungo. And my father's family stayed here. Also his brother, who was my godfather. I visited him quite often. Now they're all dead. When I heard that the Rebels still needed soldiers, I enlisted. I wanted to do something."

"My family was killed too. No one survived except me," said Dusabe softly.

"And you? How did you survive?"

"In the swamps of Lake Muhazi. You can be glad you weren't here during that time. It was horrible."

Jeanne pricked up her ears. He'd survived in a lake? She saw Eric before her and thought of the moment when they'd stood on the cloister hill and looked at the lake. About Eric's suggestion to hide there in the swamp. Would he and his brothers perhaps still be alive if they had . . . ? A feeling of guilt rose in her.

"That couldn't be!" she objected heatedly. "A person can't possibly be in the water continuously! How long were you in there?"

"About a week."

"But how? How did you survive?"

"In the reeds. And up to neck in water. In the daytime, anyway! At night sometimes I came out. After all, I needed something to eat. I got things from the fields. Manioc and sweet potatoes. Once a hippo almost got me."

"A hippo?" asked James incredulously.

"Yes. There were a couple of them in the lake. At the beginning I didn't know it. But one night I heard something moving in the water. I thought at first it was a snake. But then I saw its nose come out of the water and knew what it was. I got out of the lake as fast as I could. But the thing came after me. They can run, I'm telling you! I ran a little ways around the lake and then right into the reeds again. And I didn't move. It ran past me."

"Weren't you afraid to stay in the lake when there were wild animals in there?"

Dusabe laughed bitterly. "I was more afraid of the men outside it!"

For a long time none of them said anything.

"And then what happened?" James asked finally.

"I found out one day that there were soldiers around the lake. From then on I didn't dare come out at all. But then I simply couldn't stand the hunger any longer. I had to go out to get something to eat. When I came to the shore, there were two soldiers standing there. They saw me right away, and I thought, now it's all over. I lost hope and was going to give up. But it was the Rebels."

Jeanne had been so captivated by Dusabe's story that she hadn't noticed where James was leading them. Only when Dusabe fell silent did she suddenly realize that they were approaching the development where their house had been. She saw the destroyed houses of her former Tutsi neighbors and the abandoned houses of the Hutu. Some doors were standing wide open. Jeanne stopped in her tracks. Her heart was beating faster. There was a rushing in her head.

"I feel sick, I want to go back!" she said urgently, filled with fear.

"It's just a little way. It's not far at all now. First we'll get the *marie-angélas*!" James insisted over her objection.

As they went on, Jeanne kept her eyes firmly fixed on the road, looking neither to the right nor the left. She didn't want to see where she was. And her fear grew with every step.

James stopped. "Here it is!" he said.

Jeanne lifted her head.

And saw the orchard before her. Their orchard! Its soil overgrown with weeds. The fruity sweet air filled with the buzzing of the insects. Behind the fence, close enough to grasp, the familiar bushes whose branches bent under the weight of the *marie-angélas*. Blood-red burden. And behind the big trees, her family's house. Without a roof. A ruin.

"No!"

She was already running. Away! Just away! She fled. Followed by Jando's cheerful voice. "You wait, I'll soon catch you!" Ten paces lead. Her eyes were blind with tears.

"Dédé! Just wait! Where are you going?"

James and Dusabe caught up with her and James held her fast. She tore herself loose.

"Dédé, what's the matter?" James sounded frightened. "What's happened?"

She ran on. Didn't want to see him. Hated him to the very bottom of her soul. He was a thief like all the others.

She never wanted to speak to him again. And with no one else, either. Never again!

Earlier, when she'd been angry with Julienne, she had sometimes not spoken to her all day long. Often because of some trivial thing. If, for instance, the housemaid had intervened in an argument with Teya and taken her side. Jeanne could be stubborn. But at some point it was over. Forgotten.

But this time it was different. This was about something fundamental. Something you couldn't forget. Jeanne wanted nothing more to do with anyone. She was angry at the whole world.

"I'm going to complain," you say.

It's noontime. We've gathered around the big table to eat. Stories about school go back and forth.

"The kids in my class are so noisy that I can't hear over them. It's already hard for me anyway. Tomorrow before class I'm going to tell them so."

"No! Are you crazy?" cries someone at the table. "You just can't do that! Then everybody will be down on you!"

"Why?" you ask. "I'm not going to go to the teacher. I'm going to say it right to them. . . ."

The others protest and we debate vigorously. About peer pressure. About what you can permit yourself. About norms. And about defending your convictions.

You look at me. "What have I got to lose . . . ?" says your look.

I nod. "You have to do what you think is right. If you're certain that it's good."

The conversation is soon forgotten. A few days pass. But one noontime I think of the story again.

"Did you really say to your class what you intended to say?" I ask.

"Yes, I did."

The others prick up their ears.

"And? How did it go? Did they listen to you?"

"Yes, they were even quiet. And then they clapped. And after that it was better."

"You see!" I say in the direction of the others. Taking your triumph as my own. "You can dare a lot. You just need to have the courage to do it."

I'm proud. It was with us that you learned to express yourself freely and openly.

"For a few days it even did some good," you add and smile enigmatically.

Jeanne maintained her silence. Words no longer passed her lips. When she wanted something, she let it be known with dumb signs. But mostly she just did what she wanted. She'd completely barricaded herself against the outside. Only inside did she speak. Sometimes it was silent answers to something someone said to her. Often she talked with herself. Inside and outside were two separate worlds. The outside had nothing to do with her. Now and then, when she was alone and need not be careful, she would make a sound to herself, testing whether her voice would still obey her. And she heard a voice that was strange to her.

In the beginning, the others had tried to find an access to her and break through her silence. Especially James. He seemed to know that he had caused something bad and wanted to make amends. But her stony behavior and the hatred that blazed at him from her eyes finally compelled him to retreat once and for all.

"I'm sorry, Little Sister. I certainly didn't mean to do you any harm."

But you are harmful. Your friendship is a lie. You don't know the difference between right and wrong. You smile and kill. In one breath. And you simply take what doesn't belong to you.

Although Jeanne had cut her ties to humankind, she took in everything happening around her with hyperclarity. As if a curtain had been torn away and, out of a deep knowledge of the context, her vision for details was sharpened. Deflected by nothing, deceived by nothing. She saw everything with the incorruptibility of the child who can look at the bottom of Hell because she has been through it herself.

At the end of July it was said that the war was over, and the town began gradually to change. The camps were dismantled, the houses were restored. At first those of the Hutus. Yet only seldom was it the former owners who moved in there. People, the majority of them Tutsis who had fled to neighboring countries years before and had lived there until the war, in Uganda, Tanzania, Burundi, and Zaire, came back to reclaim "their" country. They took the empty houses. It seemed to disturb no one that they claimed strangers' property for themselves. Over and over Jeanne heard the expression: "We didn't steal the things, we liberated them!"

With disgust she decided that basically nothing had changed. Only a lot of things were turned upside down. The poor people became rich, the rich had nothing anymore. And as always, each person was only looking out for his own advantage. Relatives squabbled over the parentless children. The relatives of the father put forward their claims. The right of the men took preference. What the children wanted didn't count. No, nothing had changed!

The stores were newly opened, the hospital was there for the sick again, and the prison filled with men who were guilty of having slaughtered their neighbors.

A few weeks after the end of the war, Jeanne moved too, together with Afande Brian and his two *kadogos*. Into a large house that was situated on the main road at the Kibungo city limits. A large living room with leather sofas and glass cabinets, a dining table with artfully embroidered tablecloths, expensive rugs, shower and bath with running water, television and video equipment betrayed the wealth of the former owner.

When the *afande* asked her whether she wanted to move with him, she had neither agreed nor refused. She was indifferent to where she lived.

"Just try it out!" he had advised her. "If you don't like it, you only have to say so. Then we'll look for another solution!"

I will not say anything in any case. And you will not get me to speak!

Each one of them lived for himself. The *afande* was out a lot, and James and Dusabe had to go with him. Jeanne stayed behind under the care of the houseboy, who provided for her but left her alone. He was also extremely silent and that was all right with her.

"She can help herself to what she likes," the *afande* had explained to the houseboy. "And she doesn't need to wait for us to eat."

In the beginning, she often sat alone at the big dining room table, staring at the bare wall. And one day she just stood up and wandered outside with her plate.

Usually it was utterly quiet in the house. Except for the mornings, when the *afande* sang in the shower, or the evenings, when he had company and quantities of beer were drunk. Then the house was filled to bursting with the booming male laughter, and Jeanne couldn't get to sleep.

They laugh. They sing. They drink. They take the country for themselves. But the dead are not yet buried.

In October, school began again and Jeanne had to go. It was her old school, her mother's school. She balked. Showed her resistance unmistakably. But the *afande*, who otherwise made no demands on her, insisted on it.

"School is important. It's about time to return to normal life again."

Just half a year has passed. Half a year! And you say it's time. . . .

Jeanne was in the third grade.

Sister Angéline, an older nun, became her teacher. She had already been a teacher in the school before the war and had known Florence well. When she found out that Jeanne wouldn't speak, she accepted her silence without comment. However, she made sure that Jeanne did her written work carefully. When Jeanne sat lost in thought in front of an empty sheet of paper and hadn't even started, she would chide her.

Then Sister Angéline would place her hand on her shoulder with gentle pressure and say, so softly that the others couldn't hear her, "You must make the effort to learn something. Think of your mother!"

I must. Il y a une maison sur la colline. La bouche. Le coeur. Le coeur—impossible to say. Teya could do it. I could do math better. You can rely on numbers.

She had history with a new teacher who came from Uganda and spoke with an accent. They were again learning about the last five kings. But in more detail than before. And with different subject matter. Before the war they had taught them how the kings had oppressed the Hutus. And how with the help of the whites this unjust rule was brought to an end. Now they heard of the great deeds of the Tutsi kings. Of the battles of their soldiers. And of their traditions.

The recent history was not mentioned. Not one word about it. There was a time before. Now was the time afterward. The time in between was a deep abyss of a wound that no one wanted to touch.

The school still did not have an everyday look, and the picture of the schoolyard during recess was colorful. There was no homogeneous uniform. Many children came in regular clothes. Others wore the uniforms of their former schools.

Little groups formed everywhere. Some were the children of the people who had lived abroad—to Jeanne they were foreigners—the children of the Hutus who hadn't left, and the children who had escaped death.

Strange. Everything is strange. I am a stranger. I don't belong to this.

For Jeanne, recesses were the worst. In the schoolyard she couldn't keep people from speaking to her. Asking her where she lived. And if she had any brothers or sisters. Then she would turn her head away. She suffered. Sometimes she skipped school. Afande Brian never found out. Sister Angéline scolded Jeanne, of course, but she kept quiet about it.

Just before the beginning of the Christmas holidays there were report cards again for the first time. They were seated in rows in class according to their achievement. Not celebrated in a ceremony in the presence of their parents and the entire school as before. In the old days, the two best in their class had always received their reports on a victory pedestal. Jeanne had stood up there three times, and she had always been at least among the first five, to please her mother.

This time she was only in tenth place. It wasn't important to her.

She was glad that it was finally vacation. That she could withdraw into herself again without being challenged. Usually she roamed around somewhere or sat on one of the two low side walls that encircled the entry area to the house. She observed the people who went past her and tried to guess which group they belonged to. Recognizing the returnees from Uganda wasn't hard, for the girls and women wore long, colorfully printed pinafore dresses with sashes and puffed sleeves. The way they walked, very upright and calm, was evidence of good upbringing and polite behavior. The girls from Rwanda and Burundi weren't so easy to differentiate. They dressed very stylishly and boldly, without appreciable distinguishing marks. Nevertheless, Jeanne believed she could tell which girls came from Burundi, for they held their noses somewhat higher.

Now and then someone would ask Jeanne for a glass of water. But she didn't react to that. The rules had lost their validity. And there was a water place at the corner.

One afternoon, a few days before Christmas, she was squatting on the ground in front of the wall. Five small pebbles shifted from one hand to the other. The right hand was playing against the left. Now it was the left's turn. It threw the stones into the air and let them fall to the ground. It reached for one, threw it up, threw up the next one and caught the first before it came down again. Reaching and catching, one motion. And so it went. One stone in the air and always one more picked up from the ground. Finally all of them. The hand was not allowed to miss any stones.

As always, the right hand beat the left hand. But the left didn't give up.

Christmasy sounds murmured from one of the windows. A vigorous shower, a brief, quick downpour from the heavens, had freshened the air, laid the clouds of dust, and left behind a light of hard clarity.

Now you can see the volcanoes over the hills again.

345

The Dragon's Mouth. "*Voilà le Karisimbi*. . . ."

Inside the house there was a lively bustle going on. Afande Brian's wife was expected from Uganda. "We're going to have a lovely celebration. And it will be good for you when there's a woman in the house again," he had said to Jeanne. Her inner voice had had nothing to say to that.

Christmas with Nyogokuru. We children at her feet. Stories on Christmas Eve. During the endless waiting for the good meal. Bible stories. Nyogokuru knew them all by heart. Although she might not have been able to read at all. But that wasn't important. Nyogokuru was a book in herself.

The right hand threw a stone into the air.

At this moment James and Dusabe came out of the house. They were obviously about to go shopping.

As quick as a flash, the hand collected four stones from the ground and immediately caught up the first throwing stone. James and Dusabe stopped to watch. Jeanne acted as if she didn't notice them and continued with her game. But, for once, the right hand was allowed to throw a second time.

A piercing whistle beside her distracted her. The stone fell to the ground.

Lost! The left hand gloated.

Jeanne looked up and caught sight of two young girls coming down the street arm in arm. Both wore short skirts, whose hems ended just below the beginning of the thigh, and over the skirts T-shirts just as short. Their abdomens bare. Four long legs moved in step.

It had been Dusabe who'd whistled at the sight of them. Now he grinned impudently.

"Can't you get it a little shorter? What do you do when a breeze comes along?" he crowed.

The girls had come even with the house. They stopped and fixed Dusabe with a scornful look.

"What's the matter? Did you want something with us? You'll have to grow a little more, then," one said one pointedly.

Chuckling and with heads held high, they walked on. Arched their behinds and let them wiggle back and forth a few times.

James clearly found the scene embarrassing. "Come on!" he said roughly. He punched Dusabe in the side and pulled him away with him. The two left hurriedly.

Jeanne suppressed a giggle. Her eyes followed the girls' legs and wandered to the arms linked together.

Suddenly a jolt went through one of them. A quick turn of her head. In Jeanne's direction. A long, searching look. Then she left the other one and came slowly back. She speeded up as she got to Jeanne. Disbelief and astonishment in her face.

"Dédé? Is that you? That can't be true . . . yes, it is you! You survived? I thought—" she broke off and bit her lip. But then her eyes began to glow, a beaming smile made two little dimples in her cheeks. "Dédé! *C'est incroyable*! How marvelous to see you! You've grown!"

The sound of her voice, the familiar dimples, and above all the pale, deep scar straight across the top of her skull!

Traces of the machete that, seen up close, could not be overlooked. Jeanne saw in her mind the bloody gash and suddenly she knew who stood before her.

"Immaculée?" she heard herself ask softly.

"Yes, Dédé! I made it too! No, honestly! I almost went right past you. . . ."

Meanwhile the other girl had turned back and Immaculée introduced her. "This is my friend Sylvère. I live with her and her aunt now. Ever since that time. And you?"

"I live here with the *afande*." Jeanne marveled at how matter-of-factly words crossed her lips again.

"Oh, I see," said Imaculeé. "And what about the others?"

Jeanne shook her head. A shadow flickered over Immaculée's still joyous face.

"I saw your father shortly before his death. I am so terribly sorry about what happened to him, Dédé."

Jeanne started. What was she saying?

"You saw him again? And you know what happened to him?"

"Yes. It was a few days after the community center was overrun by the Interahamwe. Then friends got me from the hospital because it was too dangerous to stay there. On the way we met a gang. All young people. They had your father with them and drove him before them like a piece of cattle. Later I heard that they traveled around with him for more than a week. Shortly before the Rebels came they killed him."

Jeanne was staggered. She needed a moment to grasp what that meant. Her father had still been alive when she'd thought he already was dead! This realization pained her so very much that she burst into tears.

Stricken, Immaculée put her arm around her. "*Ma pauvre*! I am so very sorry. I thought you knew it!"

Jeanne wiped her eyes and slipped out of the embrace. Her lips trembled. "It's all right," she said.

Just don't cry. She would never be able to stop again. She gulped.

"And what are you doing now?" she asked, changing the subject. "Are you still going to school?"

"Not at the moment," Immaculée explained. "Just imagine! I'm flying to Europe! A few days from now. One of my father's brothers lives in Belgium. After the war was over, he came here to look for relatives and found me. Now I can go to him. Live with him. And go to school. Later I want to study. I want to be a doctor. Oh, Dédé, I am so glad to be getting out of here! Who knows, maybe there's even snow on the ground in Europe."

Snow. Yes, Jeanne had heard of that. White ice, like flour, that covered the streets. Also the houses, trees, just everything. A white world. Hardly conceivable. Aunt Colette had told them about it. And about black bread that looked like coal.

Aunt Colette! Maybe she's still alive. There's no war in Europe.

"I have an aunt in Europe. One of my mother's sisters. Maybe she's still living."

The moment she said it, something began to pulse inside her, something that she had not felt for a long time, something bright, exciting. Expectation. It rose up in her, tingling, and made a breach in the dam of hopelessness.

"Of course she's still living! Why should she be dead? Do you know her name? Do you know where she lives?" cried Immaculée.

"Yes, I know her name. And she lives in Germany."

"Germany is very big, Dédé. Very much bigger than Rwanda. Don't you know what city she lives in?"

"I don't know any city in Germany. Only Berlin. And I don't know if she lives there."

"If you know her name, they can have her searched for! Maybe she even came here in the meantime to find out what had become of all of you. Go talk to the *afande*!"

"Yes," said Jeanne. "I'll do that! Right now."

She stood up and let the pebbles drop. One by one. Clack *I* . . . clack *am* . . . clack *going* . . . clack *away* . . . clack *forever*. . . .

Something of her old strength blossomed in her. Her thoughts had a goal again: She wanted to go away! As far as possible. Leave everything behind her. Forever.

"If you don't get anywhere with it here, then you have to go to Kigali. There are people from the United Nations there. They can certainly help you search."

"Yes!" Jeanne repeated. "I'll talk with the *afande*. Right now. Thanks, Immaculée. And good luck in Europe!"

She wanted not to lose any time. Resolutely she started on her way.

You read a book.

You open it.

You follow its pages from chapter to chapter. You close it afterward and think it's come to an end. But everything is still there. You hold it in your hand. And each page is available to you, each word.

Wherever and however you want, you immerse yourself in a perception in which everything comes together at once. The perception is less limited than the experience.

This book is not at an end either. You can ramble through its pages or leap, zigzagging, back and forth. Even a bit forward, to pages that aren't written yet! And you can linger where you want to.

Sometimes I think that the history of us human beings is only a thing in self-contained motion. No more than a breath in eternity. And in that, the duration of a human life turns out to be infinitely small.

Perhaps there is no such thing as time at all. In any case, not as we see it. Perhaps there are only creation and destruction as a pair in a great whole that cannot be expressed in dimensions.

Our own limits create dimensions, poles between which we understand the world: beginning and end. We think, feel, and act sustained by the illusion that, exceeding our limits, we are constantly going forward. But I think time is not a straight line. It's a circle. Enclosing life and death within it: congruent.

While I was writing this book, usually propelled by anger and grief, sometimes also by pleasure and joy, I found—strange as it may seem to you—much of my own story in yours. Memories forgotten were suddenly there again: I sat in a little zinc tub and was being scrubbed. Not outside in the warm sun, like you, but near a warm stove on the kitchen table. And the soap burned in my eyes. And my heart burned, as did yours, with jealousy of a little sister. Your often swallowed resistance was mine!

It is always all there. Both sides of our existence. When we open ourselves, we can be connected with others.

We are twins, you said at the beginning. Yes, somehow something like that must be so. I believe our souls are related, and for a long time now, our memories.

And if ever the horror catches up with you again, then you know that I am very close by.

A girl is sitting in a huge airplane.

She is flying for the first time in her life. For she is on the way from a tiny little country in the heart of Africa to Germany. On her way to us.

From now on there will be many first times.

The first time on a bicycle. The first time in a swimming pool. The first time eating black bread. The first time on a horse. The first time in the snow. Almost as if she were a new-born.

She doesn't know anything of us yet, we know nothing of her. A time of struggle still lies ahead of us. A struggle for her right to be with us. And a time of getting to know each other. Until she knows that she belongs to us.

But she is already on the way to us. And it is certain that we are going to meet. It has to be so, I maintain.

It is this that sometimes allows me still to believe in an act of Providence.

Timeline of Rwandan History

1898 The kingdom of Rwanda becomes part of German East Africa.

1903 Baptism of Rwanda's first Catholic Christians. Almost one-third of modern Rwandans are Catholic.

1918 After World War I, Rwanda comes under the control of Belgium. Under Belgian rule, the societal order of the native groups is maintained: The Tutsis (12% of the population) belong to the aristocratic upper class and the Hutus (82%) to the lower class of farmers.

1959 In a Hutu uprising, more than 10,000 Tutsis are killed; more than 100,000 flee into the neighboring countries of Burundi and Uganda.

1962 End of Belgian colonial rule. Rwanda becomes independent. In parliamentary elections, the Hutu Party receives the majority. Grégoire Kayibanda, a Hutu, becomes president of the republic.

1962–1966 The army of the Tutsis in exile tries repeatedly to invade Rwanda and take power. The regime reacts with repression of the Tutsis living in the country. After a series of massacres, more than 300,000 Tutsis flee to neighboring countries.

1973 Military coup. General Juvénal Habyarimana becomes the new president and chief of the regime.

1975 General Habyarimana founds a one-party system with the National Democratic Movement (MRND).

1990 The RPF (Rwandan Patriotic Front), founded by exiled Tutsis, also called Tutsi Rebels, tries unsuccessfully to invade Rwanda and topple the regime. Imprisonments and massacres of Tutsis living in Rwanda are the result.

February 1993 The RPF occupies the northern part of Rwanda.

August 1993 The RPF and the regime sign a peace agreement, which provides for the participation of the Tutsis in the government. Formation of a transition government.

December 1993 United Nations peacekeeping troops are sent to Rwanda.

April 6, 1994 President Habyarimana is shot down in

his airplane over Kigali.

April 7, 1994 The troops of the MRND murder members of the transition government as well as ten United Nations peacekeepers. The beginning of the genocide of the Tutsis.

April 8, 1994 The MRND founds a transition government. Beginning of an offensive by the RPF.

April 21, 1994 The UN troops are withdrawn from Rwanda.

July 1994 Victory of the RPF, causing 1.2 million Rwandans, predominantly Hutus, to flee to Zaire.

The International Red Cross estimates the number of people killed during the genocide at 1 million.

July 19, 1994 The RPF establishes a new Rwandan government.

April 1995 Two thousand Hutu refugees are killed in fighting between RPF and Hutu soldiers.

1997 Repeated fighting between Interahamwe and RPF soldiers, with serious human rights violations on both sides.

Beginning of the genocide trials held by the United Nations.

2000 Paul Kagame (RPF) becomes president of Rwanda.

2003 Paul Kagame wins Rwanda's first presidential election since the genocide.

2005 By March, results of the United Nations trials include the convictions of twenty people, including many government and military officials, of the crime of genocide.

Glossary

A bientôt: until later

afande: the leader of a Rebel group

Allons, enfants!: Come, children!

alors: well

amapera (plural)*:* applelike fruits with red flesh

amasaka: a gruel beverage, like millet gruel

Bon, mes enfants!: Good, [my] children!

bouche: mouth

calabash: a pot-bellied container made from a bottle gourd
  or the fruit of the calabash tree

C'est incroyable!: It's incredible!

cockroaches: cockroaches, vermin. An abusive term for
  Tutsis.

coeur: heart

coeur de boeuf: tropical fruit in the shape of an ox heart

commune: the smallest administrative district in Rwanda

Compris?: Understand?

d'accord: agreed, okay

d'ailleurs: besides, moreover

Dieu soit loué!: Thank God!

donc: then, therefore, accordingly

Doucement, ma petite: Calm down, my little one

igikoma: the Rwandan term for *amasaka* gruel

igitambaro: kerchief or head cloth

Il y avait une maison sur la colline: There was a house on the hill

Interahamwe: extreme Hutu militia; literally, "the common assault"

ipera: singular of *amapera*

jamais: never

kadogo: little man, child soldier

Kigali: capital of Rwanda

Kinyarwanda: official language of Rwanda

Mais oui!: But yes!

manioc: cultivated tropical plant, whose root bulb is used to make flour

Ma pauvre!: My poor thing!

marie-angéla: small, cherrylike fruit

militia: troops whose members have only a brief military training; civilian army

milking fat: fat rubbed on a cow's udder before milking

Mon dieu!: My God!

muraho: greeting to a respected person

muzehe: graybeard, old man

Ngaho Urabeho: salute of departure

On verra: We'll see

On y va!: We're going!

Oui, je sais: Yes, I know

pour l'amour de Dieu: for the love of God

Sabyinyo: volcano in Rwanda, named for its appearance ("big, protruding tooth")

Swahili: language of central Africa, spoken in several countries

Très bien!: Very good!

umucyenyero: a dress, African wrap dress

umwitero: sash worn over the umucyenyero, diagonally across the shoulder

uraho: greeting (used by children among themselves)

Venez, enfants!: Come, children!

Voilà le Karisimbi, voilà le Muhabura et enfin le Sabyinyo: There you are: Karisimbi, Muhabura, and finally Sabyinyo. (Karisimbi, Muhabura, and Sabyinyo are the three largest volcanoes in Rwanda.)

wiriwe: good day

About the Author

Hanna Jansen wrote this book based on the true experiences of her adopted daughter, Jeanne, who survived the Rwandan genocide in 1994. Hanna and Jeanne live in Siegburg, Germany, with Hanna's husband and the Jansens' twelve other children, most of whom are war orphans.

About the Translator

Elizabeth D. Crawford's translations have earned many honors, including the Mildred L. Batchelder Award for outstanding translation of a children's book. She has been chosen three times as the American translator for the Hans Christian Andersen Honor List by the U.S. chapter of the International Board of Books for Young People. She lives in Orange, Connecticut.

'Hanna Jansen's remarkable story of her adopted daughter Jeanne is a powerful testimony of the genocide in Rwanda, and the events leading up to it. It is more important than ever to ensure that the experiences of survivors like Jeanne are chronicled for posterity, and Hanna ensures that this is handled sensitively in a way that makes it accessible to young people, without ever compromising the brutal realities of the killings that took the lives of Jeanne's family in 1994. Jeanne's story ends with her flying to Germany to live with Hanna and her loving adoptive family. But the story sadly has not ended so happily for other survivors, many who are struggling without any parents to care or provide for them. I am certain that *Over a Thousand Hills I Walk With You* will ensure that more people are aware of the realities of the genocide and hopefully will be inspired to act to make a difference to help the thousands of survivors living with, and still dying from, its consequences in Rwanda today.'

MARY KAYITESI BLEWITT
Founder and Director,
Survivors Fund (SURF)